Till Human Voices
Wake Us

PATTI DAVIS

ISBN: 1483990044

ISBN-13: 9781483990040

We have lingered in the chambers of the sea
By sea-girls wreathed with seaweed red and brown
Till human voices wake us, and we drown.

T.S. Eliot

PROLOGUE

In the dream I'm in water. Silvery bubbles stream past me and break into tiny colored prisms. Sunlight cuts through the surface like gold needles. The surface is where he is—floating there, limp and curved. A small fragile comma in a world of blue. My hands claw the water, trying to get to him. In the dream I never do. I am lost in water, trapped by distance, condemned to helplessness.

But then I wake up—to my own forever. To a world without him in it.

I did get to him. My fingers grabbed his wrist. My arm circled his waist, fingers slick on his skin, searching for a pulse, searching for life. I swam a clumsy sidestroke, his small limp body tight against me. I was desperate to get him to the side of the pool—to warm dry cement, to air. To life the way it had been that morning… yesterday…an hour ago. I remember chlorine stinging my eyes. My sandals floated off my feet. My mouth opened to scream, but I'm not sure I did. They tell me I did—the people who ran out—my husband, the men who were working in the house. I remember so much. Too much. The heaviness of Nathan's body, as if it had already absorbed pounds of water. His jeans billowing with air as I pulled him across the surface of the water to the steps. His chest horribly still and motionless like his lungs had given up on taking in air…oh God, please no. Other arms jutted out through the dry bright day to help me. None were my husband's arms.

Thomas had turned to stone on the green lawn—one leg in front of the other, as if he'd intended to take another step but had become paralyzed at the sight of our son's body. One of the workmen—drywall dust coating his hair and face—grabbed Nathan from me, and started doing CPR. Why hadn't I learned CPR? Why hadn't we started his swimming lessons already? We were just getting to that. My mind ricocheted from one thought to another.

My husband said nothing to me until after the paramedics came, and then the coroner. Until they carried our three-year old son's body away on a stretcher that was so long he was only a small shape beneath the blanket. Until an awful silence had closed down upon us like a vise.

"Who left the screen unlocked?" Thomas finally said. "It was supposed to always be locked."

In the fog of not knowing, in the sliver of an instant, along a knife-blade of fear, I decided it must have been me. I opened my mouth to speak, to shriek, but Thomas was already walking away. I watched him as he strode across afternoon shadows on the lawn, like Orion striding across the heavens, and disappeared into the Tudor-style mansion that was our home. I knew he was going inside to call his brother Peter.

My name is Isabelle Berendon. That's my married name, the name I am still called publicly. I married into a dynasty. But I believed—on that white-lace day, with swans drifting in a pond beside us and two hundred people watching—that I was marrying into love. I became a woman with impressive diamonds on her wedding finger and easy access to the best that Los Angeles can offer. Over time, I grew into a woman who looked in the mirror and saw a fool's eyes staring back at her. In this family wives are accessories. We're expected to be shiny, presentable, and never too demanding.

The Berendon family owns a chain of fashionable department stores; the gilded Berendon's sign is one of the landmarks of Beverly

Hills. During the four years of my marriage to Thomas, I learned to accept that his brother was the one he trusted and confided in. I had Thomas' name, I shared his bed; I had money and a household staff, and I was the mother of his child. That was supposed to be enough.

But standing by the blue pool where our son had just drowned, my clothes still damp and clinging to me, my shoes floating on the surface along with one small tennis shoe—Nathan's—I didn't know how to accept being left so completely alone.

Another pair of shoes—a little girl's turquoise flip-flops, decorated with daisies—were near the steps of the pool. Marjorie is Thomas' seven-year-old daughter from his first marriage, and the only relief in that terrible day was that she wasn't there. Before noon, her nanny had taken her to a friend's birthday party, and I knew by the slant of the sun that she'd be coming back soon.

I walked over and bent down for the sandals—I don't know why—probably because there was nothing else to reach for. I ended up on my knees, collapsed and helpless, weeping to a God I hated for allowing my child to die, but who else could I cry to right then?

That's how Marjorie found me.

She heard me crying from the driveway and instead of going through the front door, she opened the back gate and ran to me. I opened my eyes and looked through a film of tears at the child I had not given birth to, the child who had become mine through marriage, and who was now, at the darkest time of my life, reaching out her hand as if she could save me.

"I'm sorry," I managed to say, the words choking me. "I'm so sorry."

"Why? What's wrong?"

She didn't know. I couldn't tell her. Someone would have to…

Then Iris reached out for me. My sister-in-law bent down and helped me to my feet. I remember the late afternoon sun sinking over her shoulder—strange the details you memorize when your world has imploded. Thomas and Peter were standing near the house in a circle of shadow, far away from us as usual.

Marjorie ran to Thomas. I heard her asking what had happened. She was crying now too. I saw him kneel down in front of her and I shut my eyes into darkness. Is that what you saw when you died, Nathan? Or was it bright and golden like people say?

Iris helped me upstairs and, because I'd started shivering uncontrollably, she turned on a warm shower. Her hands gently helped me out of my clothes, held my arm as I stepped under the stream of water, and wrapped me in a thick towel when I got out.

The rest of the evening is snapshots in my memory. My mother came and at one point she and Iris were both leaning into me as if they could keep me from breaking apart. We were sitting on a bed in one of the guest rooms—the room where my mother would sleep that night, and where I would wake up the next day. I don't remember leaving Thomas' bed and walking down the hall to her, but I obviously did.

I remember my mother's warm hand on my face and arms. I remember Iris bringing me a glass of Vodka that burned going down. But nothing could thaw the deep cold in me.

Images of Nathan rose up and swallowed me whole. The first word he ever said was "bath", although he might have just said "baa" and I invented the consonants I wanted to hear. His face broke into a smile at my excitement, at the way I fluttered around telling everyone in the house. One day when I was trimming his fingernails, as my thumb stroked the velvet skin on the back of his hand, tears suddenly erupted from me. His tiny fingers and delicate pink ovals of nail were so exquisite, the love in me so huge, I could do nothing else but cry.

"How can he be gone? He can't be gone," I said to my mother and Iris that night—the longest night of my life. A vague memory fluttered in the distance: After Nathan was born and Iris helped me with challenges I never expected—like his reluctance to take my breast in his mouth and nurse—I said to her, "It's so strange that nine months ago, he wasn't here at all and now here he is, this little person."

Where was he before? Where is he now? Birth and death were ripping me apart.

It was only hours ago that I'd left him in the den, happily playing with toys, and only for a few minutes. Thomas had called out to me with some question about the construction. Workmen were re-doing the living room so more opulent parties could be given. The screen door should have been locked. It was always kept locked...

The mother of one of Marjorie's little friends lost her older son when a driver ran a red light. She'd taken him to the school bus and kissed him goodbye when the crossing light went on. She was standing helplessly on the corner when the car sped through the intersection. She saw everything—the impact, his broken body scattered across the road. He was nine years old. I didn't know her then—other mothers told me about it. She can talk about him calmly now, say things like, "When Eric was alive..."

But I've always wondered about the first night. How did she endure it? How could she have closed her eyes? The images must have crippled her. I'm not sure now how I got through the first night. A lot of it is blank, as if a merciful God erased the hours. Maybe that's what always happens—the numbness of shock is the best drug that a kindly God can offer. For a short while anyway.

The days after Nathan died streamed past with nothing to define them but darkness and dawn. I don't know how Thomas coped or what he did. Did he wander through the house in the wide lonely hours of night, the time when it seems like the whole city is asleep? Did he hide behind closed doors with sorrow burning through him like acid?

We sat in the same rooms. On most nights we slept in the same bed. But we may as well have been separated by oceans. I know my husband's anger, his blame—I'm at the other end of it—but I don't know the shape of his grief. I looked for it, but he left me alone with mine.

There were times I prayed to die. I didn't believe I could go on. Iris was the one who kept pulling me up from the undertow. You'll figure out how to live through this, she'd say, even though it doesn't seem like it now.

"But I killed my son," I told her more than once.

"No. Don't say that. You don't know who left the screen open, Isabelle," she continued to remind me—patiently, as if she hadn't already said it a hundred times before.

There did finally come a morning when I woke up and didn't feel like razor blades were slicing me each time I took a breath. It was the first moment when I believed that Iris was right—somehow I would go on. I would learn to live with the emptiness of a world without Nathan in it. I wasn't sure, though, how I was going to live with the uncertainty. What happened that day? Whose careless hand failed to lock the screen door?

It's been over seven months. Thomas and I are divorced. Now I live at the edge of the sea in what was once our getaway house, our Malibu retreat. It's how wealthy people get divorced—they divide up real estate. I stare out at the ocean for long periods of time, hoping for answers, wishing for some kind of help from God. But the tides change and I'm still hollow.

I live with my lover, my partner, the last person on earth I would have imagined loving in this way. I live with Iris.

1.

It's early. In a half-sleep state, I hear our bedroom door creak open and Marjorie pads across the floor in bare feet. She climbs up on the bed between me and Iris and I blink my eyes at the gray light. The lapping sound of lazy shallow waves comes through the open window; it's low tide. Iris opens her eyes and closes them again. She isn't a morning person.

Now that Marjorie has my attention, she gets down to business. "When I get married, will I marry a man or a woman?"

I scrunch myself up on a mound of pillows. The clock says 5:47. "I don't know, sweetheart. As long as it's someone you love, that's what matters."

Her eyes bore into me—not harshly, but in a way that lets me know she isn't going to leave without some answers. "Did you love my father?"

"Yes," I tell her, wondering if I'm being truthful. "Until...well, until things changed. We changed. Sometimes that feeling doesn't grow along with you. Not in the ways you hoped it would."

"Was it because Nathan died? Is that why you don't love Daddy anymore?"

Iris sinks further down into the pillows, her face hidden by a curtain of blond bed-messed hair. I feel like punching her. Why isn't she helping me?

"I think things changed before that," I admit. When in doubt, tell the truth.

"But now you and Iris love each other…" Marjorie says.

"Yes, we do. The thing about love is, you can't always figure out why it comes along when it does. You just know it has, and you can't say no to it. Your heart tells you. You should never argue with your heart. It's smarter than your brain."

She nods and gets off the bed, apparently satisfied for the moment. After she closes the door softly behind her, Iris finally opens her eyes and pushes herself up in the bed.

"Thanks a lot for your help," I tell her.

"Isabelle, she was reaching out to you. You married her father. You gave her a family—one with two parents, something she didn't remember having before. She was only three months old when her mother died. She loved being Nathan's big sister, she loved feeling like there was a complete family there. And when Nathan died, her world fell apart too. And then everything else turned upside down…it's a lot for a seven year old to handle. She came in to talk to you, not me."

"Except I don't know how to answer her questions."

Iris reaches up and brushes my hair off my face. "Yes you do. You did fine. Besides, I don't think it was about answers. She just wanted you to hear her. She wants to know there's room for her—past all the sadness inside you. She's trying to make sure you still love her even though you miss Nathan. Do you?"

I hate it when Iris asks me direct questions like that; she usually does it when I don't have direct answers.

"Yes. Of course I do. It's just that…I still feel so raw. And I think a part of me is scared to love her as much as I want to. What if something happens to her?"

"You know what I think? I think loving anyone takes a lot of courage. Love is not for sissies."

"Well, I can't argue with that," I tell her. "You know, I think it's really weird that you take so long to wake up and then once you do, you can be logical five minutes later. Most people need coffee first."

After the first Mrs. Berendon died suddenly of an aneurysm, Thomas relied on Iris to fill the void with his infant daughter. He made no effort to expand his role as parent, so Marjorie had only known Aunt Iris as a mother figure when I came along. Iris and I often joked that Marjorie acted like she'd hit the jackpot with two mothers once Thomas and I married.

So we probably shouldn't have been surprised when she confronted her father with a child's determination to have her way and announced that she wanted to live with Iris and me. Thomas didn't try to change her mind.

The first night we spent in this house, with the surf crashing outside and a bright moon gilding the sea, Marjorie looked at me with eyes clear as summer and circled her hands around my wrist, tugging as if she were intending to pull me into another room. But that wasn't it; her intention was to pull me into a future she'd decided upon.

"I don't want to be your stepdaughter," she said. "I just want to be your daughter."

I don't believe I had ever called her my stepdaughter, although it's possible that once Nathan was born, I'd made her feel like that sometimes. I'm just not sure anymore.

"You're definitely my daughter," I answered, feeling Iris' gaze brush across me from the other side of the room. "No question about it."

But there is a mote around my heart. Iris knows it, and my fear is that Marjorie senses it. A ribbon of water I won't yet allow her to cross. My son's body is there.

Losing a child is like no other loss—it erases whole parts of you, parts that were once willing and soft and open. Love might come to you in other ways, but the thought of loving a child again is as frightening as walking straight into a hurricane. It becomes a matter of self-preservation to keep some small bit of remove.

I wanted to let my son go in the way that mothers know they must—in the long unfurling of years. I thought I'd hear tires squealing as he drove away in his first car; I thought I'd get collect calls from an east coast college. And hold my breath when he brought a girlfriend home for Thanksgiving.

I'll never know the stages that parents complain about, yet weep over when they've passed. The tantrums, the pouting, the first day of school when you can't believe your child will be away for all those hours. I'll never know how he would have wrenched himself from me—every child has to—sometimes in anger, often just in frustration. How would Nathan have gone about defining himself? He'd have grown up with a famous name, which is like growing up with a famous building around you. You struggle to find yourself inside that architecture, and at times it seems nearly impossible. Would he have burst through walls and rooftops to claim his individuality?

Sometimes when the light hits a certain way, I think I see a shadow on the wall—a small, slightly bow-legged boy, still uncertain on his feet, still happily tumbling into furniture as he tackled the challenge of walking. On nights when the moon rides along the backbones of scattered clouds, I see his face looking up at the stars. I used to imagine what I would someday say to him about the sky's artistry. I imagine it still.

Parents never stop calling out to their children. I understood that the moment I gave birth to Nathan. Children leave—they have to—but we hope, no matter where they are, that they'll hear our voice on the wind, lift their heads, and turn toward home. There is a mysterious music to ancestry; eventually, most of us hear it. I expected this would happen with my son when he was older, when he had put miles between us in order to grow into who he was meant to be. But I'll never truly know who he would have become. He'll always be three.

He left the warm water of my womb in a fiery blinding passage. I remember the white ceiling, the white-hot pain, the rush after it was done and the squalling of a tiny being who had been inside me for so long, I was shocked that he was now unattached. I wept at the sheer miracle of it. All the kicking and turning that had filled my belly was flesh, bone, blood. A tiny pink mouth opening to cry. So much was still ahead of him. They say babies miss their small watery world when they explode into wide dry space.

Water took Nathan back.

But there is another child who watches me with her father's blue-green eyes and an openness all her own. Our children are not always the ones born to us; sometimes they arrive in our lives from the twists of fate and circumstance. Families are formed and re-formed for many different reasons. If one is very lucky, the family they're part of has been formed from love.

Despite all we've endured, Iris and I are lucky. We crashed into a love neither of us could have imagined and we didn't run away. Now we are, essentially, Marjorie's parents, since I don't think her weekly visits to Thomas can count as parenting. We are the ones she'll rebel against, hurl insults at, slam doors on, and hopefully return to after all that fieriness has burned itself out. Eventually, she'll fall in love and our combined histories will take the fall with her. We never fall in love alone; we bring everything along with us—our shadows, our parents' shadows. Everything.

Children start with bedtime stories, but in time grow impatient for stories stitched from history. We discover ourselves by discovering those who came before us. There is a point in childhood—we all reach it—when we look into the eyes of a grown-up and all we want to see is the truth.

"We're condemned to tell the truth," Iris once said to me. She said it in a brittle tone. She said it when we were a news story, a scandal. When our pictures were printed in tabloids and our lives were held up to glaring lights as if they were X-rays that needed to be analyzed for breaks and shattered bones. When religious zealots sent us hate mail and gay rights organizations sent us invitations to meetings. She said it because sometimes living your life truthfully is the hardest thing you can do.

2.

I am the daughter of a dancer and a shoplifter. These facts were mentioned frequently when Iris and I became fodder for gossip columnists who attacked us gleefully—two wealthy socialites simultaneously divorcing their husbands to be with each other. To live and dream and sleep with each other.

"To be with each other in the Biblical sense, although the Bible certainly didn't endorse this," a newscaster on FOX News said.

"You have to wonder," another reporter sniffed, "what kind of secret lives two women in their mid-thirties have been living up until now. You don't just hop on a different pony in the middle of the race."

"You don't?" I asked Iris when I heard that. I was trying to avoid the TV commentaries, the news items, the blogs. But short of going to a cave in the Himalayas, I couldn't avoid any of it. "What about realizing you love someone, even though that person isn't the gender you're familiar with? What were we supposed to do, Iris? Keep living a lie?"

"Of course," she said, laughing one of those harsh laughs. "People do it all the time. Especially people in our station of life. We should have fucked each other in private, never let on in public, and stayed with our husbands, who only fucked us on every other Wednesday."

We were living in the Beverly Hills hotel then, at the worst of the publicity scandal. We'd taken separate rooms but hardly ever stayed in them. We'd eat breakfast in thick white robes and read the newspaper that had been left at the door, hoping we weren't in it. Mornings were always a toss-up. Going on line was always risky.

"I'm starting to hate my I-Pad," Iris said. "But I have to go on it. And then I find me. And us. I'm not looking—I swear. But still I find us."

Iris escaped the brutal analysis of her family. She was born into wealth—a family remarkably similar to the one into which she married—and that gave her a certain amount of immunity.

Despite the fact that Iris had never in her life had to worry about money, I would still choose my family over hers, especially on the maternal side. Her mother has a shrill voice, hard as walnut shells. And when she's angry she sounds like she's auditioning for the Green Berets. In the early days of our scandal she left a voicemail that I heard before Iris.

"Well, you certainly did figure out how to humiliate us beyond all reason! I hope you're proud of yourself! You have no idea how to treat other people!" She then slammed down the phone. I swear she reminded me of Jack Nicholson in A Few Good Men.

"Your mother called!" I said sweetly to Iris, who was upstairs getting dressed. "Might want to listen to the message first before calling her back."

I was standing beside her when she phoned back and said calmly, "Got your message, Mother. How clever of you to have figured out this was all about you and ruining your life. I thought I'd been so subtle in my intentions. I did toy with the idea of prostitution and heroin addiction, but it's so unclean and heroin wreaks havoc with your teeth. So I settled on falling love with Isabelle instead."

"Your father and I are devastated. I just hope he doesn't end up in the hospital with a heart attack."

He didn't.

My mother, on the other hand, looped her arm through mine and said, "I always hoped you'd find someone who could take your breath away. I knew Thomas didn't."

Our families are always part of us. They're etched on our bones like scrimshaw. I grew up poor, just like my mother did. But the love she's given me is worth more than rubies.

If Iris and I had never become a scandal, few people would have cared about my background. Most wouldn't have looked past my incarnation as Mrs. Thomas Berendon. Privilege is a starting point, a reality unto itself. Generally speaking, people don't care what came before.

I was raised by a father who didn't know how to be one and a mother who tried stoically to fill in the emptiness left in his wake every time he walked out the door. I was a daughter with something to prove and a lot to hide. A girl determined to escape from her splintery neighborhood by the freeway, with its sagging chain link fences and postage-stamp lawns. I used to practice walking like the elegant women I saw on television. They glided into rooms, crossed their legs at a careful angle when they sat down on chintz sofas. When I was eight I made a necklace out of tightly rolled tin foil and pretended it was diamonds. I tied an old curtain around my waist to resemble a long evening skirt. My mother smiled at my efforts. My father said things like, "Have you snapped a twig in your head, girl? Got bats in the belfry or something? You're walking around in sandwich wrapping and a curtain!"

There is that old adage, Be careful what you wish for. Maybe I should have heeded it. Decades later, when I met Thomas Berendon, was it the young girl dreaming of another life who quickly melted under his charms or a woman who simply fell in love? I've asked myself that often lately.

It's a strange exercise wondering why you fell in love with someone long after you've fallen out of love with them. It's like looking into a funhouse mirror—you're never going to get a true reflection. But still I feel I owe it to myself, and to Marjorie, to try and understand why I loved Thomas, or if I ever did. Was it all just illusion? I can't truly see him as I did then—too much has changed. But I can squint back through time and study the memories.

Thomas seemed to fill up a room just by walking into it, often without saying a word. He had a smooth presence about him, a confidence that didn't need to shout or lean hard, it was just there. When he turned to listen to me, his eyes saw no one else. I didn't lie to him about my upbringing but I didn't tell him everything—not at first. I told him my father died from a heart attack while mowing the lawn. My father wouldn't have had a clue how to even start a lawn mower, much less use one. But the heart attack part was true.

Later, when Thomas and I were a confirmed couple, I told him the truth about my father and our sad little home. He pulled me against his shoulder and said, "I understand." I might have fallen in love with his shoulders. Muscular and strong from workouts with a private trainer and weekly tennis games, they seemed like they could hold up the world. Or at least my corner of it. I knew I was falling out of love with him when one day I looked at his shoulders after he'd gotten out of the shower and I felt nothing. No heat between my legs, no flutter of desire in my stomach.

Love is often just a matter of perception. I saw in Thomas a man so unlike my father, I could leave my upbringing in the dust of a road I never needed to walk down again. I could shed the small scrappy life my father had trapped us in—a life my mother tried to accept and pointlessly tried to dream beyond. I swore I'd be different. I would never stay up past midnight waiting for my husband's footsteps in the hall, the smell of Johnny Walker trailing him, ripe as sweat. Not for me the desperation of wondering how to pay for groceries because he lost another job. Or the sullen, hung-over mornings when his very presence felt dangerous.

I was thirty-three when I became Mrs. Thomas Berendon, and I felt like I was finally and completely free from Isabelle Haller, the girl with tape holding her shoes together and bus fare in her pocket. I had been granted membership into a new kingdom with a handsome prince at my side. It looked like a happy ending. It looked like love. But a year into my marriage I started to realize that Thomas was actually very much like my father. Both men were killers of dreams. I was Thomas' property, another acquisition. I wasn't supposed to take up too much space or have too many things to say. I wasn't supposed to look past the walls of the palace.

When Iris and I became the scandal of the month, I was written about as the former peasant, the one who grew up on the outskirts of West Los Angeles, with the freeway hovering nearby and old ladies in polyester house dresses watering sad little lawns.

"An unorthodox, lower-class upbringing," the papers said about my childhood, as if that explained something about falling in love with my sister-in-law. "Isabelle Berendon came from a bohemian mother and a father who lived outside the law."

While it is true that Frank Haller skirted the law and almost never purchased what he carried out of stores, he did choose things with his family in mind—socks for me, earrings for my mother, even food occasionally since he was aware that groceries were expensive. Once he pulled up behind a market while a truck was unloading dry goods; we ended up eating Rice A Roni for two weeks straight. He attempted to get real jobs, and sometimes he was actually hired. Predictably, the employers would realize their mistake within a month and he'd be fired.

Looking back on him now, I tend to see him through softer eyes. But growing up, I saw him as the con artist he was, the betrayer of my mother's trust. My bitterness toward him was a jigsaw puzzle and he made assembling it so easy, providing me with pieces that were always a perfect fit. He was never there, and even when he was, he wasn't really. He was the man in the shadows, drifting in and out of our house according to his own selfish timetable. Eventually, he became only a shadow.

We never knew what his story would be when he came home—a new job, a lost job, a haul of stolen goods. He generally filled his time with gambling, drinking, stealing and scheming. "Between jobs" was his usual description of his life. He would puff himself up when he said it too, as if it were a badge of honor. He had dark wavy hair that never appeared combed and his eyes matched the black coffee he poured into his favorite mug when he wandered in just after dawn. He was tall and wiry and in my dreams I still see the bones of his shoulders curved toward his knees when he thought no one was looking and he sat slumped in a kitchen chair. Those were the moments when I longed for him to fill in the outlines of a father. He never did. I have never missed my father, but all my life I've missed finding myself in my father's eyes.

Frank Haller could walk through the door with just about anything—a cut crystal flower vase, a gold bracelet, or a case of Ajax cleanser. One day he arrived home with a car—a bright yellow Volvo.

I had just turned fifteen and was getting ready to leave the house for school when he walked into the kitchen, slapped the pink slip and keys on the Formica table and announced he'd won a car in a card game. The kitchen smelled like coffee and French toast; he smelled like Scotch and cigarettes.

"A card game?" my mother asked, her voice taut as stretched wire.

"We got a car, Catherine. Don't ask a lot of damn questions," he said. "Jesus, a little gratitude, maybe? You're always complaining you have to take the bus…"

We were, up until that moment, a one-car family, the "car" being a rattletrap old pickup truck that never sounded as if it would start up. Since my father always used it for himself, my mother and I were left with public transportation.

He poured himself a mug of coffee and walked out of the kitchen, down the hall toward the bedroom. That was the one thing I could count on with my father—the sound of his footsteps in the hallway. He was always coming or going.

My mother was standing at the sink, sun shining through the window—bathing her—as if it could burn away the hours of a long empty night. "It seems legal," she said to me. "With the pink slip and all."

My beautiful, disillusioned mother, with her long dancer's legs and her long red hair—she's always made me think of wind and water. Everything about her seemed to flow and glide—through, grief, loss, even humiliation. I see her like that still, although she is slower now at sixty-three and her hair is streaked with gray. She still teaches a few dance classes at a Community Center—modern, interpretive dance— but she no longer demonstrates the movements. An old black and white photograph of Catherine Haller hangs in the hallway of the Center. She is in profile, in black tights and a sheer, pale long-sleeved top; her back is arched and her right leg is stretched out straight and high. Her arms are stretched up also—to the ceiling, the sky, the stars she would point to on clear nights. "There are pictures in the stars," she'd tell me. "Stories, too. Of gods and horses. Even chariots." My mother was always catching the scent of flowers in harsh city winds, always looking beyond the peeling paint of her life for artwork in the sky. She could make even the most ordinary events seem magical, but she was never able to transform the story of her own life.

I wished, when I was a child, that I would grow up to resemble my mother. Maybe my dark hair would lighten and my body would stretch out into the lithe, leggy shape that would make even passing strangers think, "Ah, a dancer." But it wasn't to be. My father's char- coal eyes stare back at me from mirrors, my hair is his also. And my legs betrayed me by several inches.

The morning after my father presented us with the yellow Volvo, my mother came into my room and woke me up. She had already applied mascara and lipstick. She smelled like patchouli oil and fresh laundry— a mixture of scents I will always think of as uniquely hers. Beneath her robe I saw the lace detail of the one silk camisole she owned.

"Isabelle," she said, "Get up and put on something nice. You and I are going to go shopping."

"For what?"

"Whatever we find." She was smiling as if she had just checked the calendar and discovered it was a holiday.

It was a Saturday in November—a crisp blue-sky morning with white, muscular clouds rolling along with the wind, colliding sometimes and blocking the sun.

"Your father went to work," she added, ironing out her voice as if this were a perfectly normal thing to say. As if we were a tidy, properly folded family.

"And which job would that be? Another card game or staking out a store that's expecting deliveries?"

"Don't be a smart-mouth, Isabelle. Your father tries to do his best. His friend Don got him a job at a moving company for a few days. They were short-handed."

"A moving company? As in moving people's possessions? Gosh, I wonder what he'll bring home from the job. Maybe he'll really score and nab a Picasso," I said as I climbed out of bed—unhappily, since it was a weekend and I wanted to sleep longer.

"Stop it, Isabelle. Now get dressed. I have breakfast on the table for you."

An hour later we were driving along Wilshire Boulevard toward Beverly Hills. My mother was wearing beige slacks and a black sweater; she looked sleek and elegant to me even though I knew she had bought the clothes at a discount store. I had unearthed a gray skirt in my closet and had chosen a white sweater that was long enough to cover some threadbare patches on the skirt. I opened the glove compartment, looking for signs of the car's previous owner. Nothing.

"Why are we going shopping?" I asked my mother. "We don't have money."

"I've saved a little from teaching. We have a new car, so I think it's important to celebrate—be a little extravagant. We won't go overboard, we'll just treat ourselves."

It was my first trip to Beverly Hills, and clearly I had entered another country. The sidewalks sparkled, the cars were expensive and meticulously polished, with the dignified colors preferred by rich people. Our yellow Volvo, bright as a sunflower, stood out like a tacky, tasteless relative come to visit. Slender women in clothes plucked from the pages of magazines walked leisurely past store windows. My mother didn't seem to care how out of place we were. She left our car with a uniformed parking attendant and we strolled out of the lot into a world where we didn't belong. Everything felt unfamiliar; even the sunlight along Rodeo Drive seemed silkier, more golden than it was in our neighborhood.

We walked into a linen shop where my mother looked at a display of sheet sets, soft as a cloud. They cost more than both the beds in our house.

"Oh my word," she said. "I never dreamed sheets could be so expensive. Feel this, Isabelle, the fabric is like heaven."

"Except a lot more expensive," I pointed out.

A saleswoman with polished gray hair and sedate gold jewelry came over to us. "May I help you?" she asked, and something in her tone alerted me to the fact that she already knew the answer.

"No, no. We were just taking a look at your beautiful things," my mother answered, moving then to a table of delicate, lace-trimmed pillowcases.

The woman followed us, her eyes sharp and watchful as a raven's. I looked at my mother's un-manicured hand caressing the scalloped edge of a dainty towel and I saw it through the woman's eyes. A hand that couldn't afford pampering, a rough, lower-class hand that could easily steal. But my mother was unaware of the choreography that was going on—our steps being mirrored by the steps of a woman who had earned her fashionable black pumps, her tasteful white silk shirt, her pearl earrings by punching a time card every morning. She catered to women a thousand times wealthier than she would ever be—women who could get every tell-tale wrinkle on their faces erased by plastic surgeons and who never had to glance at a price tag in any store. Women who didn't know what time cards were. She had learned to smile at them and scrutinize people like us. Underneath, she hated all of us.

When another customer came in, the woman left us…but not without whispering something to a younger salesgirl who then trained her eyes on us. I felt like saying, "Hey, wrong members of the family. My father's the thief, not us. And he isn't here."

But he was. He was always there. He had branded us, clothed us in his thievery—literally and figuratively. The lines got blurred over time. What had been bought? What had been stolen? Did my mother buy my boots for me or did my father present them to me? We lived off a thief's cunning ways; we wore the spoils of his own private war –the one he'd declared on a world that wouldn't let him in.

That day on those clean sidewalks, I knew my father would always be twisted in my shadow. He would follow me everywhere. You can't argue with shadows.

My mother led us into an air-conditioned shoe store that smelled of sanitized hides. A pair of suede boots with the texture of velvet cost nearly as much as one month's house payment. I had seen my mother write out checks to the bank on the first of every month. It was the one thing that made me suspect she didn't have as much faith in my father as she claimed. The house was hers—in her name only. She had bought it with the money she got when her father died.

"I had enough for a down payment," she explained to me once when I asked her point-blank who owned the house. "Your father and I were just engaged. It would have been inappropriate to invest in something like a house with my fiancé. And later…well, I just left things as they were."

I never asked about it again, because I knew it was my mother's way of protecting the two of us. Loving my father, forgiving him with an almost religious fever, didn't mean she was blind to his flaws. He could just as easily lose the house in a poker game as bring back a pile of cash from that same game. When it came to our future—hers and mine—my mother did not gamble.

We went into a small boutique with cashmere sweaters folded perfectly on round tables, scented candles filling the air with perfume. She turned and walked out without lingering at any of the tables.

The morning was getting hotter. I was sweating inside my white sweater and we had found nothing in any store that we could afford. Even a scarf was too costly. And the angle of people's eyes, especially store personnel, made it clear we were not welcome.

It seemed to me that my mother was growing smaller—whittled down by this crash course in elitism. Her graceful dancer's stride was shortening into a staccato trot. She clipped along the sidewalk, and I transformed my heartbreak into rage at my father. It would become the acrobatic pattern of my life.

"Mother, let's go home," I finally said.

"We should do something here," she told me. "Otherwise it's a wasted trip. Let's at least get something to eat."

We ended up eating in a coffee shop, incongruously located on a street with lavish salons and designer stores that opened only by appointment. I think we were the only two people in that eatery younger than sixty.

"Mother, look around," I whispered to her. "We've stumbled into the pasture where the elderly of Beverly Hills have been put out to graze."

"Oh, Isabelle, the way you talk," she said. But I could tell from the way her eyes swept across the tables that she agreed.

"We don't belong here," I continued. "And you know what? Who cares? It's stupid to spend thousands of dollars on bed sheets."

When our check came, my mother carefully counted out some bills from her wallet and then added a tip that was overly generous by anyone's standards.

I put my hand over the crisp ten dollar bill she was leaving for the bottle-blonde waitress. "That's too much," I whispered.

But she pushed my hand away with a force that surprised me. "That woman is like us," she said, her jaw set in a determined clench. "It's the least I can do after we came here and are leaving with nothing to show for it. This is my money and this is how much I want to give her."

"Okay," I answered, meekly giving in.

That night, she set three places at the dinner table and miraculously my father came home in time to join us. She said nothing about our trip to Beverly Hills, so I didn't either. I listened passively to my father grumble about rich people and how cheap they are with the people who work for them. This was apparently his justification for the sterling silver tray he brought home with him. He took payment into his own hands—literally. He was his own bastardized version of Robin Hood: steal from the rich and give to yourself.

3.

I'm sitting out on the deck of the home that still feels new to me. A cold afternoon wind is streaming off the ocean; it's pulled clouds in with it. I hear the deck door open and Marjorie runs over to me.

"Hi, Mommy," she says, draping herself across my lap.

"Hey, you. How was ballet class?"

"I can almost get up on my toes."

"Really? That's terrific!"

Friday is Marjorie's day for ballet class after school and Iris and I trade off picking her up so she can show off for each of us at different times. Today Marjorie is wearing pink tights that match her ballet slippers and a black stretchy top. Her long sandy-colored hair is pulled up into a ponytail and her eyes scan the sea. She comes back over to me and drapes herself across my lap. My arms reach for her, my hand strokes her back, her shoulders. My love for her reminds me of Nathan—the way a surge of emotion rises up from my belly into my throat. But now there are tears in there too, not just the rush of joy that I used to feel.

"Can I go out and play on the beach?" Marjorie asks me.

"Go change into something warm first."

She races back into the house and I hear Iris' footsteps crossing the hardwood floor of the living room. The day Thomas and I were married, Marjorie—in her frilly white flower-girl dress—said to me,

"Now I get to call you Mommy." When Nathan was almost two, he suddenly said Mommy. It's likely that he just imitated Marjorie, but it was a day I'll never forget. It stings me now sometimes, this word out of her innocent mouth. I hear the echo of my son's voice. She still calls Iris by the name she always has—Aunt Iris—and Aunt Iris is now bending over me, kissing me on the neck.

"Been sitting out here long?" she asks, smiling at me and crossing her arms against the push of cold wind.

"Yeah. Daydreaming I guess."

Iris nods, hesitates. "Marjorie asked me today if I think Nathan ever looks in on us. If he knows she's taking ballet and living at the beach. She said she tells him about things at night before she goes to sleep. I had the feeling she really wanted to be talking to you about this."

"She can," I tell her, momentarily distracted by the play of sunlight in her hair.

She crosses her arms against the chill. "Can she?"

Before I can respond, Marjorie runs past us in jeans and a green sweatshirt that's a size too big for her. She races down the steps of the deck onto the sand and runs toward the water's edge.

"Stay on the dry sand—the water's cold!" I call out.

"I will!" Her voice is a lilting childlike sound on the wind.

Iris goes inside and then comes back out wrapped in a woven shawl—blue, the shade of an early night sky. We sit beside each other and watch Marjorie running along the sand, picking up long strands of seaweed and trailing them behind her, trying to make them rise into the air like streamers. She stops sometimes and gazes out across the water—I know she's looking for dolphins. She will never go into the swimming pool at her father's house anymore, but she has no fear of the ocean. She'll cradle a starfish in her hands and gently carry it back into the surf so it won't dry up and die. She will watch, mesmerized, as pelicans dive for food. One day when we found a pelican wounded from fishing line wrapped around its neck, she sat beside it for an hour until the wildlife rescue people came. Iris has joked that she's going to grow up to be a marine biologist, which would be fine with me.

I used to worry about teaching Nathan that wealth doesn't define people. I wanted him to follow his desires, his passions, not just adopt a map drawn by heritage. I wanted him to pause at simple things— sunsets, cloudbanks. I wanted to instill in him an instinct to see past the trappings of his life as a Berendon, to look at other people with kind eyes, no matter how ragged they might be.

Marjorie was also born into a life of pampering and excess; she learned to crawl on Aubusson rugs and was pushed in the most expensive pram by a nanny hired to watch over her. The same promises I made to myself about Nathan I now make about her. But long before I even met Thomas, Iris was already training Marjorie's eyes to look past her glossy life.

Iris was the untamed princess in the Berendon kingdom; I saw that the first time we met.

I'd had only a few dates with Thomas when he invited me to a party in a Beverly Hills mansion—one of those gatherings you read about later in society columns, complete with photographs of smiling guests holding champagne flutes. It was so early in our relationship that I found Thomas' precision, his adherence to schedules, reassuring, even attractive. I arrived at his estate for the limousine ride to the party and then watched him get annoyed when Peter and Iris were more than ten minutes late.

He scowled as their car pulled up. This was my first glimpse of the woman who would become my sister-in-law and my friend... the woman who I would eventually fall in love with: a lean blonde woman in a sleeveless black cocktail dress and strappy sandals walking calmly across the flagstone driveway completely unaffected by her brother-in-law's obvious irritation.

"Iris didn't want to come," Peter said by way of explanation as we climbed into the limousine.

"These parties are a prolonged form of torture," she said, smiling at me and extending her hand. "I'm Iris. Isabelle, right?" Her voice, I noticed, was one of those fortunate velvety ones that could probably tame a grizzly.

"Yes. Nice to meet you," I told her, wondering what Thomas had said about me.

Trying to sound amused, but not quite succeeding, Thomas said to me, "Our Iris is a bit rebellious. She didn't even return from her honeymoon with Peter. Instead, she took off on her own to Peru to climb Machu Pichu."

Iris Berendon, one of those naturally beautiful women who need no embellishments, ran her fingers through her hair, looked out the window, and couldn't have cared less.

At the party, I felt alone and awkward. I saw myself as a fraud, an imposter. At that time, I was working for a wealthy man as his personal assistant and I had given myself a crash course in the accouterments of wealth. I decorated my employer's home, bought clothes for him at fashionable stores and I could name all the trendy designers of the moment.

But on this evening I had entered an exalted kingdom populated by people who were fluent in several languages, who summered in the Caribbean or the Hamptons, who traveled on private jets and bought yachts just because they were bored. There is no substitute for lineage and breeding; without it, one is always a mediocre student hoping to avoid getting called upon in class. I lingered by the buffet table, feeling more comfortable in the proximity of the hired help. It was Iris who rescued me.

She crossed the living room, brushing past women sleek as greyhounds, and put a hand on my wrist.

"How are you?" she asked me.

"Other than feeling hopelessly out of place?" I said. "I'm not sure. At the risk of being nosey, has this always been a normal part of your life?"

Iris laughed. "I might argue with the word normal. But yes, I grew up rich. Right from the Tiffany baby rattle to the BMW at graduation. I escape when I can, for purposes of sanity. I've traveled through India, I went to Egypt to see the pyramids, to Africa..." she lowered her voice to a whisper. "Without my husband and without a limo in sight."

She made me think of a smooth current, and I suspected that she would flow through life just as easily if she were poor.

"I'll tell you a secret," Iris continued. "Everyone here feels at least a little out of place. They've just had years of training in concealing their insecurities." She tilted her head toward a raven-haired woman in a pale green pants suit. "See that woman? It's pretty widely known that her husband beats the shit out of her—usually on her legs and torso so the wounds don't show. She always wears pants and long-sleeved tops and she'll probably never leave him because he's beaten out every bit of self-confidence she ever had. And that guy over there? Who looks like he could be on a billboard for fitness equipment? He has AIDS. He probably won't make it to this party next year. Everyone has stories written under their skin, Isabelle. Don't let their skin fool you."

A man with a leathery tan, hair dyed a coppery color and heavy-lidded blue eyes interrupted us. "Iris, darling. How are you?" He kissed her cheek and then brushed off the spot with his thumb, like a woman does who has left a smudge of lipstick. God, maybe he left a smudge of tan on her, I thought.

"Gaston, this is Isabelle," Iris said.

He gave me a scrutinizing look, apparently to determine if I was worthy of anything more than a perfunctory greeting. Deciding I was not he said, "Hello," in a curt tone and then wheeled around, his back firmly facing me, to address only Iris.

"We're going to take the yacht to Mexico this summer. Maybe you and Peter could go with us."

"Probably not," Iris said, backing up from him, moving toward me and slipping her arm through mine. "Peter vomits on boats."

Gaston scrunched up his face. "Oh my," he mumbled. "Well, anyway...I'm waiting for my other half to arrive. She said she'd be here at six, but you know how Denise is with time. Enjoy yourself." With that, he swirled away into the living room and was folded into another group of people.

"Is that true?" I asked her. "About Peter?"

"No," she said, smiling mischievously. "I just like to tarnish his image sometimes. In small ways. Nothing that would alert the Feds or anything. So, you want to know Gaston's story?"

"Sure." I was finally starting to relax and enjoy myself.

"His 'other half' as he so fondly referred to her, had her stomach stapled so she could lose weight for him and hopefully stop him from screwing every twenty-something chick within a five mile radius. It didn't work"

"The surgery or the marital outcome?"

"Both. His wife throws up all the time—some kind of unexpected side effect—and he still can't keep his dick in his pants."

I suddenly felt more at ease in that gathering. It was just a lot of people with things to hide. I could relate to that.

We should always pay attention to the people who rescue us. They usually know their way across the sea better than we do. They are better navigators and have a better ear for small craft warnings.

I've remembered that party because Marjorie will someday slip on a cocktail dress and walk across one of those marble foyers into a grand house with guests air-kissing while glancing over shoulders for someone more exciting. I hope she doesn't take any of it seriously.

Right now, she's happily playing on the beach, sweeping her arms through the air and dancing away from the shallow, white-foam waves. Iris and I walk out to the sand to try and convince her it's time to come inside and she runs toward us, her cheeks red from the cold and her hair full of wind. So far, she isn't stained or molded by privilege. She has a good chance of living a life her heart can be proud of. A life like Iris'—born to wealth but wide open to life.

4.

The last time I saw my father he was handcuffed and getting into a police car. I was seventeen and had just come back from a date with Chet Rubin. Chet had gotten a Volkswagon for his eighteenth birthday but he hadn't yet mastered every aspect of driving it. The car lurched into a parking space near my house, front wheels bumping the curb.

"Why are those cops outside your house?" he asked.

I stared at the blinking red and blue lights from three police cars and noticed a fairly new white Ford pickup parked directly in front of our house. I still felt the warm print of Chet's hand on my breast and I tugged my bra down even though it was already in place.

"Probably just a misunderstanding," I said, knowing I would be proven wrong. One cop was opening the driver's side door of the truck and peering inside. The other cops were going to the front door of our house. Moments later, illuminated by the lights of the police cruisers, my father was led down the walk in handcuffs.

"Oh my God! Did he steal that truck?" Chet asked.

"I don't know," I muttered. My voice was a small splinter in my throat.

"Pretty dumb place to leave it," Chet said and laughed—a self-conscious, awkward laugh.

I did the only thing that seemed appropriate. I slapped him hard across the face, got out of his car and slammed the door so hard I

24

was hoping I'd jarred something loose. I resolved to not speak to him again—ever—even if we brushed past each other in the school hallways. And I kept my promise.

I never saw if my father ducked when he got into the back seat of the squad car or if one of the cops put a hand on his head the way they usually do so he wouldn't bash himself on the hard metal frame. I never turned around, never met his eyes. I of course didn't know it at the time, but I would never see him again. I walked toward my mother standing in the doorway, framed by warm yellow lamplight from the living room. Her shoulders were straight and her chin was tilted slightly up, as if pride were a dress that she could keep in place with her defiant posture.

She put a heavy arm around my shoulders as the police took her husband away. Her eyes fought hard against tears. "He'll be home soon," she said to me. It almost seemed like she believed it.

But this wasn't my father's first offense and the court had no mercy on a fool who would leave his beaten up truck in a Walgreen's parking lot, hotwire a newer one and brazenly drive it home. He was given a five-to-seven year prison sentence.

Less than a year after my father was sent away, my mother and I stopped talking about when he would come home. We stopped thinking of our family as having three members in it and began our new life as a family of two.

Then on a sunny fall day, we learned we would always be a family of two. My father was never going to come home again.

It was late September and Santa Ana winds scraped the sky; the air smelled like dust. The heat seemed to have weight and everywhere you went, tempers were short. There were more sirens, more sounds of screeching tires, angry voices…nothing to look forward to except an easing up of the winds and the occasional lovely sunset, which was really just the sun sinking into the smog.

I was a senior in high school, newly turned eighteen, and I had gone to get a cup of coffee with a few classmates after school that afternoon. I took a later bus home than usual and as I walked from the bus stop to my house I saw that the chain link fence bordering our property had been strung with black fabric. I recognized it as Halloween decorations from years before. Over the front door was a large black bow, fashioned from a witch's costume my mother had made for me a decade earlier when I still went trick-or-treating.

My first thought was that my poor mother, sad and lonely in my father's absence, had lost her mind. It was seven weeks until Halloween and she wasn't the type to get an early start on anything.

"Hello, dear. Home from school?" our next door neighbor, Mrs. Middlington, called out in her sing-song voice as she often did whenever she spotted any of her neighbors. She was kneeling beside her front door, pulling weeds out of her narrow flower bed. She maneuvered herself to her feet, which took several minutes.

"How are you, Mrs. Middlington?" I said, elevating the volume of my voice so I wouldn't have to repeat the question, although that rarely proved effective.

"What?" she said, cupping her hand to her ear.

"I said how are you?" I repeated, at an even louder volume.

She was now at the fence that separated our two lots. "Oh, fine, fine. I must get one of those gardening benches. My fifty-seven year old knees just creak and complain something awful." Mrs. Middlington was, in fact, in her late sixties, but no one ever let on they knew her true age. "Listen, dear—I think something happened to your father."

"What do you mean?" If he had been released from prison and was coming home, black ribbons hardly seemed appropriate.

"I'm not exactly sure, but your mother was crying earlier and she apologized to me for the smell of burning sage. She said it was an important ceremony."

That's when I knew. I thanked Mrs. Middlington and ran into the house.

The sage gave it away. My mother believed in purifying the air and placating the spirits whenever anything somber occurred. I was five when our cat Nimby died and my mother burned sage for two days, certain that the ritual would ensure Nimby's reincarnation as a figure of royalty in some peace-loving, neutral country. "I dreamed about her in the Swiss Alps," she said one morning over Cornflakes, ignoring my father's eye-roll and the disdainful shake of his head.

When I walked into the house I could barely see at first through the smoke of burning sage. Squinting, I saw found my mother in the living room arranging an altar of sorts—photographs of my father, candles, a bracelet and earrings that he had once stolen for her.

"Mother…"

She came over to me and slipped her arms around me. "Oh, Isabelle. This is a sad day. I should have known this morning that something awful was going to happen. There were three black crows on the lawn."

She smelled of patchouli oil, which was her usual scent, but she seemed to have doused herself with it. I detected another more subtle scent, though—something emanating from her blood, her spirit. It was sorrow—deep, unreachable sorrow that grows in the dark and sends out roots to claim everything around it.

"Your father left early this afternoon," she told me, her eyes shiny with tears, red along the rims.

For a second, I wondered if maybe I'd been wrong in my assumption. "Wait—left the world or left prison?" I asked.

"The world. Well, the prison, too, strictly speaking. He's gone, sweetheart. His heart just gave out. It didn't want to go on. I got the call a few hours ago. They're going to send his ashes."

"Send them? Through the mail?" I envisioned a package arriving with postage due—a pouch of ashes. This couldn't possibly be the standard procedure of delivering a loved one's remains.

"Well, you know what I mean," she said.

"No. I don't."

"Isabelle, your father and I both requested cremation." She said this as if it were something we had discussed, which we hadn't. "The prison is going to take care of it and I expect they'll send someone with the ashes."

"But what will they be in? The ashes, I mean."

There are passages in life when time seems to spin out in crazy patterns. This was one of them. My questions were irritating my mother and were probably irrelevant at the moment, but they were all I had to hold onto. I curled my toes inside my shoes. It felt like I'd been standing there for a long time, although it must have been only ten minutes or so.

"An urn, I expect," my mother told me. "Or a box. I really don't know, Isabelle." Something vague and frightened passed across her face. "I guess I thought they would have sent him home—whole, you know. His body. So I could take care of it. Maybe he filled out some kind of request in prison for what should happen if he dies there... maybe he wanted to make it easier on me."

"Yeah. Maybe." I didn't believe that last part for a second. When had my father ever made anything easy on us?

As the sun moved across the sky and set in an ocean we couldn't see from our freeway-shaded neighborhood, my mother began lighting candles. Everywhere. Outside the sky was a rusty orange and the Santa Ana winds rattled the loose window screens, rumbled against our front door. Inside our small house, candlelight flickered across the cottage cheese ceiling, duplicated itself in the window glass.

My mother opened a bottle of red wine, set it on the altar, and got out the only two good wine goblets she owned.

"These glasses were your father's anniversary present to me one year," she said. "I can't recall which year."

Neither could I, but I was sure he hadn't paid for them.

She put them down carefully on the altar and motioned me over. The smoke from the burning sage was getting thicker; I was concerned we'd both run out of oxygen.

"Mother, I think we should open some windows."

"But what about the candles? The wind will come in."

"Yes, but the smoke will go out," I explained. "I can't breathe."

She relented and opened several windows half way. The candles stayed lit, although they danced wildly. She pulled up two pillows for us to sit on and we took our places in front of the altar. I knew the ceremony; we'd done the same for Nimby, except for that one we'd used milk instead of liquor. As wind curled around us, my mother poured wine into our goblets, said a prayer to the spirit of our departed loved one and then asked for a moment of silence.

But something else was different about this ceremony—not just the addition of wine. This was not for a large, cinder-gray cat who had lived a long, relaxed life with few worries and regular afternoon naps. This was my father—her husband—who died of a heart attack in a cement and steel prison, as alone as anyone can be.

I listened to my mother blame herself for all that she believed she had done wrong in her marriage, and I said nothing. I thought there was only one thing she'd done wrong, and that was marrying my father in the first place. I watched as tears filled her eyes and traveled down her face. My eyes stayed dry.

Later, when the bundles of sage had burned themselves out and the candles were sputtering, when we had finished the bottle of wine and were both a bit tipsy, my mother said, "Someday when you fall in love with a man, don't ever forget that a man's pride is everything to him. It's a woman's responsibility to nurture his pride. It's more fragile than you realize. Promise me you won't make the same mistakes I made."

"Okay," I assured her. But I made another promise to myself. I pledged to never marry a thief and a liar.

I went to bed that night—finally—with the wind screaming outside. I wish I could say I wept for my father; I wish I could say that grief slipped into my veins like an injection and flowed through my bloodstream. But I can't. I didn't know how to mourn my father's passing. He'd drifted through my life the same way he'd drifted through the rooms of our house. He was a constant adventure, always bringing home unexpected things, always hatching up schemes and plans to make money, and always failing. I can't remember his eyes ever lingering on me for more than a few minutes. He was the man in the hallway; he was a shape in the kitchen, gulping down coffee in the morning. He was the empty chair at the dinner table most nights of the week, or the sound of the front door opening long after midnight followed by footsteps on the floor. He was sounds and glimpses—pieces of a man. Who should I cry for? That was the question haunting me as wind swept the darkness and kept me awake. I finally squeezed out some tears, but I think they were for my mother, for a life that should have been better.

It was just before two in the morning and Id obviously dozed off because I woke from something—sleep, a dream, I'm not sure—to hear my mother talking softly out in the living room. I crept out of my bedroom and went down the hall. I found her sitting on the couch with only two candles left burning. One of the windows—one that didn't have a screen—was wide open, and a white pigeon was sitting near her, perched on the back of the arm chair.

"Mother," I whispered. "What are you doing? There's a bird in here."

"I know, dear. Your father and I are talking. Go back to bed. It's all right."

The pigeon blinked his eyes at me and seemed not at all startled by the intrusion of another human being.

"My father?" I asked.

"Uh-huh. He flew in through the window when I opened it. Just like he'd been waiting out there. I'll see you in the morning, Isabelle."

There was nothing for me to do but go back to bed and leave my mother to her dialogue with the bird who she believed was my father. We never spoke about it after that, but the next morning she seemed content, not as torn apart by sadness as she'd been the night before. It's often better to allow people their beliefs, their fantasies, no matter how outlandish they might seem.

I knew that morning that I had woken up much older than the barely-eighteen year old girl I'd been the day before. In the shifting of life and death, in the soft ministrations of that windy night, in the chaos of candlelight and burning sage, I had become my mother's mother. Feeling protective of her, I was now even angrier at my father for dying. He'd abandoned us, left us alone and vulnerable in a world that always seemed too big for us. My mother, with her daydreams and her strange notions, would keep trying to weave a life for herself that made sense. But loneliness would snip off every thread.

I remember looking at her face during the brief memorial service for my father two weeks later. Her eyes were downcast and heavy—in part, I suspect, because only two other people showed up—neighbors who probably took pity on us. We put the urn of ashes in a drawer on a cement wall and my mother touched it gently with her hand. I saw in the soft surrender of her mouth the death of every dream she had held onto and it broke my heart.

A few months after my father died, I invited a girl from school to sleep over at my house. Other girls at school did such things, and I wanted to fit in. Her name was Emily and for much of the evening, things were uneventful and normal. We tried on clothes, assembled outfits, painted our toenails and watched reruns of old TV shows. But late in the night, when the house was dark, the sound of my mother's voice humming a slow melody trailed through the rooms and woke us.

"What's that?" Emily asked.

"Nothing. Go back to sleep," I told her. "My mother's just singing. She has insomnia."

But Emily got up, tip-toed into the living room, and found my mother in a white nightgown standing in front of the open window. Her face was tilted to the half moon and she was humming a melody. Something was in her hands and I came up behind Emily just as my mother reached toward the windowsill and deposited whatever she had been clutching. The silver of the moon and the blue-white glow from the streetlights shone through her nightgown; her lithe dancer's body twisted as she sensed us behind her and turned to face us.

"Mother, what are you doing?" I said. I didn't want Emily to ask.

"I'm putting lavender on the windowsill so your father will fly back in. It was a half moon when he came before."

The next day at school, Emily and a cluster of girls were laughing as I passed them in the hall. I knew it was about me. "Does your mother do witchcraft and cast spells, too?" one of them said to my back as I walked away quickly, stiffening my spine into a shield against them. I blamed my father. Who else could I blame? Certainly not my mother, floating inside sheer white fabric, leaving lavender on the windowsill, believing her husband would return on wings.

I knew that in the dark rivers of night, his hands must have fallen soft and fluid on her skin. But all I could see was the memory of his hand reaching into the collection plate at church, the few times we went, and taking money out.

I knew my father's back—its outlines, its own particular curve. I knew it because he was usually leaving. When did he start leaving my mother? I know it happened—in small, steady ways. I know it because I found her one night when I was a child, sleeping in a pool of moonlight all alone.

I was about eight, I think. I woke up and the stiff, breathless silence in the house told me my father wasn't home. I crept out of my bedroom and found my mother in the living room, stretched out on the rug. The light from a full moon was pouring through the window and it looked like she was floating in a silvery river.

"Hi," I whispered. I was afraid the scrape of my voice would disturb the moonlight, or her place within it.

"I'm bathing my bones," she said, opening her eyes and smiling at me. "The moonlight is very healing. It's magic. It seeps into your bones and keeps them white and clean. Just like the moon itself."

"So you'll have moonbones?"

She laughed. Her hand reached through silver for mine and I eagerly grasped her fingers.

"Yes, my darling, you're so smart," she said. "Bathing in the moonlight will give you moonbones. Lie here with me so we'll both live forever."

I did. I bent against my mother in that white pool on the floor of a house that could barely recognize the sound of my father's footsteps. And I did believe we would live forever.

5.

Fog, light as smoke, rests on the water. I'm the only one awake as a milky sun lifts itself into the sky. It's Saturday and neither Iris nor Marjorie will stir for a while. Sometimes dawn is my enemy, and this is one of those times. I woke up from dreams I don't quite remember, but they've left me knotted up with sadness. I'm trying to undo the knots—tip-toeing through the house barefoot, making coffee, hoping daylight will push back the remains of the night. I carry a steaming mug of coffee into the living room so I can nestle in the armchair by the window and watch the ocean.

Something out at sea catches my eye and I realize there are probably a dozen or more dolphins out there. Graceful arches in the gray-blue water, they leap above the surface and then knife smoothly down through the currents. If I were out there drowning they are the ones who would come save me—there are many stories about that. If Nathan had wandered into the ocean instead of into an architect-designed swimming pool, he might still be alive. Did he call out for me? Or did his lungs fill with water before he could say anything? Did his eyes look around, wild and terrified, at the pale drift of emptiness around him—no one coming for him, no one realizing he wasn't safe in the house with his toys? I try to remember my hand pulling open the screen door sometime that morning—a neglectful hand that failed to snap the lock down when closing it again. I can't dredge up the memory of the aluminum handle against my skin, but I must have done that—my palm feels crossed with the scar.

I hear Marjorie's light steps coming down the stairs and across the floor. I know she's gone into the kitchen; I leave the dolphins and my tortured questions to go find her.

She's tugged open the refrigerator and is pulling a plastic bottle of orange juice from the shelf in the door. She's in her white pajamas with small ducks along the seams and I suddenly wonder how long it will be before she decides they're too childish for her.

"Let me get a glass for you," I tell her, kissing the top of her head.

"Aunt Iris is still asleep."

"I know."

I also know what's coming next, as Marjorie pulls a chair out and sits at the round breakfast table, stretching her arms across the oak surface and twisting her head around to look at me.

"Do I have to go to Daddy's house today?"

I put two glasses of orange juice on the table and sit in the chair beside her. "Marjorie, we go through this every Saturday. You know that's the day your father gets to be with you. Why do we always have to have this conversation?"

"Because I don't want to go. He doesn't know what to do with me. Sometimes he just rents some videos and leaves me there with the housekeeper."

I slide my chair closer and put my arms around her. "I know, sweetie. But I can't order him around as far as what to do when you're there. It's his day with you—it's the one day he asked for. He's doing the best he can. Hey, you know what? I saw dolphins out in the water—why don't you go into the living room and watch them while I fix some breakfast."

When Iris comes downstairs I'm alone in the kitchen stirring oatmeal. Part of me is far away in another kitchen, another time, with a father who didn't know what to do with me either.

"Where's Marjorie?" she asks me, kissing my shoulder as she heads for the coffee-maker. She smells like sleep and toothpaste.

"Watching the dolphins. She doesn't want to go to Thomas' today."

Iris shakes her head. "Every Saturday…"

"I know. There really isn't anything I can do about it. Except listen to her and then tell her she has to go anyway."

"I wonder why Thomas even insists on these visits," Iris says, sitting at the kitchen table and cradling the coffee mug in her hands.

"Image. It wouldn't look good if word got out that he doesn't make an effort to see his daughter."

Iris and I have an easy familiarity with raising Marjorie; we've essentially parented her together ever since I married Thomas. We were the ones who joined other parents at children's birthday parties, who took Marjorie and a few of her friends to Disneyland. We helped her with crafts projects for school and shopped with her for clothes and toys.

With Nathan, too, Iris was the one by my side after he was born—not Thomas. He and Peter left for New York on a business trip two days after Nathan's birth. Iris was at the house every day helping me and keeping Marjorie company so I could grab some sleep whenever Nathan quieted down and dozed off. It was she who took charge when Nathan refused to take my nipple and nurse, arranging for someone from the hospital to come and literally train my baby to do what I thought was supposed to come naturally.

"Should I take it personally that he doesn't want my breast?" I asked the woman who was patiently coaxing his mouth toward me.

"Oh no," she answered sweetly. "This is more common than you know."

"He's probably going to grow up to be a butt man, though," Iris quipped.

I think it was the first time I'd laughed since giving birth.

Marjorie comes into the kitchen for her breakfast and sidles up to Iris. "Does my forehead feel hot?" she asks.

Playing along, Iris puts a hand on Marjorie's forehead, then feels her cheeks. "Nope. You're fine. That was a nice try, though. Tell you what, if you come down with malaria while you're at your dad's, you can cut the day short."

"What's malaria?"

"Something you're not going to get," I tell her.

Saturdays also belong to Iris and me; we can be alone as the new lovers we still are. I drive Marjorie into Brentwood in the morning and then return to a day with just the two of us in it. Sometimes we take long walks on the beach; other times we never leave the house, tumbling back into bed or sprawling on the couch for hours. We don't have to worry about Marjorie coming in; doors can stay ajar and our voices can carry through the house with no one else to hear them.

Love-making is a singular event, but if love is truly part of it, it's much more than that. It alters the landscape, spreads itself out across boundaries and time. Nothing feels the same anymore.

As two women making love, Iris and I are citizens of a new country, yet strangely it's as if we've come home. We laugh about it sometimes, rising from the tangle of our bodies, our faces flushed and damp with each other's scents. Neither of us knew how to do this—make love with another woman—but some kind of knowing took over...takes over...every time.

Early on, I felt I could never get naked enough with Iris. There are many versions of nakedness. Emotional, psychological, spiritual...skin is only one of them. But skin is an important one, not to be discounted or trivialized.

So with that in mind, I walked into a beauty salon one afternoon and asked for a Brazilian bikini wax, although I asked for slightly modified version. How much more naked can you get than that? At least on the skin-deep level. You're being turned nubile again, smooth and silky as a newcomer. Which I was, so the whole thing made sense. The slender Korean woman who proceeded to remove almost all the hair from between my legs, except a thin strip in the front, was professional and remarkably detached given the gyneco-logical nature of her task. My awkwardness about the whole thing—legs up in the air, her hands between my legs stripping me bare—at least provided a distraction from the pain.

I said nothing to Iris; I simply let her discover my new nakedness the next time we were together. It's my commitment to you, Iris—that's how I saw it—I want to be bare and new for you. We were still at a nervous, scary juncture—we had declared our love for each other and we were trying to stand brave against the onslaught. But the cost was high for everyone, the complexities enormous. The outside world was leaning in hard. We were being judged, punished, ridiculed by some, gossiped about by everyone. We were, after all, sisters-in-law and while not celebrities, we were well-known because of our husbands. Still, when we were alone together, we were happy and playful as colts.

On the day of the unveiling, I said nothing as we stripped off our clothes. I just let her discover what I'd done. I saw the look in her eyes, but she didn't say anything either.

Iris moved across my new silky bare skin, tender enough to absorb every stroke of her fingers, every impression of her tongue. My nerve endings tingled wildly. When we were finished—flushed and coated with sweat—she backed up, kneeled above me and looked at the narrow rectangle of hair between my legs—all that remained of what I used to have.

"I like it," she said, smiling at me. "I only have one reservation. Visually? From the front? It makes me think of Hitler."

I looked down and immediately saw what she meant—that distinctive strip of dark hair. Laughter sent us back into the twisted, undone sheets and into each other.

Days later, Iris decided we should be equally naked. Apparently she had resolved the visual problem. Skin to skin—there is a lot to be said for that.

A few weeks ago on a Saturday afternoon we were walking along the beach at low tide, a crisp breeze flapping around us.

"If you had to come up with a definition of love, what would it be?" Iris asked me.

"Is this a trick question?"

"No. I'm serious," she said. "How would you describe love?"

I looked past her to a flock of pelicans flying low over the water in the shape of a perfect V. One pelican broke off from the others and plunged into the water after a fish. Another followed. Then another.

"That," I told her, pointing at the birds. "Plunging in, following your flying mate."

Iris looked at them, smiled, and slipped her arm around my waist. "I like that. I can't compete. So I'm going to steal your definition."

"Okay. As long as I get properly credited."

My mother once said to me, "Love is like a pomegranate."

I was eleven or twelve, I think—not terribly interested in love and not too familiar with pomegranates.

"A what?" I asked her.

"A pomegranate, dear. You know, the fruit that's hard on the outside and has all those little seeds inside that burst in your mouth when you eat them?"

I nodded, wondering where this was going.

"Love is like that. Sometimes it looks plain and leathery on the outside, but if you're patient and you open it up—if you taste each seed and let the taste linger on your tongue, you get the sweetness."

We all have our own definitions. I like mine better. I think love is plunging down through the water's slick surface—down into depths where sunlight might never reach, where the push of unseen currents is in control and survival depends on trust.

There are different kinds of drowning.

I learned that several weeks after Nathan died. There was a moment when I leaned toward Iris ever so slightly, fell off the path and into the deep. Water closed over my head. Afraid, I tried to fight. Then I realized how easily I could float...and breathe. Way down beneath the surface is where life is.

6.

Maybe the future is always folded like tight petals inside the present. Especially in relationships. Maybe Thomas and I were steadily leaving each other even when it seemed like we were building a life together. Maybe Iris and I were melting into each other long before we knew it.

I do think about a starting point in loving Iris, but even as I do, I'm aware that it felt like a continuation—an intimacy that changed form. She knew my body long before she "knew" it in the Biblical sense. She stood beside me as I studied my naked self in a full-length mirror a week after giving birth to Nathan.

"Oh my God," I moaned, lifting up the loose skin across my abdomen. "I'm a Bloodhound."

Iris laughed and then felt bad about laughing. "I'm sorry," she said. "I know how you feel now, but -"

"No, you don't," I interrupted. "You've never had a baby."

"Okay. True. But I can imagine how you feel. It's only been a week, though, Isabelle. You'll see—your body will rearrange itself."

She was right. My body did. But is that what the two of us were doing all that time? Rearranging ourselves?

Still, I do think of us as having a beginning.

A couple of weeks after Nathan died, on a brutally sleepless night, I left the bed I shared with Thomas and crept down the hallway in our too-quiet house. I went into a room that should have had a child in it. But there were only cruel reminders—fluffy animal toys, plastic wind-up tractors and cars, clothes he would have outgrown in another month. It's impossible to be careless with what's left behind after someone dies. We might horde their things, lie down with them and breathe them in, or we might turn into slightly crazed soldiers and scoop everything into piles because to keep anything around is to turn the knife once again and shed more blood than we already have.

I pulled clothes from the closet, raked others out of drawers, I shoved toys into pillow cases. I was frantic, desperate to staunch the flow of pain. At some point I collapsed, unable to hold myself up. The center of me folded in on itself.

Thomas found me at dawn, lying on the narrow bed in what had once been our son's room, inhaling Nathan's scent from the blanket and pillow. My husband, who had barely spoken to me since the day our son died, stood over me, suffocating me with his shadow and his silence. He was wearing the maroon silk robe I'd given him that past Christmas. I don't know if I wanted him to touch me, to sit down beside me, or simply to cry with me…we were such strangers to each other by then, it was hard to know what I wanted. I'd been trapped in a cave for weeks—that's how it felt—painting messages on stone so someone someday would know I'd been there.

"What are you going to do with his things?" he asked me finally, his voice flat and hard as sheet rock.

I had no idea. I just couldn't leave them there, in a room that no longer had Nathan in it. In a house where I still thought I heard his footsteps.

Thomas walked out and left me there, with my child's things all packed up and my sorrow flapping around like bats trapped on the wrong side of night.

I walked downstairs and called Iris, clenching back tears and asking where I should take Nathan's clothes and toys. They still smelled like him. I didn't know who else to call.

"Let's take them to the battered women's shelter," she said. "There are a lot of kids there. Women come with babies, toddlers. Nathan's things will be going to children who have nothing and who can really use something to make them happy. It'll be a good legacy for Nathan, don't you think?" She was right. I could imagine a child's face breaking into a smile at the expensive toys and clever games that parents in my world take for granted.

A month earlier, Iris had started doing volunteer work at a somber, hard place miles from the luxury of her life. A place women flee to from homes that held them hostage, clutching shredded clothes and shredded dreams. Often they come with children who have known nothing beyond late-night screams and bruised mornings.

Ah, but they leave with much more, Iris has said. They leave with terror crawling up their backs, drilling into their bones. They leave with welts on their flesh and the taste of blood in their mouths. They leave with old scars and new wounds, with missing teeth and missing years. They leave with a wall in front of them, because any idea of a future slams them right back into the past.

"They leave with futility," she said. "Not a good foundation for anything. It's our job to try and give them hope about all the tomorrows ahead of them."

Later that afternoon, Iris came to get me. It was a flat overcast day, no breeze stirring beneath a tarnished-silver sky.

"I already loaded the stuff into my car," I told her. "It was too hard to keep looking at everything."

We got into my Jaguar and Iris gave me directions that included shortcuts along residential streets so similar to the neighborhood I grew up in, I felt caught between two worlds. We were the conspicuous Jaguar cruising past small stucco houses with Hondas and dented pick-ups parked in front. We were the car I once would have scowled at, standing by my chain link fence in a polyester shirt and cheap jeans, grinding my Pay-Less shoes into the dirt. Rich bitches, I'd have mumbled.

Now I was the one behind the wheel of a luxury car, with my beautiful blond sister-in-law beside me—two wealthy women with famous last names, one of them drowning in grief. But no one would know any of that by watching us drive by. We just looked like two women who'd strayed into the wrong end of town.

"I've started going out on some domestic violence calls with the cops," Iris told me. "They sometimes need one of us from the shelter to convince a woman to leave."

Up until then she had been answering phone calls, often from women sobbing through broken teeth, standing at pay phones with terrified children clinging to them. I suddenly felt frightened for Iris.

"Are you sure you should be doing that?" I asked her. "I mean, what if the husband or boyfriend is armed?"

"We don't go in initially with the cops. The place is secured before we even get out of the car. I'm not saying there isn't any danger, there probably is…but someone has to help these women. You know what? At the end of my life, I'd like to think I did something worthwhile and didn't just spend my days getting pedicures and shopping."

"Amen."

She made sure we weren't at the shelter long, knowing that the haunted eyes of women and children beaten by fists, baseball bats, and lives that had turned out wrong would shred the composure I was trying to maintain. We unloaded my car and left boxes of clothes, pillowcases stuffed with toys, at the front desk with a dark-eyed woman named Maria who was probably younger than she looked.

Schools were letting out by the time we got back into the car to head home. I angled my eyes away from children boarding yellow buses, the lines of cars outside—parents picking up their sons and daughters. Marjorie was in a car pool, but my one day a week as the driver of four six year olds had been suspended following Nathan's death. 'So you can have time to cope with your loss' is what one of the other mothers said…as if that were a possibility.

"Will Thomas be home when we get back?" Iris asked, after we had been quiet for what seemed like a long time.

"Probably not. Why?"

"I just didn't want you to be alone," she said.

I laughed—one of those rough, threadbare sounds that isn't a laugh at all. "Alone is what I've been since the moment I found Nathan, Iris."

We had just gotten to the intersection of San Vicente Boulevard and Bundy, and had just passed another school. I was moving into the right turn lane for our climb into the hills north of Sunset, when a black BMW cut in front of me, tried to make the right turn even though the pedestrian crossing light was on. The idiot had to slam on the brakes to narrowly avoid hitting a boy on a bicycle. The kid gave the driver his middle finger and continued on his way. I was not as gracious.

I jammed the gear shift into park, got out of the car and ran up to the BMW.

"You mother-fucker!" I shrieked.

The driver's side window was down. I was face to face with a sandy-haired man in the vicinity of forty who smelled of cigarettes and had one of those spray-on tans.

"Jesus, lady—what's your problem?" he said.

"You're my problem, you arrogant stupid fuck! You almost hit that boy! What the hell's the matter with you? You're in such a god-damn hurry you're going to kill a child?"

Horns were honking at us. I was holding up a long line of cars. Iris came up behind me, grabbed me by the shoulders and wheeled me around to face her.

"Isabelle, come back to the car. Get in the passenger side. I'm going to drive."

I let her lead me back. The man in the BMW got in a parting shot. He leaned his head out of the window and yelled, "Fuck you, too!"

A woman behind my Jaguar leaned her head out. "Fuck both of you!" she screamed. "Move it!"

Iris was completely calm. "Put on your seat belt," she said when we got into the car with her behind the wheel.

I did as she said but I was still furious. "That asshole could have killed that boy! And he didn't even care! Mother-fucker! I hope he drives into a tree! Except I don't want him to hurt the tree."

Iris was just driving along, watching the road, waiting for me to wind down. The thing about losing control around someone who remains calm is, there does come a moment when you feel completely foolish. I shifted in my seat, looked through the window, and waited for her to say something.

Finally she said, "The guy was definitely a jerk. But I don't think that was the best way to handle it. Besides, your upset isn't really about Mr. BMW, is it?"

She pulled over, two streets away from where I lived, in front of a modest house—at least by Brentwood standards. She undid her seatbelt and twisted around to face me. I felt trapped in the belt so I undid mine as well.

"Isabelle, you're going through the worst thing anyone can experience and you're pretty much going through it alone. No one should have to do that. I watched Thomas do this same thing when Allison died—he just cut himself off from his own emotions, from other people's emotions… Marjorie was left alone to grieve the same way you've been."

It was strange hearing the name of the first Mrs. Berendon. I knew it, of course, but whenever Thomas referred to her, he would say 'my first wife' or 'Marjorie's mother'. He never once said Allison, at least not to me. It was as if her name had been tossed onto the casket with the roses and lowered into the ground along with her body.

"I'm starting to wonder if he even has any emotions," I said to Iris.

"They're down there somewhere, but he's sealed them up pretty well. If you'd known Papa Berendon, you'd know why. The guy was a tyrant. Ran his house like a military camp and was even worse in business. Underlings, as he called nearly everyone, were not allowed to meet his eyes. If they did, they were fired. Thomas and Peter had to come up with some kind of survival skills. It was so surprising when the old guy died of a heart attack. First hint anyone had that he actually had a heart in his chest."

I felt the break inside me seconds before the deluge of tears came—like tiny twigs snapping. Then all the sadness I'd been holding onto tumbled out. I fell against Iris, crying in messy surges. In all that chaos—in the sobs that sounded like they were coming from someone else, anyone but me—there was also a warm wash of relief. Safety, I remember thinking—that's what this feels like. Strange because I couldn't have imagined feeling safe with anyone while sobbing like that. I was leaving a wet stain on Iris' white shirt—tears and black mascara.

Finally, the deluge ended. I pulled back a little from her body, but I didn't want to—couldn't make myself—and I sank back into her. Her hands were warm and strong on my back. I felt my breasts pressing against hers and my fingers slid down past her shoulders to the clasp of her bra. My hand froze and so did everything inside me. I knew I had to move away, and I did…we did. Her arms loosened and I breathed myself away from her. Then a whole chattering chorus of questions streamed in. What was this? Just a foolish desperate moment, gone now? Or something deeper, something unexpectedly unearthed? It wasn't just that we were two women, we were sisters-in-law. That's about as complicated as you can get. And yet…

When we pulled back, our eyes met without blinking or turning away. I saw flecks of brown in the blue of Iris' eyes, the faint etching of laugh lines at the corners. I saw everything about her and I saw nothing else except her.

There are moments that change everything—you know it when you're in one of them, you just don't always know how you got there. A whole life can be lived, or lost, or born in a matter of seconds.

Once when I was eighteen, I drank too many beers with a girl-friend in her house when her parents were gone. Laughing and drunk, we thought it would be fun to try making out, just as an experiment—to see where it might lead. But we couldn't stop laughing, so it went nowhere and we didn't really care anyway. It was just a game.

But this—with Iris—this didn't feel experimental or casual. Certainly there was nothing to laugh about.

We kept driving, continued on to my house, and went down the long driveway without saying a word. Then we both got out of the car, avoiding each other's eyes. Iris handed me the keys. Before walking over to her car, she looked back at me and said, "Talk to you later."

"Yeah…Thanks for going with me."

I walked into the house and stood in the foyer for several minutes, listening to the quiet around me, breathing in the careful air of well-appointed rooms that were dusted and cleaned daily, the lingering perfume of fresh lilies arranged perfectly in a vase at the foot of the stairway. Through the double-height windows and the skylight above the stairs, it seemed to be getting grayer outside, but maybe it was just the day growing late. No children have ever played in the downstairs of this house; there have never been squealing voices and racing feet, laughter and bickering and small bodies tumbling onto the polished wood floor. There is a large playroom upstairs and the children's bedrooms are huge. Thomas believes in keeping children in their place. The quiet was familiar to me—yet on this day it seemed strange, alien.

No thought of love entered my mind. I hadn't picked up that piece of the puzzle yet. I only knew I suddenly felt the heat of someone breathing next to me, even though she wasn't there. And I wasn't used to closeness—I'd spent my life charting a careful course around it, confident that I could place people where I wanted them.

A child who grows up in a house where anything can happen, where all bets are off, learns early on to protect her heart from intruders. My father had taken a dancer whose dreams seeded the clouds and had slowed her steps, pulled her down to gravelly roads as surely as if he held a string around her. I listened to my mother walk the floors at night, waiting for my father to come home. I saw the wound in her eyes when he brushed past her in the morning, smelling like the night before. I swore I'd never be hurt like that. I'd install checkpoints, boundary lines. No one except my mother and my child would enter the inner sanctuary of my being. That's where damage can be done. It was an unacceptable risk to me.

I married Thomas, in part, because he never tried to intrude on me. I was safe from invasion—secure in my own private country. In the best of times, Thomas and I were America and Britain—allies, but with a nice wide ocean between us. That's how I'd always thought about love—passion was a delicious benefit, but negotiation and protection were vital. I believed one of my greatest accomplishments in life had been defending myself from surprises.

Then on a silver-backed day in March, when giving away my son's things broke something open in me, Iris walked calmly across the border as if she'd always been there. Part of me smiled at her easy entrance. Part of me wanted to send her away with a police escort. The rest of me stood mute, wondering what was happening to me.

I once had a lover whom I stayed with because I liked the light through his bedroom window. I was twenty, working as a waitress in a diner instead of going to college, which my mother couldn't afford. He was scrambled eggs, no bacon, and dry toast with strawberry jam—conventional, but with eyes that looked like fucking. So I did. After work, when the afternoon was dipping toward evening, I'd go to his second floor apartment for conventional, predictable sex on his queen size bed. I've always found queen size beds to be indicative of a certain personality trait. They are beds with a message. They say:

I'm open to having sex, but then you have to leave because it's too crowded for sleep. He was a cartoonist; sketches were strewn about on the floor—silly faces grinned up at us while he slapped his body against mine and I listened to the bed springs creak.

I didn't love him at all, and the sex was not what his eyes had suggested it would be. But I loved the pale gold light that spilled through his window—late sunlight splintering through a huge pine tree on a neighbor's property. One day, I arrived and the tree had been cut down. I never went back. Without that light through the branches, his touch wasn't even tolerable.

As I said, I don't like surprises.

With Iris' eyes on my mind, I stood just inside the front door for a while, trying to adjust to the fact that I lived there, trying to return to my life as I knew it—as Mrs. Thomas Berendon. Footsteps interrupted my daydreaming. Carla, a soft-spoken woman who'd been with Thomas for many years—long before I became lady of the house—approached me deferentially.

"Mrs. Berendon?"

"Hi, Carla."

"Can I get you anything?" That wasn't really what she wanted to know. She wanted to know why I was still standing there so long after I'd arrived home.

"No, I'm fine. Do you know where Marjorie is?"

"Yes, ma'am. She's outside in the yard."

I found Marjorie in the garden, across the wide green swath of perfectly mowed lawn. She was sitting on the swing set, rocking back and forth a little; I wondered if she had been pushing herself high into the air moments earlier and had grown tired or if she'd just come out there to sit.

"Want me to push you?" I asked, bending down and kissing her cheek. A gust of wind swept her hair across my face.

"No."

I sat down beside her in the other swing. "Did you just come out here to think?"

She glanced at me and then looked away. "Sort of. When people die, can they float on the wind? Like birds?"

"Maybe. Maybe they are the wind," I said. "Sometimes I look up at these trees, at the branches swaying and the leaves moving, and I imagine that it's Nathan who is doing that—just having a big laugh getting the tree to move."

Marjorie smiled at me and then looked away, up to the highest branches of a tall eucalyptus tree. Then she turned serious. It was as if the next gust of wind took her smile with it. "I miss him," she said quietly.

"Me too. All the time."

"Are you going to have another baby?" She directed her question to the pale sky instead of to me.

"No." I owed her that much. I owed her the truth. I expected her to ask why but she didn't.

We were silent for a few minutes, both of us rocking back and forth on our swings, and then I had an idea. "Hey, Marjorie? Why don't we get the kite out of the garage and go fly it. The wind's strong enough I think."

Daylight left the sky over Brentwood as a red kite swooped and dove on the darkening wind currents. Anyone who saw us would have thought they were watching a mother and daughter at close of day, laughing and flying a bright red kite. They wouldn't have known that the little girl woke some mornings with tears dried on her face and the woman holding her hand was not her mother, but was trying to be.

They wouldn't know that, late that night, the woman would slide across miles of bed and climb on top of her husband, work herself against him until he was inside her, not because she wanted him there but because she was desperate to remember the woman she once believed herself to be.

7.

In bright morning sunlight, I'm let through the iron gates of Thomas' house. He changed the security code after I moved out so every Saturday I'm forced to push the buzzer and say, "It's Isabelle and Marjorie." Marjorie sits tense and still beside me, staring glumly ahead as we approach the house.

Thomas answers the door himself, dressed in tennis whites and carrying his racket. He ignores me and bends down to kiss Marjorie on the cheek.

"Are you on your way out?" I ask him, trying not at all to warm up my chilly tone. Sunlight bounces off the marble columns that border the front door; his light brown hair gleams. His arms are lean and chiseled, and I find myself glancing at the muscles of his thighs. Once upon a time they could make heat bloom in me. Now I hate it that I even remember how his legs felt inside the grip of mine.

"We're both heading out." He says this more to Marjorie than to me. "We're going to the Morrow's house. You like it there, right Marjorie? They have a big yard and a standard poodle who likes to chase tennis balls. You have a great time there, right?"

Reluctantly Marjorie nods and says, "Uh-huh," in a barely perceptible voice.

She steps across the threshold into the house she no longer wants to visit, and Thomas puts his hand on the door, getting ready to close it.

"I'll have Phillip bring her back tonight, as usual," he says to me and then shuts the door, as if announcing his driver's responsibility for Marjorie's safe return should be suitable. That's it, business concluded. The son-of-a-bitch just dismissed me and then shut the door in my face.

I stare at the polished mahogany door for all of three seconds and then ring the bell. Thomas opens it immediately.

"What?" he says.

"You closed the door in my face. Could you at least try to be somewhat civil?"

He steps outside and pulls the door almost shut behind him. He's glaring at me with what I interpret to be pure hatred.

"Civil? Why should I be civil to you, Isabelle? You tore apart this family. You killed my son -"

"Our son."

"Oh, yes—your maternal instincts. Where were they that morning when you didn't lock the screen?"

I feel my face getting red; my hands start trembling. But it feels more like fear than rage. This accusation has festered between us, but has never been put into words. Until now.

"Are you absolutely certain it wasn't you, Thomas?" I ask him. "Or someone else in the house? You're so invested in blaming me I doubt you've ever shed a tear for Nathan. Do you even know what grief is?" I can't believe I've actually said this—aimed so deliberately at his jugular. Well, he started it.

But there's something else I can't believe—in a matter of seconds I've crawled past my guilt to consider the possibility that I might not be guilty at all.

Thomas doesn't respond to my attack. He turns and goes back into the house, closing the door more emphatically this time. I suddenly realize that he isn't sure who is to blame. Only two maids were in the house that Saturday and they would have had no reason to venture outside. The workers were in another part of the house. But still...

As I drive down the long tree-lined driveway, raked free of leaves by the daily diligence of several gardeners, I think about how this property—this estate—has been so many things to me. A home, a prison, a refuge, a maze of rooms and hallways where sorrow and secrets took up space, where Nathan laughed, crawled, stood, grew, and left us wandering about lost in the wasteland of missing him.

The day Marjorie and I went kite-flying, we returned home just before dark. Thomas was already there, sitting in the living room with the evening news on, ice cubes clinking in a glass of vodka, his mouth a stern straight line.

"Where have you been?" he asked, glancing from Marjorie to me.

"Flying a kite at the park," she answered.

"It's nearly dinner time."

I leaned down to Marjorie, brushed her hair back from her neck. "Why don't you go upstairs and wash your hands, okay?" I told her.

When I couldn't hear her footsteps anymore, I met my husband's ice-flint eyes. "You could try being glad to see her, Thomas."

"I didn't know where you were. Carla just said you'd driven off."

"I told her we'd be back soon and we were. Were you worried about us or just concerned about your schedule? God forbid dinner should be late by five minutes."

"Stop it, Isabelle."

So I did. We said little to each other at the dinner table. We said nothing to each other after Marjorie went to bed. Thomas went into the library and I watched an episode of Law and Order that I'd seen before, but I liked knowing the criminal would be found guilty, led off in handcuffs and for a few minutes the world would seem a little safer.

I, however, did not feel safe. I still saw Iris' eyes inches from mine. I had the unnerving feeling that her fingerprints were beneath my skin. I didn't understand what had happened in my car. Or maybe I did but didn't want to. How can one snip of time feel so much like an endless free-fall?

I was already under the covers with the lights turned out when Thomas finally came to bed. He smelled like soap and toothpaste. He smelled like a man I once knew, once wanted. The night fell down between us. I listened to his breathing grow slower, deeper, and I knew even without rolling over that he was lying on his back, left arm bent beneath the pillow and his head. Thomas could go to sleep in that position and wake up exactly the same way. His attachment to organization never wavered.

When I did finally roll over to look at him he was so dead asleep he didn't stir at all. I crossed the miles of dark space between us and slid onto his body. As I moved downward from the bars of his ribcage to the pulse point on his stomach he woke up, startled. It sounded like words were about to come from his mouth but he gasped instead as I took him in my mouth and went to work. I was efficient, deliberate, and when he had what I wanted I straddled him and plunged him into me. This was not love-making, this was fucking—fierce and ruthless, with only conquest as a goal. But it wasn't Thomas I was trying to conquer, it was myself I was desperate to reclaim. 'This is who I am' was the blood-beat in every thrust of my body. There was no love there, just fury. No passion, just the flailing of a soul overboard, trying to make it back to recognizable land.

He gripped my arms. I sat above him fucking him with the half of my body commissioned for that task. But I was a divided country. I never bent toward his face, never approached his mouth, never met his eyes. I tried to quiet the thoughts in my head, silence the high, clear siren song and the bass notes of fear so I could hear again the mid-notes of a life that felt like mine. I failed.

Lot's wife followed her husband, who was described as "a righteous man", out of Sodom just before it crumbled. Despite God's command to keep walking and not turn around, she did. She looked back at the life she was leaving—the low stone buildings, the red-dirt streets, the doorways that let in summer and the smell of warm hearths in winter. We all know how that turned out—she became a pillar of salt right there in the road.

My husband is not a righteous man and he was not the one I was tempted to follow. But like Lot's wife, I had to look back at all I was abandoning—the home I called mine, the life I stitched myself into, the woman I grew to be—a wealthy man's wife, a mother and stepmother.

Every choice comes with a cost.

A pillar of salt is a tough one—no antidote for that. Although in these modern times there are probably clever scientists who could figure out how to take that poor flaking woman and turn her human again. But who are we once we have been re-configured? Would Lot's wife have returned to Sodom if she could have? Would I?

The sound Thomas made when he came resembled a choked-off scream. I climbed off him and slinked back to my side of the bed, like a wolf leaving a carcass she's just devoured.

It was no good—I still wasn't who I'd been yesterday. I couldn't shake the feeling of Iris' breasts against mine. I turned over on my stomach and took some comfort in the press of the mattress.

"What was that about?" Thomas said after a few minutes. He was still lying on his back.

I didn't answer him.

My dreams that night took me back to a day from my past—a day I didn't even realize I'd remembered. But dreamland is a huge field of composted soil—you have no idea how much is still alive there.

I was about to turn thirteen and my father presented me with my birthday present two weeks early. We were all going to drive to Malibu and go horseback riding.

"Why?" I asked him.

"Because my friends who own a horse-riding place are giving us horses to ride for an afternoon. How many kids get that for a birthday present, Isabelle? You could say thank you, you know. I've told you umpteen times I do the best I can for you."

"Umpteen isn't a number," I snapped back.

His friends were two women—Madge and Hazel—who sometimes joined his poker group. Madge and Hazel lost one night and instead of forking over the cash, they offered my father a free horseback ride for the family. Frank Haller had his own peculiar bartering system.

There was a heat wave punishing Los Angeles that week, but that didn't deter my father. We drove up the coast to a run-down piece of property inland from the ocean and stepped out of the car into dust and circling flies. Madge and Hazel turned out to be two fiftyish lesbians with men's haircuts, men's clothes, and packs of cigarettes in their breast pockets. They slapped my father on the back and then led out four over-ridden, sad horses. Madge was going to be our trail boss.

For an hour, we plodded along, coughed up dust, listened to my father and Madge talk about gambling and the track and God knows what else. I didn't care how Madge and Hazel chose to live their lives, I just wanted the day to be over, which is why I didn't even know the memory of those women was still in me.

But apparently it was, because in my dream, I was Madge—or at least a reasonable facsimile of her. Same Elvis-style haircut, same manly clothes…and I was standing on a dusty piece of land looking at the back of a blonde woman as she rode away from me on a slow, worn-down horse. I never saw the woman's face in my dream, but I understood her to be Iris.

I woke up angry. I had the unsettling, albeit unreasonable, thought that I'd dreamed my own destiny. That to continue thinking about Iris as I had been would turn me not into a pillar of salt, but into Madge. Anger is strange thing—it can be amorphous, undefined, but there's a strong desire to give it structure, focus, a reason for existing. By breakfast time, I'd decided I was angry at Iris.

It didn't help when Thomas peered at me over his cup of coffee and said, "You do remember that Iris and Peter are coming for dinner tonight."

I hadn't, actually, but I nodded mutely, avoiding his eyes and wishing I could hop a plane to someplace with no extradition.

I tromped through the day, angry and aimless. The murky sky was a perfect mirror of how I felt inside. In the afternoon, I decided to go for a hike. I put on a pair of unfashionable sweat pants, one of Thomas' T-shirts and a plaid flannel shirt I'd once used to help Marjorie paint an art project. I laced up hiking boots I hadn't worn in years and drove to Pacific Palisades where a wide fire road winds for miles through the Santa Monica Mountains.

I hiked up to an overlook where I stood staring out at the Pacific Ocean. I'd just walked several miles without recognizing my own footsteps. Nor did I recognize the person inside my skin; it was the same skin I had yesterday and all the days before but that was where the familiarity ended. I asked the sea and sky and breeze who I was supposed to be now. None of them answered.

Late in the day I returned home. I smelled dinner cooking as I went upstairs; I glanced into the dining room, saw the table already set with polished silverware and crystal goblets. I felt like an intruder who would be discovered at any moment and asked to leave. Even Marjorie pulling me into her room to look at a drawing she'd done of a turtle didn't pull me back to the woman I was supposed to be in this house, this life.

Cocktails began without me. I could hear Iris' voice drifting up from the living room and I fought hard against the softening effect it had on me. I reminded myself it was she who did this to me—reached for me, reached into me, jumbled everything inside and left me stomping around, a stranger to myself.

When I finally went downstairs, still in my hiking clothes, all eyes turned to me and I wasn't oblivious to the looks of puzzled surprise.

"Hi, how are you?" Iris said, bravely jumping into the silence with both feet.

"Okay. Hi, everyone."

I went to the bar, poured myself a glass of Chardonnay and sat in the armchair farthest from the others. Marjorie came down wearing a dress, which Thomas had told her to put on, and she looked at me strangely as well. Although it might have been a look of envy—why did she have to get dressed up and I could sit there in my sweatpants and baggy plaid shirt, my hiking boots coated with dust?

I said almost nothing while we were at the dinner table, punishing Iris with my remove, my incarnation into someone I didn't want to be. I didn't really taste the grilled chicken or the asparagus spears. All I tasted was anger. She did this to me…

We always think we can make a clean get-away—pounce on the first available moment and escape. But it hardly ever works out that way. Marjorie excused herself halfway through desert, saying she was full and wanted to go back up to her room. Then Thomas and Peter said they were going to walk outside and smoke cigars. I'd wanted to run away quickly from Iris, but suddenly there we were, pushing back from an empty table, glancing at each other across candlelight as the maids came in and started clearing away dishes.

"Isabelle, can we talk?" she said softly.

I moved toward the doorway, addressed her over my shoulder. "There isn't anything to talk about."

She came after me, grabbed my arm and turned me toward her. "Hey!" her voice was strong but muted—a talent honed from growing up in a formal home where privacy can never be counted on. She pushed me toward the living room and I shuffled ahead of her, my hiking boots squeaking on the polished floor.

From the living room windows, I could see Thomas and Peter standing out in the garden, the necklace of city lights behind them, the orange tips of their cigars glowing in the night air. Our husbands,

I thought, touching on the betrayal that was closing in like a foregone conclusion.

"Isabelle," Iris said, and I turned from the window to find her less than two feet from me. "This is weird for me, too." She was wearing a sky blue cashmere sweater and black pants. A single diamond on a chain hung just above her collarbone. I'm usually cashmere and diamonds too, except now I was channeling Madge.

I didn't say anything.

"Why are you acting like you're mad at me?"

"I'm not," I answered, unconvincingly. I was having trouble locating the anger I'd clung to all day.

"Yes, you are. You've been snubbing me all evening. And at the risk of stating the obvious, you're dressed like a lumberjack. I have no idea what that's about, but...look, what happened in your car yesterday is confusing to me too. It just seems like we should talk about it."

We weren't going to get a chance to then. Thomas and Peter walked back in and went to the bar to pour themselves some brandy. The evening ended as it had begun—with distance and detours and a knotted tangle of things not spoken.

Except I was aware of this: As soon as I'd allowed myself to meet Iris' eyes, all my fury drained out and I was cracking wide open to her again.

I slept a dreamless sleep that night.

8.

On the third day I rose and didn't feel like Madge anymore. As I dressed myself in Ralph Lauren, the significance of the time span didn't elude me. I felt like I was experiencing my own Resurrection. Not that I could remotely claim holiness of any kind, but life is full of various crucifixions, large and small. All any of us hope for is a resurrection at the other end.

My mother was in the living room reading the morning paper when I arrived at her house unexpectedly. She was dressed in a loose, ankle length lavender skirt and a white long-sleeved shirt; a string of silver beads hung around her neck.

"Isabelle, what a surprise! Good morning…"

"Morning. Sorry, I should have called. Are you on your way out?"

She motioned me in. "In a little while. One of my former students is choreographing a dance routine. I told her I'd come and see how it's going. Are you okay, dear? You look…I don't know…weighed down."

"Yeah. That's a good description."

She moved the paper off the couch and we sat down. My mother has a way of looking at people sometimes that says, Don't rush, I have all the time in the world. That was the look she was giving me.

I told her what had happened in my car. I told her how I fell into a woman I'd known for years—my sister-in-law—as if I'd never known her to be anyone other than this new person. The person who had come to change everything I thought was true about myself, my life. I told her I hadn't realized how lonely I'd been until right then, pressed against Iris with my face, my tears, the soft ache of sorrow spilling onto her…and how in the midst of all that, a desire so hot it burned me found its way through. But not just desire—love.

As I talked I looked for shock or judgment in my mother's eyes and saw only calmness. But of course that's why I'd come here. I knew instinctively that she'd listen and soothe, pick up the broken threads and start mending.

"Isabelle," she said when I stopped for breath. "Do you know you've never used the word love to me when you've talked about Thomas? Not even when you married him. This is the first time." She reached over and held both my hands in hers. "We can't choose who we love. And it doesn't matter if it's someone you've known before and never been in love with. People are always changing. You're seeing Iris differently because you're different…she's different."

"But a woman? My sister-in-law? This is insane."

My mother smiled. "Love and sanity aren't always the best of friends. You can turn away from this if you want, you can run and hide and tell yourself it isn't true. But if you really have fallen in love, nothing is going to change that. You can't make it not true. Sometimes we don't fall in love with the most convenient people."

I wanted to ask my mother if that's how she saw her marriage to my father—as an example of falling in love with an inconvenient person. But I wasn't sure she would want to tell me the truth about that.

"Mother, do you remember that day when Dad took us horseback riding in Malibu? For my thirteenth birthday? Do you remember Madge and Hazel?"

My mother laughed. "Oh yes. You were quite miserable. It wasn't a whole lot of fun, I have to admit."

"I had a dream that I turned into Madge."

Now she laughed harder. "Sweetheart, you're just scared, and for good reason. This is not an easy thing. And it's going to get harder, I'm afraid…but you're not going to turn into Madge, I promise."

You should have seen me yesterday, I thought, but didn't say.

"I don't know what to do," I said instead.

"Oh, I think you do. You need to talk to Iris and then you both need to choose between your hearts and your heads. We all want the world to be happy for us when we fall in love. We want approval, smiles all around. But sometimes it doesn't work out that way. That's when you have to be really certain that your heart is telling you the truth and then it doesn't matter if anyone else understands. You have to be willing to pay the price, too, which in your case will be a high one, I'm afraid. But Isabelle, a lot of people go through their whole lives and never meet anyone who they love deeply, completely. It's not something to be tossed away out of fear—it might never come your way again."

When I left my mother's house, I felt lighter, less ravaged by fear, but the fear was still in me. It had just changed forms—from a lion to a lamb. I called Iris from my cell phone and a small part of me hoped she wasn't home. She answered on the second ring.

"Iris, can I come over? And talk?"

"I'm here."

I knew Peter was at work because Thomas was. The Berendon brothers were predictable, presiding over their empire like paranoid monarchs. They kept long hours and paid close attention to minutiae.

Iris was barefoot, in faded jeans and a green T-shirt. She wasn't wearing a bra—something she could get away with since she has the enviable breasts of a woman who's not had children. She hugged me quickly, her hands squeezing my back.

"You okay?" she asked.

"I'm not sure."

Something I couldn't decipher passed across her face. "Yeah. Me neither," she said, letting out a long, slow breath; I wondered if she had been holding in that one breath for three days.

We went into the sunken living room, where Iris' style argued with Peter's. She had decorated the room with slouchy, slip-covered furniture mixed with eclectic pieces like a chipped paint sideboard and vintage chandeliers—very Shabby Chic—but Peter had won out with the corner bar. There were mirrored walls and slick glass shelves displaying all varieties of tumblers and goblets, a counter crowded with liquor bottles, and a decorative beer keg that had no beer in it but was a necessary emblem to ensure his place in the high-testosterone, high-fiving men's club.

We left a few cautious inches of space between us on the couch.

"We need to talk about what happened in my car," I said. "Since I guess we both feel that something did."

Iris nodded slowly. "Yeah, we do. I think it was definitely an uh-oh moment."

"An uh-oh moment. Well, that's one way of putting it. Sounds so innocuous, though. Was it innocuous?"

Her cheeks flushed. "No. At least not to me. I didn't want to let go of you, Isabelle, and more than that…I wanted to keep going. You know what I mean?"

"I think so, yes. I did, too."

There was a surge of relief in saying it, letting the words hang between us. But then we both just sat quietly, not knowing where to go from there. Finally Iris broke the silence.

"I'm not gay. Or even bi…"

"Me neither. It's just confusing how something could all of a sudden be this different between us. We've been friends for four years, how could we suddenly -"

"Fall in love?" Iris said softly.

I felt my face flush. "Yeah. I mean people talk about that happening and I'm sure it does, but with another woman when you've never had any desire in that direction? And on top of that we're sisters-in-law? I just don't know how this could happen."

I could hear my mother inside my head saying, "Well, it did."

"The only thing that doesn't feel confusing to me," Iris said, "and this is really the truth—is that for the first time in my life I felt totally comfortable and at home with someone, and so filled up with love it felt like I'd burst open. I've never felt that way with Peter—he was just always there, and familiar. Our marriage made sense. I guess I told myself that not everyone finds love in this life, and you just accept what you have found."

"I never really wanted to love like that," I admitted. "It was way too vulnerable and scary. But I haven't thought about anyone except you since the other day. And, strangely, that's the one part that isn't scary. The consequences of this, on the other hand, frighten the hell out of me."

"It would make it easier if this was just curiosity, huh?"

"Yes, but…"

"I know," Iris said. "It isn't." She paused, looked around the room and then back to me with the eyes that had become my undoing. "When I went to Thailand a few years ago, I went to this island with a guide—an interpreter—I wanted to see the Moken people. I'd read a lot about them—they're called the sea gypsies of the Andaman Sea."

I was puzzled by this turn in the conversation, but I had to assume she was going somewhere with it.

"They're so completely unaffected by modern civilization," she continued, "so pure in their thinking. They have no word for 'when' in their language—they just let time wash over them. And no word for 'want.' I've wondered since then if I could be like that, not wanting anything ever. At all. Not even recognizing the idea of wanting as being worthy of a word. After yesterday, I'm absolutely sure I could never be a Moken."

So that's where she was going. I nodded and tried to imagine not wanting Iris. "I'd definitely be run out of that village," I told her.

"It's not just the gender part. Like you said, we're sisters-in-law. I mean, have you ever heard of anything like this happening before?"

"I haven't gotten around to doing a Google search on it. And I doubt anyone has done a survey. We could pretend it didn't happen and just go on like before—I mean it is an option."

I thought about what my mother said about love, but I needed to ask Iris. I needed a clear view of how she felt.

"I don't want to go on like before," she said softly.

I suddenly wished it was night. I imagined jumping into the car with Iris and just going—headlights streaming past, the road wide open in front of us, leading to wherever we wanted to go. But we weren't lucky enough to have that kind of freedom. Maybe no one really is.

"I don't know how exactly to handle this, and I want to think about it before …you know…saying anything," Iris said. "It's one thing for us to get our heads around this, but Thomas and Peter…"

"I know." That was it—the moment when I knew our lives were going to change forever.

"Have you ever been this surprised by another person?" Iris asked me. "By your own feelings for someone else?"

"I banned surprises from my life years ago. I'm not fond of them."

Iris slid closer to me. Now there was only a thin ribbon of space between us. "I was once really shocked by liking this guy who was totally not my type," she said. "I was in college and he was a football player—a real jock. It wasn't love or anything—I mean, we were completely mismatched. I speak three languages, I'd read all of Shakespeare by the time I graduated high school, and he was trying to get through a Jackie Collins novel—stumbling over three-syllable words. But I swear I could not get enough of him. I'd have fucked him on the football field at half time if he'd asked me to. It was like I was possessed. I actually went to football games just to watch him run and throw and…whatever the hell they do in that game.

"Then one night we went out for a drink—he had condoms stuffed in his jacket pocket for later—and I mentioned a Mike Nichols film that I'd just seen. He said, 'Who's Mike Nichols?' And that was it. Cut. The End. I never had sex with him again. I mean, I just couldn't fuck a guy who didn't know who Mike Nichols was."

I didn't say anything for a moment, wondering if there was more to the story but there apparently wasn't.

"That's your example of being surprised?" I finally asked.

"Uh-huh. I know it's not the same as this. As us. But it's the only example I have. I guess I haven't been surprised too often since that's the only thing I can compare this to."

There was something delightful in Iris' telling of that ridiculous story and I couldn't help laughing. Iris laughed too and somewhere in that wash of relief our eyes met and we leaned toward each other. I'm not sure if one of us initiated our first kiss or if we just met in the middle, both of us pushed by a longing we were still struggling to understand. We were shy, tentative, but reluctant to stop.

We did stop, of course. And I thought my mouth must look different—bruised and reshaped with the imprint of Iris. Only seconds had passed, but the lives we'd been living for years were dead on the vine.

"So we really can't walk away from this, can we?" I said.

"No. But I'm scared."

"Me too. Iris, were you ever in love with Peter? Really in love?"

She shrugged and looked away. "Maybe a little, sure. Mostly in my head more than my heart. I've known him for so long. We knew each other in high school—we'd date, break up, then get back together. He never stopped waiting for me…he took my virginity on graduation night." She laughed a thin, papery laugh. "At Princeton we took the same classes, kept dating and sometimes breaking up, seeing other people. Then eventually…it just seemed like we were supposed to be together, like it had been pre-ordained. When we got engaged, it sort of felt like we already had been for years. I told myself I loved him, but maybe I was just used to him. He was an easy habit."

Before I could say something about Thomas, I heard my cell phone ringing from inside my purse. I'd tossed my purse onto an armchair and I lunged for it, managing to find the interrupting contraption by the fifth or sixth ring. I thought, if this is Thomas calling me right now I might actually feel some shame, which so far I hadn't. But it was the headmistress of Marjorie's school.

"Mrs. Berendon, I phoned your husband at work, but he said he was going into a meeting so I should call you," she told me. "I'd like to talk to you about the drawings Marjorie's been doing."

"Oh. Okay, I can come now."

When I hung up, I looked at Iris—my sister-in-law, the woman I had just kissed, the woman I wanted in every way possible. "I have to go to Marjorie's school. The headmistress is concerned about some drawings she's been doing. I don't really know what this is about."

"Should I go with you?" Iris asked.

"No. I'm afraid we might have big scarlet A's emblazoned on our chests. I'll call you later and tell you about it."

When I was shown into Mrs. Corcoran's office, she had four of Marjorie's crayon drawings spread out on her desk. They were harsh, bleak pictures of drowning. One was of a boy beneath blue water, arms wild and reaching. But the other three were darker, more frightening. The water wasn't blue, it was gray and black. Spindly arms were coming up toward him from below, pulling him down.

"I'm worried about Marjorie's state of mind," Mrs. Corcoran said. "A loss like this—what you've gone through, all of you—is so hard. I don't think Marjorie knows what to do with all the emotions boiling up in her."

Mrs. Corcoran is, I would guess, in her mid-forties. But she looks much older. It's her drab sweaters and skirts, clothes that my mother would say "have seen better days." It's her sensible shoes and the way her eyelids slope down as if she's given up on excitement, spontaneity—resigning herself instead to one day lumbering after the next.

"I'll talk to her," I tell her.

"I can recommend a counselor, if you like. Grief for children can be...well, complicated."

"I'll talk to my husband about that. But I think we'll try to work on this between ourselves first."

Marjorie was called into the office and when she walked in, she looked from Mrs. Corcoran to me with panic in her eyes.

"It's okay, sweetie," I told her, folding her into my arms. "We're just going to leave early today and talk. Hey, I didn't know what a good artist you are."

We drove to the park in Brentwood where we'd flown a red kite just days before. It was one of her favorite spots—a place I thought she might want to have her seventh birthday party weeks ago. But she'd adamantly refused to have any kind of party. As we walked across a wide green lawn to a bench beneath the trees, I thought about that and wondered if I should have been more alarmed. It had seemed so logical; none of us were in the mood to celebrate, but maybe I missed a clue that was right in front of me.

"Mrs. Corcoran is concerned about how sad your drawings are," I said to her.

Marjorie nodded and watched a squirrel scampering up a tree trunk. "I am sad. You are, too."

"Yeah, I am. Every day."

"Will we ever be happy again?"

I knew if I let go of all that was holding on tight in me I could crumble. I put my arms around Marjorie and hugged her tightly, trying to breathe away the tears that pressed into my eyes.

"We will," I assured her. "It just takes time. Marjorie, why did you draw all those arms underneath the water in that one picture?"

She squirmed away and looked at me. "Because I think Nathan was really scared. And that's how it must have felt—like arms pulling him. But maybe when he died—I mean after—he woke up in the sky. Do you think?"

"I bet he did. Can you draw that? Him waking up in miles and miles of blue, sitting on clouds?"

"Yes…"

We sat on that bench until the sun moved to the center of the sky. We talked about Nathan, pulled out memory after memory, laughing sometimes at how silly he could be, at the faces he would make. How he would start running and then not be able to keep up with his legs. He hardly ever cried when he tumbled down. We watched squirrels and listened to the breeze slip between branches. Time drifted and for a while we were outside of it. When hunger reeled us in and we decided to go get some lunch, we had—at least for that day—remembered how to be happy.

9.

On Saturdays, there is always a tug of guilt when I get back to Malibu. I've left Marjorie pouting unhappily at Thomas' while I cheerfully rush back to the one day of the week that belongs solely to Iris and me. Today, when I return, the house is quiet and I wonder if she went back to sleep.

"Iris?"

"Upstairs."

She's sitting up in bed with the newspaper around her, still in the oversized shirt she likes to sleep in. Her hair is tumbling around her face in a lovely blond mess. I want to tell her that Thomas finally accused me to my face of killing Nathan; I want to tell her that in doing so he left himself unmasked and I saw his uncertainty. That for the first time I'm actually considering the possibility that my hand might never have touched the screen door at all. I might be innocent. I will tell her, but later...

I peel off my clothes and get back into bed, pushing the newspapers aside and kicking the bedclothes down. A slant of sunlight falls across Iris' collarbone until I smother it with my mouth. I can hear the rumble of traffic from the highway, the crash of waves from what sounds like high tide, but all of that falls away and I'm a happy prisoner, hearing only our breathing, seeing only Iris' pale skin and half-closed eyelids, inhaling her, tasting her—oblivious to everything outside this bed. It's always like this—a starvation only she can feed. Sometimes I wonder if we will grow into a tired old married couple…with perfunctory sex scheduled for every Wednesday after our evening martini…done and over in a few minutes without even wrinkling the sheets. I suppose that could happen, but I can't imagine it.

Some people think lovemaking between women is a surface affair, a shallow substitute for the way a man enters a woman, pushes deep into her, makes her stretch and expand—literally—the tissues and muscles do exactly that.

But penetration is a matter of viewpoint. We're all more porous than we think we are. And the skin is the body's largest organ. I melt into Iris' skin, into the mold of her body, so like my own that even the first time, it was like coming home.

After our first kiss, we didn't touch each other for more than a week. Except in our minds…and in whispered confessions that made us blush. We started spending nearly every day together—lunches, taking Marjorie to the park in the afternoons, even going to museums and art galleries. We never stole away to kiss or embrace. But we came to each other in daylight with the night's fantasies trailing after us. Sometimes a glance of our eyes would make us blush.

"You and Iris are spending a lot of time together," Thomas said to me one evening.

We were having martinis in the living room before dinner. An orange sun was dropping heavily outside the windows and I looked past him at the colors painted on the sky—playing for time, trying to figure out if he knew. Had he seen something in our smiles, our eyes, our attitude?

"Well, we've always spent time together," I answered cautiously.

"I just noticed you were spending more. It seems like it's helping. You're feeling better, yes?" He actually was being sincere.

"Yes, I am," I told him, feeling an unfamiliar slice of pain for Thomas—for the wound I knew I was going to inflict.

I made love with my husband for the last time that night. Gently, quickly, with tears pooled in the corners of my eyes. I was saying goodbye, I was saying I'm sorry. Only he didn't know it yet.

Before he and Peter were told, Iris and I decided to consummate our relationship. We made our plans on the phone and if anyone had been listening in, it would have just sounded like two sisters-in-law making innocent plans to walk on the beach in Malibu.

The beach house was empty on Tuesdays and Thursdays. The maid came on the other weekdays and occasionally on Saturdays if Thomas had scheduled a Malibu weekend for us. So Iris and I drove up the Coast Highway on a Tuesday, knowing and not knowing what we were heading for. We knew how to be pirates, but we had no idea how to be lovers.

We were shy as we climbed the stairs to the bedroom. We had singed the sheets in our separate beds while we lay beside sleeping husbands we could no longer love—husbands who didn't yet know we had already left them.

"We're both virgins at this," Iris whispered midway up the stairs, as if someone else could hear us.

"I know," I answered, not bothering to whisper. "It's weird, huh?" she asked.

"It is…"

I had wondered about our combined inexperience and now it was a nervous twitch in my stomach. Would we fumble around and feel horribly embarrassed? There is technique and there is passion; the best lovemaking usually combines both. As it turned out, I needn't have worried. Never underestimate passion…it pulls you under and leaves you stripped bare of everything except desire.

Each part of me knew what to do, and seemed to have been waiting for permission to do it. My tongue memorized her taste, knew the map of her, the soft pink heat of her. My lips formed perfect circles around her nipples and knew the nerve path downward along her stomach muscles to the delicate v-shape below. We rolled and tumbled across the high thread-count sheets, perfectly in sinc. My legs fell open, trembled against her shoulders as her mouth let me know she'd figured out some things too. My hands held her head as if it were a dance we had done a thousand times. I wanted to claim every part of her, leave my scent on her and bathe myself in hers. It seemed as if I had always loved her like this, although that wasn't true.

Outside that room was a life we were going to have to step into, claim as ours. For a little while, we let ourselves forget about that—we played and laughed and explored, carefree as innocents who don't have a thought about tomorrow.

On the way home from Malibu, the future arranged itself in front of us and we turned serious and deliberate. We agreed to tell our husbands that night; we synchronized the time, so neither brother would know before the other.

"Late enough that Marjorie should be asleep," I pointed out.

"Yes. God, this is so surreal," Iris said. "Like we fell asleep and woke up in a different world."

"Maybe we did."

That evening at the dinner table, the enormity of it all hit me with the force of an avalanche. Thomas, Marjorie and I sat at one end of the long, polished table that could comfortably seat ten. I looked at my stepdaughter expertly cutting her chicken as she had been taught to do. I looked around the lavish room with its crystal chandelier, ornate sideboard, huge antique mirror. It was February, dark fell early, and outside the French doors a thin crescent moon floated in a scattering of stars. I would never sit in this room again— across from Marjorie—never listen to the music of her voice fill up the dinner hour since Thomas and I had so little to say to each other these days.

She looked at both of us when she asked, "Can we go out to the beach this weekend?"

"I can't," Thomas said. "But you two go out there. Take Iris along with you."

I thought I would cry at that moment and it took every bit of strength I had in me not to. I suddenly realized I might never see Marjorie again. Once I left Thomas, once the truth was out, he could forbid both Iris and me from seeing her.

She was looking at me, waiting for an answer. So was Thomas.

"Isabelle?" he said.

"Yes...sorry...I was just trying to think if I had anything this weekend. Maybe we can...I'll have to see."

Later, when I put Marjorie to bed, I hugged her tightly and whispered into the shampoo-scent of her hair, "You know I love you, right?"

"Uh-huh. What's wrong? Are you sad tonight?"

I couldn't look at her so I kept holding her against me. "Yes. Tonight I'm a little sad. Sometimes it's just like that."

"Me too. Some mornings I wake up and miss Nathan so much, I know it's going to be a sad day."

I kissed her forehead, her cheek, her hands, and managed to pull a smile up through the dread that was choking me. Missing her was already a chasm inside me.

"You sleep tight, okay?"

She nodded and smiled at me. "And I won't let the bed bugs bite."

"Absolutely not."

I wandered through the rooms of the house that evening—the well-appointed rooms that I'd had nothing to do with—they had been decorated and arranged long before I arrived. I'd wondered many times if the first Mrs. Berendon had chosen the antiques, the drapes and area rugs, the lamps and artwork. Since no one in the house ever mentioned her, I'd never asked. Thomas was in his study. I noticed one of the phone lines was lit up as I walked through the living room and approached the room I'd not stepped into for months. I could hear, from the kitchen, the soft murmur of voices—"the help" was how Thomas referred to them, as if they had no other purpose in life except to attend to his needs.

A single lamp was on in the den and in the play of light and shadow, I saw again my three-year old son, sitting on the floor rolling a plastic truck back and forth. I walked across the room, stepping carefully around his ghost, and reached for the door that led out to the pool. I searched for a recollection, an imprint of that day when life as I'd known it came tumbling down. I still couldn't recall opening the door, yet I knew that people often block out traumatic memories. I would not be abandoning my son in this house—I'd be taking him with me. In the territory of the heart, no one ever dies.

I switched off the lamp when I left the room and walked out to the pool through a different door. I stared into the water where a coin-edged moon was reflected in the calm surface, and I tried to still the turbulence inside me. I had fallen in love—deeply, completely—with the most inconvenient person in the world. Nathan died in this water, I thought, and now I'm looking into it as if it can baptize me into a new life.

It was nearly nine-thirty, the time Iris and I had agreed upon. My footsteps on the stairs seemed louder than they ever had before.

"Thomas," I said to my husband's back as he was unbuttoning his shirt in the bedroom. He turned, sensing something in my voice. "I have something to say."

"Yes?"

"Our marriage, our relationship…we're not really working anymore…together, I mean."

Relief flooded his face. "No, we're not," he said.

He thought this was going to be simple, amicable even. My heart hurt for him, although he will probably never believe that.

"There's more, though. I've fallen in love with someone else." There was no other way to say it except that stark declarative sentence.

He frowned, confused. "When could you even have met someone else?" he asked. "You've been spending nearly every day with Iris."

I just looked at him, letting my eyes tell him. There was a slow dawning, a tightening of his features, a clenching of his jaw.

"No," he said. "You're not telling me this. No! Are you sick? Twisted? What the fuck's wrong with you?"

"I'm sorry. We fell in love. I don't know how it happened, but it did."

Thomas wheeled around as if he was lost and trying to find his way in the wilderness. When he looked at me again he was red and shaking with rage. I thought he was going to hit me. But he turned, picked up a chair and hoisted it in the air. He aimed it at the mirror and I reflexively put my hands over my ears, anticipating shattering glass. But something in his own reflection, or mine, or maybe just the undertow of shock made him drop his arms and the chair.

But then the rage returned. "If you wanted to screw around with another woman, why didn't you just go pick someone up at a bar?" he shouted. I knew he was going to wake Marjorie.

"I didn't want to be with another woman. I didn't want any of this to happen. Neither of us did. We fell in love…"

"You fell in love." He said it icily, bitterness dripping from each syllable. "And I suppose you consummated your 'love.'"

I nodded yes and he looked around at our bed. "No, not here," I told him. "We went out to Malibu."

He shook his head hard, like he was trying to wake himself from a nightmare. I saw him fill himself up with breath before he yelled, "Fuck you! Get out of this house! Now! You've torn this family apart!"

He turned furiously and went into the bathroom, slamming the door so hard I thought something would fall off the walls. I didn't walk out immediately. I went into the closet, got a gym bag and stuffed a few clothes in it. I got my purse, my cell phone, a jacket. I'd go to a hotel—strange that Iris and I hadn't planned for this part of it. When I left the bedroom, I heard Thomas vomiting in the bathroom.

Marjorie's door was open and she was huddled in the doorway, crying.

"Where are you going?" she asked me, the words thick in her throat.

I knelt down in front of her. "I'm sorry, Marjorie. I have to leave right now. I know this is going to be really hard for you to understand..."

I didn't get any further. Thomas exploded out of the bedroom, saw me there and yelled, "Get out of this house!"

There was nothing I could do. Marjorie ducked back into her room and closed her door. Thomas stood in the hallway, a coil of fury and pain. And I ran out to my car, drove down the long driveway, through the elaborate gates, and only when I turned onto the softly-lit street did I pull over and wonder where I should go.

My hands were shaking as I called Iris' cell-phone from mine.

"Peter just drove away," she said when she picked up. "He's probably on his way there."

"I'm stopped on the street. I needed to call you and...I have to check into a hotel. The Beverly Hills Hotel, I'll go there. I can't go to the Bel Air, I got married there." My voice didn't sound like mine, it was ragged and shaky.

"Okay. Beverly Hills Hotel. I'll see you there. We'll get separate rooms, though—that'll be better for the moment."

There is nothing subtle about a woman with a famous last name checking into a hotel a few miles from her home late at night. I got the discreet but knowing look that hotel personnel are so adept at giving but I couldn't help thinking, You have no idea.

Iris and I did get separate rooms but we slept together. It was a long, restless night punctuated by bouts of crying. We would talk for long stretches, slip into a half-sleep stupor and then cling to each other again.

"I broke into a thousand pieces when Nathan died," I told her. "And you picked up all of them."

"In a way, you did the same for me. I've traveled around the world trying to figure out who I'm supposed to be here on this planet for whatever time I've been given. I never really felt worthwhile until you broke down in my arms after Nathan died and I thought, this is it. I'm right where I'm supposed to be."

"Do you think this began then? Without us realizing it?" I asked her.

"I don't know. I think who we love is unpredictable. It just claims us and we have nothing to say about it."

"You sound like my mother."

"That's not a bad person to sound like," Iris said. "Isabelle, I have a confession."

"Uh-oh."

"No, it's not a bad one—I don't think. I found myself wishing the other day that you were a man. It would just remove one of our huge complications, you know? It was just a weird thought."

"Well, I'm not going to do that, Iris. It's terribly painful and it never looks real."

We both laughed and the air around us suddenly felt lighter. "I didn't mean that, silly. It was just a thought," she said. "Not a wish, for God's sake."

"I know. And I might have had the same thought, except you're so attractive as a woman."

Two days later, we were a public scandal. We stopped answering the phones in our hotel rooms; if we went out we'd be accosted by photographers who would jump in front of us, leering behind their cameras. I will always believe that our husbands fed us to the press. Thomas and Peter were used to being in control. It was not in their nature to wait for the story to leak out. Their war strategy was to get in front of a story, especially one like this, so they could assume the mantle of the sympathetic husbands who had been cruelly betrayed.

We still didn't know what we were going to do, but we had to live somewhere other than the hotel. Iris had always kept her trust fund money separate from Peter's wealth, so we knew we could afford to buy a house. But before we could set that in motion, I got a phone message from Thomas' attorney.

"Thomas is giving you the Malibu house," he said bluntly. "Since the two of you already desecrated it."

I wanted to respond to the word desecrate, but I clamped my mouth shut.

"And he is going to honor the terms of the pre-nup," he continued. "You can pick up a check at my office. We're starting divorce proceedings immediately. It will take six months to be finalized. There is one more thing—Marjorie wants to live with you and Iris."

"She...she does? What did Thomas say about that?"

"He isn't going to try and keep the child where she doesn't want to be. Is that acceptable to the two of you?" The man sounded like he couldn't wait for this conversation to end.

I didn't need to ask Iris about this, I knew the answer. "Yes, of course."

"Fine. I'll have someone at the house contact you about arrangements. Good day, Mrs. Berendon."

The Berendon brothers filed for divorce at the same time. And on that same day, two women welcomed a six year old girl into their newly formed family. Families are hardly ever the result of design and planning. There is always an element of chance, of fate. The best you can hope for is that love is the red cord binding everyone together. On that front, Iris and I didn't worry about a thing.

10.

It's almost noon, but with Marjorie gone it doesn't matter. The whole day can feel like morning if we want it to. We are lying on the bed, both on our backs, staring up at the ceiling and waiting until our breathing slows down. The phone rings and we glance at each other with the same unspoken question.

"Let it go to voicemail," Iris says. "We'll hear who it is and if - "

Before she can complete the sentence, my mother's voice fills the room. "Isabelle? Are you there? Isabelle?"

I plop across Iris to pick up the phone. My breasts are against her thighs, which is an inappropriate position for talking to one's mother, no matter what the mother-daughter relationship is like. I grab the phone and slide off Iris onto a more respectable area of the mattress.

"Hi, Mother."

"Oh, you're there. Hello, dear. I was wondering if you would go with me to a doctor's appointment on Monday."

Something in my stomach tightens. My mother never goes to doctors. On her fiftieth birthday she swore off the entire medical profession with the exception of her dentist, and I suspect if she could find someone to clean her teeth with crystals, she'd dump him too.

"Okay. What flavor of doctor are we going to?"

"A shaman," my mother says, as if it's the most logical thing in the world.

"A shaman," I repeat, giving Iris a wide-eyed look and enjoying the smile she gives me in return.

"Yes, dear. My friend Tina swears by him. She had receding gums and the dentist was going to take skin from somewhere else in her mouth and do some kind of…well, never mind, it was very ugly sounding. Then she found Savasa. And she's fine now. I mean, her gums are fine."

"Savasa? It sounds like a brand of beer. Mother, are your gums receding?"

"Oh, no. Nothing like that."

Iris gets out of bed and walks into the bathroom. I'm momentarily distracted by the way she passes through sunbeams and shadows. "So, what is your complaint?" I ask my mother. "Because if it's something major…" I don't really want to go there; I make my thoughts skid to a stop. Don't crumble now, Mother. I've lost my son. I need you to stay whole and healthy. I need you to stay forever.

"It's a little embarrassing." I can hear her blushing through the phone line.

"You're embarrassed to tell me but you're going to go confide in a shaman who probably got his name from some obscure yoga pose?"

"I'm bloated," she tells me abruptly, in an are-you-happy-now tone.

"Oh. Well, I guess that's a harmless enough reason to go see someone like that. Where did he get his training? At a commune in Marakesh?"

"Isabelle, please mind your manners when we're there."

Later, I do an internet search of shamans. Nothing I find is very encouraging, and none of the sites offer any remedies for bloating.

Monday morning, I drive Marjorie to school before going to get my mother. Marjorie has never complained about adjusting to a new school in Malibu, but I have wondered at times if it's been harder than she admits. Is this child so determined to make a new life here that she'll ignore whatever problems arise?

"Is Grandma sick?" she asks when we pull into morning traffic. "Is that why you're taking her to a doctor?"

"No, her stomach is just bothering her. She'll be fine. And he isn't really a doctor. He's more of a therapist...sort of. Grandma doesn't think much of medical degrees."

Marjorie doesn't call Thomas' mother Grandma, which I must admit has always given me a perverse sense of pleasure. When she was a toddler, long before I knew her, she started calling the elder Mrs. Berendon, with her waxy looking silver hair and stern jaw, Mootie, and the name stuck. I have no idea where she heard it.

"Daddy is seeing a doctor, too," Marjorie says.

"He is?"

"Uh-huh. A doctor for his head. I heard him talking to Mr. Morrow about it. They didn't know I could hear them. Daddy said the doctor told him to write about that day...you know...the day Nathan died."

We are approaching Marjorie's school, but I pull over before we get to the entrance. "So he's seeing a psychiatrist?" I ask her.

"I guess. Yeah. He told Mr. Morrow he's trying to remember everything about what happened that day. So his doctor told him to keep writing it down over and over and see how much he could remember."

I pull up to the entrance, kiss Marjorie goodbye and watch her walk into the school. So Thomas is trying to figure out if he was the one who left the screen unlocked—I know that's what he's doing, and I know if he ever decides it was him, he will never tell me. Blaming me is too important to him.

I pick up my mother a little before ten. The yellow Volvo is long gone but she does have a car—a dark blue Honda, which she avoids driving as much as possible because she says there's too much traffic and the other cars on the road are too big.

She gives me the address and directions, which land us at a driftwood colored house in the heart of Venice. Two teenage boys in hoodies and baggy jeans eye us coldly as get out of my silver Jaguar. Emphatically, I push the alarm button on my key chain, wishing the sound were louder.

"Look at the lovely flower beds out front," my mother says as we walk up the path. "And window boxes, too." She stops to admire pansies intermingled with clusters of white alyssum. Jasmine vines are tangled together in one corner of the small yard, waiting for warmer weather before they bloom again. "I always say you can trust a man who gardens."

"Mother, I've never heard you say that."

"Well, I've said it to myself. Many times."

We walk into a house that's ripe with the smell of incense. What would normally be the living room has been arranged as a waiting room, apparently with the assistance of a feng-shui consultant. One of those fake rock fountains you can buy at Home Depot is in the corner and a round end table is laden with chunks of rose quartz. I suppose I was expecting a man in some sort of headdress—a turban perhaps—but when Savasa breezes in from another room, he looks like a Jewish guy from Queens. I'm tempted to ask what his real name is, but I don't. He's wearing Gap khakis and a pale blue shirt. I glance at his feet, expecting to see sandals and socks, but he's wearing Nikes.

"Mrs. Haller?" he says in a voice much more robust than his slight build would suggest.

"Yes. Hello—it's so nice to meet you after our lovely phone conversation." My mother is smiling, shaking his hand warmly, almost as if this is a first date.

I have one of those moments when you see someone through a clearer lens—as if you have been merely brushing past them for years but suddenly, in that instant, become acutely aware of details. I am looking at a sixty-three year old woman whose face has settled into itself, the features arranged around lines drawn by life and time. Her shoulder-length hair, while still red, is streaked with white, like clay soil after a light snowfall. Today, she is dressed in a loose green skirt the color of pine trees, a white shirt and a hand-woven vest a friend bought for her in Peru. Silver bracelets adorn her wrists. To my knowledge, Catherine Haller has never opened a fashion magazine; she is a committed bohemian and will remain one until she dies. I didn't appreciate her uniqueness until I entered a life of women so perfectly sculpted by scalpels, so observant of fashion trends that they seem to have walked out of the pages of Vogue. I used to stand back at parties I attended with Thomas and wonder about the blood flow of the women around me.

"This is my daughter, Isabelle," my mother says, and Savasa shakes my hand firmly. I catch the look in his eyes. He knows perfectly well who I am. He might call himself a shaman but I'll bet he reads gossip columns and probably has a subscription to People magazine.

In his inner sanctum, where he leads us, there is nothing as crass as an issue of People. The morning sunlight is barely visible through the Venetian blinds, which are slanted down so the room remains shadowy and dim. I have the feeling Savasa doesn't want his clients to think about time, hence the shades positioned to block out the passage of the sun. He leads my mother to a reclining chair and runs his hands across her body, although without actually touching her. He keeps his palms about a half inch away like he's trying to divine water beneath the surface of her skin.

"Ah-hah," he says after a moment. "You complained about your stomach when we spoke on the phone."

"Yes," my mother tells him. "It's bloated. It aches a lot. I've never had that problem before."

"It's your heart," he pronounces in a somber tone, stepping back from her and surveying her like one would a painting.

"Her heart is bloated?" I ask. I'm ready to drag her out of here. This is ridiculous, and I can't wait to hear what he's going to charge.

He glances disapprovingly in my direction, then ignores me and returns to her. "Your heart is heavy with sadness. All the grief you've been holding just sinks down. It has to show up somewhere. I think your belly is full of tears."

My mother nods slowly, contemplating this. I can hear the sound of water from the plaster fountain in the other room, the hum of traffic from the street outside. For some reason, my mind wanders to the flocks of tiny white birds that cluster along the tide line at the beach and then lift off in unison, spurred by some invisible communication. I want the sorrow my mother has inside her to lift off, fly away on a hundred small wings.

"We've had…some sadness in the family," she says softly, turning her eyes away from Savasa to the window shaded against the day.

Savasa nods solemnly. I'm sure he knows exactly what she's talking about. Our travails have been discussed on the evening news, blogged about, emblazoned on the front pages of tabloids. He takes her right hand in his, lays his other hand across her wrist. "Your pulse is tired and heavy. I want you to go home and meditate on this image. You are entering a dark cave, full of unknown things, strange sounds. You must go deep into the cave, you can't turn back. And once you have entered total blackness, you just have to sit there and be alone with yourself. Accept the pain that comes up, accept the memories. Don't run, even if you want to. Then come back here for another session and we'll do some work on your chakras that will lead you out of the cave, back into clearer space and sunlight." He reaches over to the table and picks up a small, round piece of polished black rock. "Here," he says, handing it to her. "This is tourmaline. Its energy is very powerful. Keep it with you at all times. Even when you sleep, put it under your pillow."

"Oh, like a tooth," my mother tells him, and laughs—nervously, I think. "For the Tooth Fairy."

"If you like," Savasa answers. "Whatever image works."

My mother's eyes are glistening with tears as she thanks him and stands up. The fee is one hundred and ten dollars, which I pay as I knew I would. I don't mind—money is something I have plenty of now—but I still don't like wasting it and this is looking like waste to me.

"I feel better already," my mother tells me when get in the car.

"Because he told you to go in a cave with a piece of black rock?" I ask her, my voice going up about half an octave.

"Isabelle, he's a shaman. He comes from a family of shamans and healers. For eighteen hundred years, this has been a tradition with his people. It's a genetic gift that runs in his family."

"Oh, for God's sake. Who could you possibly get to do that kind of family tree?"

My mother shifts in the seat, angling herself toward the window. "Fine. If you want to be cynical, go right ahead. It's not healthy, you know, that attitude."

We drive in silence for more than a few minutes. I feel sixteen again—sullen and resentful. Finally, as we are heading down Pico Boulevard, I ask the question that tugged at me back there in that dim room.

"Mother, when you told him there had been sadness in our family, were you only referring to Nathan or did you mean my divorce too? Did you mean Iris and me?"

She shifts back around to face me. "Oh, Isabelle, of course not. I'm so happy that you finally fell in love. I wondered if you ever would. I knew you didn't really love Thomas, but…well, it wasn't my place to say anything."

"Okay. Just needed to ask."

"But you know," she says slowly. "There are some kinds of love that require work."

"As in love between two women?"

"No, dear. As in you and Marjorie."

I turn onto the street where I grew up, where I always run into an earlier version of myself. The shadow of a girl walks down the sidewalk, practicing an attitude she hopes will keep the world at bay—a walk that says, Don't mess with me—I don't need anyone.

"I think I just need some more time—after Nathan," I tell my mother as I pull up to the house.

She doesn't say anything until we are walking up the front steps and her key is in the lock. "Sometimes you have to push your way past the sadness, Isabelle. So everything doesn't fall apart. Or fall away. Marjorie needs you—she lets you know that in so many ways."

"I know, Mother. I'm trying. At least I think I am."

She unlocks the door and turns to me, smiling before she kisses me on the cheek, dismissing me with her eyes.

"I'm going to lie down for a bit, otherwise I'd ask you to stay and have some tea. But I'm awfully tired."

As I walk back to my car I think about all the times I've offered to get her another house—sell this place so she can move to a nicer area. 'Thank you, dear, but no. This is my home,' is always her answer.

The city has closed its jaws around this small neighborhood. Mrs. Middlington is gone and a young couple with a new baby is living next door. There is no flower bed, no narrow little lawn with a whirly-bird sprinkler attachment on the end of a hose. Just weeds. Most of the houses have bars on the windows now and occasionally graffiti is sprayed on the curbs and sidewalks.

But to my mother it's home and you can't argue with where someone feels they belong. It's like arguing about who someone has fallen in love with—same thing. Belonging isn't a decision; it's a condition of the heart.

In the flat blue noontime of a seasonless California day, I drive back to my home—Iris.

11.

On short notice, Iris and I manage to get Kim, Marjorie's usual baby-sitter, so we can go out to dinner. Kim is a student at Pepperdine, the Malibu university run by the Church of Christ. She seems to embody the clean-cut religious identity of the institution, except for the hickies on her neck, which I'm fairly certain the Church of Christ wouldn't approve of. Although they're probably Christian hickies, so they might give her a pass.

Nobu, Malibu's expensive sushi restaurant, is frequented by those of us who don't need to worry about the amount of the bill. At times when I walk into restaurants like this I still feel like an imposter. The girl I once was is right beneath my skin—the kid in stolen clothes from the house by the freeway, the girl whose father died in prison. It's usually a fleeting feeling, and it is on this evening as well. It's a reminder, though, that we never leave who we were in the past.

Still, within minutes, I fold comfortably into the candlelit room.

Iris and I are cheerful gluttons, ordering more sushi than we can eat and an expensive bottle of Chardonnay.

"So let me get this straight," Iris says, after I tell her about my morning with my mother. "She's having digestive problems, and this guy told her to go into a cave -"

"A metaphorical cave," I interject.

"Right. With a chunk of tourmaline."

"Uh-huh. Although I think she's also supposed to put that under her pillow."

"And this will help her stomach, except she doesn't actually have a problem with her stomach, it's more an issue of the heart," Iris says, with forced earnestness.

"That's basically it, yes. According to him, her belly is full of tears."

"Does this guy have any kind of degree?" Iris asks, as she maneuvers a piece of salmon sushi into the grip of her chopsticks.

"Gee, Iris, I'm not sure. There might have been a framed document between the rock fountain, the photo of a swami and the altar of crystals, but it was hard to see through all the smoke from the incense. What kind of degree could he have? A certificate of shamanism?"

"Just asking," Iris says, pouring more wine into her glass.

Her eyes catch someone behind me and I turn to see Harlan Brandt coming over to our table. Harlan is a successful Hollywood producer and is also our next door neighbor on the beach. Openly gay, he lives with a much younger actor—Bruce Devore, whose blond, chiseled-body handsomeness might make a casual observer assume that a vacuous mind is the inevitable companion. But Bruce can shatter that assumption in a matter of seconds. When my mother met him, she gave him a penetrating look and pronounced, "You are smart as a fox—I can tell."

"I think the saying is sly as a fox," Bruce responded. "And I'm that, too. Smart and sly And I so appreciate the compliment. You are a very astute woman."

Bruce waves to us from a nearby table as Harlan comes up behind me and puts his hands on my shoulders.

"How are my neighbors?" he asks us.

"We're good," Iris tells him. "Hanging in there."

He leans down and angles his face toward mine. "Yes?"

"Yes," I assure him.

"I've been in New York but I'm back now for a while. I'll organize a little dinner gathering soon."

"We'll hold you to that," Iris tells him. "I never forget an offer of a meal."

"Enjoy," Harlan says and heads back to his table.

"You know, I wonder if we would ever have gotten to know Harlan and Bruce if our lives had stayed the same," I say to Iris.

"Doubtful. In typical Berendon fashion Thomas kept the high-profile people to himself. Didn't he?"

"Oh yes…"

I've never told Iris, and I will certainly never tell Harlan, what Thomas said when it was decided Iris and I would take the beach house: "Perfect. The two of you living next door to two fags. A match made in heaven."

"Fuck you," was my response. Not that Thomas cared what I said to him at that point.

I met Harlan before Iris did. He came by a few days after we had moved in, on an afternoon when the sky was sharp as blue glass. Iris was working at the women's shelter and Marjorie was not yet living with us. I was still foggy with grief; I would spend hours doing basically nothing, just staring out the window or pacing from one room to the next, chased by thoughts of Nathan, certain that if I rounded a corner he would be there and it would all have been a bad dream. By afternoon, I'd decided to do one productive thing—bake banana bread. I'd just laid out all the ingredients in the kitchen and had discovered that the carton of eggs in the fridge were no longer good.

When a male voice called, "Hello?" from the beach side, I had one contact lens in, the other poised on my finger. I was getting ready to run to the market. I put my left lens back in the case and went out to the deck. Harlan Brandt was standing on the steps.

"Hi," he said. "I thought I'd be neighborly and welcome you. Is this a bad time?"

"Oh, no," I stammered. "Except I only have one contact lens in and my eggs are expired."

"Oh my, I'm so sorry," he said in a heavy, slightly puzzled tone. "About your eggs. You and Iris were planning on having a baby?"

"No, no—not my personal eggs. I didn't mean that." I could feel my face getting red. "The eggs in the refrigerator. I was going to bake banana bread."

Harlan smiled, relieved. "I see. I love banana bread. Well, I just wanted to introduce myself. I'm Harlan Brandt. We've waved to each other—before—when you were here with Thomas. But we were never properly introduced."

"Right. My ex-husband didn't always introduce his wife."

Thomas used to lean over the balcony to chat with Harlan, never thinking of introducing me, leaving me lingering awkwardly behind him, like a Geisha, although Geishas never showed awkwardness .

"Come in, Harlan. I don't really need to go to the store right now. But I do need to put in my other lens so I can actually see you."

He sat down on a deck chair and waited for me. When I came back outside, he said, "I'm very sorry about your son. It's always hard to know what to say, but I didn't want to step around it like…well, you know. Like people tend to do."

"Yeah, I do know. It's actually a relief to talk about it."

We ended up sitting on the deck for hours, starting with tea and moving on to wine as the day grew late and the tides changed. Shallow waves lapped close to the deck when the tide was its highest. We were like two old sailors steering our memories across rough seas, finding our way into safe harbors—old friends who had traveled down the years together. Except we had just met. It happens like that sometimes—although not often. The wind turned velvety, the sky filled with sunset, and the butter melted on the kitchen counter. I'd completely forgotten about making bread.

I talked to Harlan about love—the subject I'd only discussed with Iris until that day. Love—that thing that had claimed me, turned me upside down, unzipped and undone me. Iris was never far from me, I told Harlan—she was always next to my thoughts, my dreams, my day. She inhabited the night—all of it—every star, cloud, planet and shadow. No lover had ever claimed so much space before. Until her, I was a champion of incomplete relationships. I kept my husband at bay even while I lifted my white wedding veil and took a vow to be his.

"I can relate," Harlan said. "I spent years telling myself I was looking for love, but I found such creative ways to avoid it. Or sabotage it. You know how it felt when I fell in love with Bruce? It was like what my terribly nearsighted friend said after he had lasik surgery on his eyes. He wept because suddenly he could see clearly. He wept at the beauty of vision. It was just like that."

"Lasik for the soul," I offered.

"Exactly," Harlan said. "Lasik for life. Let's make T-shirts with that on it. Although no one will know what we're really talking about. On second thought, let's keep it between us."

When we get home from Nobu, Iris pays Kim and I go upstairs to check on Marjorie. I find her awake, huddled under the covers with a flashlight. Carefully, I lift up a corner of her cave.

"Hello, in there."

She scrambles out, holding a picture book in one hand and the flashlight in the other. "I wasn't sleepy yet."

"I can see that." I sit on the edge of the bed and fluff up the pillows so they will look like an inviting place for her head. "Did you have fun tonight?"

"Uh-huh. We watched Finding Nemo and had chocolate ice cream."

Marjorie is somewhat addicted to Finding Nemo. By my count, this is about the fifth time she's watched it. "So we've solved the mystery of why you aren't sleepy," I tell her as she flops over on her back and I pull the covers up under her chin. "All that sugar from the ice-cream. You're wired up on glucose."

She reaches out and plays with the sleeve of my sweater. "Remember Nathan's birthday party when he got chocolate icing all over his face?"

"I do, yes." The image is as fresh as it was that day—his small face smeared with chocolate, his hands—also covered in icing—flapping wildly in the air. He was having so much fun making a mess, I felt like a traitor cleaning him up.

"Maybe they have chocolate in heaven," Marjorie says. "You think?"

"It's possible. In fact, I'd bet on it. It's heaven, they have everything delicious. You should sleep now."

She nods okay and I kiss her goodnight, knowing the minute I get down the hall she'll be back under the covers with her flashlight.

"Goodnight, Mommy," she says softly as I slip out the door.

Will there ever come a time when that word doesn't wound me? When I don't hear behind it the thin, high voice of my son? It's just two syllables, a jumble of nouns and consonants, but it cuts into my veins. A word shouldn't have that much power.

The only light falling on Iris and me a little later is a filigree of moonlight. She holds me prisoner with deep kisses as we roll across the sheets.

I would tumble down hillsides with Iris, not bothering to map out the land below. As long as I was fused to her, breathing in her breath, slipping across her skin, I'd be content. I'd be happy. She is the only map I want. I know the thin white scar above her kneecap where she cut herself on glass as a child. I know the soft skin on the back of her neck, pale and hidden from the sun by her hair. I know the ridge of her collarbone—my tongue has traced it, my fingers have read it like Braille.

Something cracks open in me tonight when her mouth finds my breast. I find myself suddenly crying, my tears as much a surprise to me as they are to her.

"I'm sorry," I manage to say.

She slides up and nuzzles her face against mine. "What is it?"

"Nathan. I just thought of Nathan. I loved nursing him, and I guess when you -"

I don't finish the sentence. I don't need to.

Iris rearranges us, lying so I am curved against her, harbored in her arms. I cry in a soft stream and she lets me, not bothering to speak because there is nothing to say. There is an artistry to cradling a lover's sorrow and Iris is a master at it. I didn't know, before, how different it would feel. After Nathan died, I wept into white pillows late at night with Thomas fast asleep next to me,but a million miles away. I took long showers, mixing tears with streams of warm water and fooled myself with thick terrycloth towels when I stepped out and told myself I felt better. I stared too long out windows, seeing nothing and hearing only the awful quiet of a house without my baby in it.

Grief isn't meant to be a game of solitaire.

The moon moves across us as my tears give way to a tiredness so intense I think sleep might swallow me whole. The last thing I'll remember of this night is the scent of Iris' skin and her hand, light as a leaf, on my shoulder.

Iris offers to take Marjorie to school in the morning and I willingly agree. My eyes are puffy from last night's tears. I'm distracted and vague—I'd probably be a hazard behind the wheel. I kiss them both goodbye, drink a cup of coffee and pull on some clothes to take a long walk on the beach.

The air is dry and the sky over the ocean is glazed with smog; the Santa Anas are marshaling their forces. Cruel winds that they are, they're getting ready to siphon every molecule of moisture from the air and sweep the city's pollutants out over the Pacific.

I walk north from our house toward Malibu Colony. This is not the first time I have been a Malibu resident. Ironically, when I met Thomas I was working for a man who lived in Malibu Colony and who has since moved. I was his live-in assistant—his keeper, his shopper, his scheduler.

Oddly, I was directed to this well-paying job while lying on the examining table in my gynecologist's office.

"So, no college for you, huh? What are your plans then?" Dr. Korzenborn asked as I lay open like a wishbone, my feet in the stirrups.

Dr. Korzenborn was white-haired, grandfatherly, and had an annoying habit of conducting entire conversations while staring into my vagina. But he was my mother's doctor (she hadn't yet turned fifty, so she hadn't yet dismissed the medical profession), he had delivered me, and he charged us very little for check-ups. So I forgave him for inappropriately directing small-talk to my cervix.

"I've been working in a restaurant but I'm looking for a better job," I answered, scrunching my chin down so I could at least direct myself to the top of his head.

"It's fine, Isabelle."

"Not really. I haven't found a new job yet."

"I meant your cervix," he said.

"Oh, that's good." I sat up and he gently pushed me back down so he could examine my breasts—also an odd way to have a conversation but preferable to the other end of my anatomy.

"I have a friend whose son is looking for a Girl Friday," he said as he pinched my nipples. "You know, a helper."

"Yes, I know what a Girl Friday is. What does this man do for a living?"

"He's a mathematical genius," Dr. Korzenborn told me, which didn't exactly answer my question. He motioned me to sit up so he could tap on my back. "He was a child prodigy, actually. Turned his gifts onto the stock market and, my Lord, has he made a bundle. He lives in a beach house now, but he doesn't seem to have a clue about everyday life."

This was how I ended up arriving at the gates of Malibu Colony in my mother's yellow Volvo with my brand new driver's license, wearing a skirt and sweater that I hoped would convey dependability.

The guard at the gate eyed me suspiciously, as if I must be lost. I gave him Campbell Lockett's name and he grudgingly checked his clip-board, gave me a pass for the dashboard and waved me in.

I pulled up in front of an ocean-side house and found the gate standing open. Looking in, I saw a short brick pathway across a small garden area that had no plants in it. The front door of the house was also ajar. Either he's opened it for me or he really likes the airflow, I thought.

"Hello?" I called, venturing down the path past empty terra cotta pots and a decapitated cement swan—its head tossed a few feet away. It looked like some ferns had once grown in one corner; now there were just brown, dried-up fronds.

"Come on in," I heard. It was a man's voice from somewhere inside the house...which, when I walked in, looked as bare as the garden graveyard outside. There was one round table in the living room and two hard-backed chairs, a cheap stand-up lamp in the cor-ner—no sofa, no armchairs, no paintings or prints on the walls.

An attractive, dark-haired man emerged from the hallway. I noticed how thin he was—one of those guys who forgets to eat, I guessed. "You must be Isabelle," he said, offering me a hesitant handshake.

"Yes. Hi—Campbell?"

"Uh-huh. Well, let's sit down."

We took our seats on the two uncomfortable chairs and faced each other. Questions tugged at our polite smiles. I assumed he was supposed to start—wasn't this a job interview? But he didn't seem to know that.

Finally he said, "So you're here to snap my life into shape, huh?"

"Well, I need a job, and apparently you need a Girl Friday?"

Campbell laughed. "A Girl Friday? That's funny. Especially since I need help with all seven days of the week. Isn't assistant a better label?"

"Yeah, okay. But...look, I have to be honest. It's not like I have a résumé or references or...anything, really. I've never been an assis-tant before."

He smiled and seemed to feel a little more relaxed. "Well, I don't have any experience in being assisted, so this will probably work out fine. I have a little trouble with the daily aspects of life. I know numbers, math, the stock market. But a grocery market? Haven't a clue. My mother's been dropping off food and essentials, but she's getting tired of doing that. Do you drive?"

"Yeah—that's how I got here," I told him. It's L.A., I felt like saying—everyone drives.

"I don't," he said. "I never learned. Maybe I should get a car and you can teach me."

"How do you get around?"

He shrugged as if it was no big deal. "I go to New York a lot—I don't need to drive there. And when I'm here, I hire a car and driver. I need furniture, too, as you can see. I'll just give you my credit card and you can go shopping for me."

He was so lucky I walked through his door. If the Bad Witch From Oz had crossed his threshold, he'd have lost his shirt.

"Campbell, I'd love to work for you if you want me to. But may I point out that you're really lucky because I'm a trustworthy person—I'm not going to rip you off. Someone else could have walked in here and…well, you're kind of an easy mark, if you don't mind me saying so."

He smiled. "I know. I'm a bit naïve. My mother blames herself. She says I never matured properly, possibly because she named me after a can of soup."

"Oh. Really? Campbell isn't some old family name?"

"Nope," he said, shaking his head emphatically. "She had morning sickness and Campbell's tomato soup was the only thing she could keep down. So, the name was decided upon before I ever arrived."

I drove back to my mother's house that day as a newly employed person. I was to report back to Malibu Colony the next morning, only not in the yellow Volvo. Campbell was sending a car and driver for me with instructions to go car shopping for him.

"What's he like?" my mother asked.

"He's kind of like an idiot-savant."

"Oh my," she said. "You're working for a disabled person? Isabelle, I know you need a job, but you don't have training for that."

"He's not disabled, Mother. He's just kind of strange. Limited, I guess you'd say. A genius at numbers, but so far he's flunking Life 101."

This is how I entered a world of carefree money—a world full of people who never worried about price tags or credit card balances. Campbell Lockett opened a portal for me into this rarified realm and I gladly took up residence. But if you are an assistant, there is a caveat: You are, when all is said and done, an employee. Personal assistants get the perks, the lifestyle, the shopping trips (with someone else's credit card.) They make decisions, place phone calls to billionaires and occasionally celebrities. But they can never forget they are completely dependant upon the person who writes the checks. It's a tennis game for the ego. It can all change in one mercurial moment.

Fortunately for me, Campbell was not fickle when it came to other human beings—dim, at times, and somewhat clueless, but always loyal. I quickly transformed his house into a tastefully decorated home. He returned from a trip to New York and walked into a living room with plush sofas, sisal rugs, end tables, graceful yet masculine lamps, sleek, modern-looking Roman shades on the windows. I had stocked his refrigerator with food, bought some new clothes for him, and even put some vitamins on the kitchen counter since I thought he looked a bit pallid.

Our life progressed from there, the two of us weaving a tighter rope until eventually I moved into his guest bedroom, took his house as my permanent residence, and pointed out to my mother that she needn't be sad, she now had beach access in Malibu whenever she wanted. Campbell depended on me for social scheduling, shopping, organizing his trips, and bolstering his often-wavering confidence. I was mother, assistant, friend and confidante…and I was learning a great deal about living in the world of the extremely wealthy.

It all seems so long ago. I went from an assistant to Mrs. Thomas Berendon; then I became a mother. Now I'm a woman who has buried her child—they don't have a name for that, which is strange. On this dry, wind-scraped morning, in this new incarnation of my life, I end up on the beach of Malibu Colony, slowing down in front of the house I once lived in. Campbell sold it years ago. A family lives here now, although I don't know them. A golden retriever is on the deck and children's toys are scattered on the sand in front of the house. There are plush drapes framing the living room windows, and large potted plants bordering the steps up to the deck. A bright blue umbrella is perched above a round wooden table surrounded by chairs. I'm sure the narrow front garden is green and lush. I'm sure the house is always full of voices and footsteps…life.

Everything changes. People leave, drift away. People die. But when someone dies who is supposed to have so much more life to live—when it's a child, when it's your child—you feel like the earth suddenly altered itself around you. You're an alien on a planet that was once familiar. You stop in front of a house you once lived in, or a street you once knew, you look at a photograph or a letter on faded stationery and you can't recall who you were then and how you got to who you are now. You wonder where all those years went. What would you change if you could? You tuck your history under your arm and head on down the road, hoping for the best.

In the end, we all become bundles of stories; we take them with us every time we go out the door. No wonder our footsteps seem to grow heavier with time.

As I turn to walk back home, I feel the first gust of hot desert wind. Sand is already being strafed and blown about, stinging my legs as it hits me. Soon all the footprints on this shore will be erased and, with winds this fierce, new ones will only stay for a few moments.

12.

For the next two days, the Santa Ana winds batter us. The sea is full of whitecaps and no one is hearty enough, or foolish enough, to walk along the sand. The beach looks deserted. I hate this weather, and no amount of cajoling from Iris can take the edge off my mood. Whenever these hot winds blow off the desert and rush toward the sea, canyon residents and people living along the coast start sniffing the air and checking the sky for signs of smoke. Fires usually come along with these winds. And even if they don't, the fear of fire creeps across every face you see.

Marjorie has a ballet performance at the little dance studio she goes to after school, and I'm grateful for the distraction from the weather. Iris was supposed to go with me but there was an emergency at the women's shelter, so I sit with other parents who are watching their daughters leap about in tutus, trying valiantly to balance on their toes. I should have asked my mother to come with me; she'd have loved watching these seedling dancers.

I have only seen a few photographs of Marjorie's mother, and that was an accident. They tumbled out of a book Thomas was lifting down from a shelf. Marjorie has her jaw line, I think, and her slender features. She has her mother's full lower lip, a mouth that can just as easily pout as cajole. But she has Thomas' blue-green eyes—not only the exact shade of his, but also the beguiling almond shape.

It was Thomas' eyes that first nailed me on an overcast afternoon in Beverly Hills when I was clothes shopping for Campbell. In the men's department of Ralph Lauren Polo, my hands reached for a cashmere sweater while the gaze of a handsome man in a dark gray suit checked them for a wedding ring. He then surveyed the rest of me. Thanks to Campbell, I was wearing Cole Haan boots, a Donna Karan sweater, and expensive jeans.

He might have decided that I was a rich man's daughter, or the beneficiary of some old-money trust fund. I never did ask Thomas about his first impression. He clearly didn't know that beneath the expensive clothes, the facials, the pampering, the quickly learned manners, a girl-from-the-wrong-side-of-town still heard echoes of the freeway in her sleep.

He caught up with me on Rodeo Drive and introduced himself— Thomas Berendon. I would never have recognized him, but I certainly recognized the name. Berendon's flagship store was a stately presence in Beverly Hills and several other stores were lofty additions to malls and shopping areas around the country.

"Excuse me," he said, and lifted his sunglasses so he could fix me with the eyes that would be my undoing. "I don't mean to be forward…"

"But you're going to be anyway?" I asked him.

He smiled at me and for a brief moment I inhabited the role I wanted to be playing. I actually felt as if I were to-the-manner-born. I had him fooled. And I liked it.

We went for coffee and Thomas was charming and attentive, leaning forward and absorbing me with his eyes whenever I talked. Sometimes now I try to remember him like that—to feel something of what I felt that day, just to see if I can. But I don't know where that man went, or if he was ever really there at all.

For forty minutes, Marjorie and her ballet-school classmates proudly show off what they've been learning. When it's over and they smile and curtsy, I and the other parents move onto the floor like a tide. We extend arms, kisses, compliments. We gush and gloat and sweep our children into big strong embraces as if there isn't anything bad in the world that can hurt them. As if life is a long easy stream with occasional pirouettes thrown in for fun. I take Marjorie for ice cream afterwards and when we walk back to the car, it feels like the winds might be lessening. Or it might just be that my mood has improved.

Iris greets us at the door, having just gotten home herself. She's holding a piece of white paper but says nothing about it until she gets a full report from Marjorie about the ballet performance.

"You'll come to the next one, right?" Marjorie asks as she heads upstairs.

"Absolutely. I promise," Iris assures her, and then turns her attention to me. "Your mother left a note in the mailbox."

"Really? She doesn't usually just drop by." I reach for the note but Iris has unfolded it and is shaking her head in bewilderment as she studies it. "This is really odd, Isabelle. 'I came by with some cows but you weren't here. Couldn't wait, I'm married.' Is she okay? This makes no sense at all. Should we be concerned?"

"That's probably not what it says," I tell her, snatching the note from her hands. "The only thing that's worse than my mother's spelling is her penmanship. She once wrote a note excusing me from school that said, 'Isabelle is sick. Please execute her.'" I quickly scan the note and decipher the true words. "Okay, this says, 'I came by with some news. Couldn't wait. I'm hurried.'"

"I'm hurried?" Iris repeats.

"I know. Not grammatically correct. But the good news is, she wasn't bringing us cows."

Marjorie bounds down the stairs dressed in jeans and a sweatshirt. "I'm going out to the beach," she announces without stopping for an answer.

"Just for a little bit," Iris calls after her. "It's going to be dark soon."

The sun is setting in a rusty orange haze formed from the city's smog that the Santa Ana's have blown in our direction. Iris and I go into the living room so we can watch Marjorie through the windows. I open a bottle of wine and pour two glasses before going to the phone to call my mother. She answers on the second ring, and something in her voice makes my breath catch. She sounds old, tired. Maybe she was napping and I woke her.

"Hi, Mother—I just got home and found your note. I wish I'd known you were coming out here..."

"Yes, well. It was a spur of the moment thing." There is a long pause and I find myself measuring her breathing. "Isabelle, I didn't want to tell you this on the phone but I suppose now I should. I have cancer, dear. Incurable cancer. Ovarian. Although it's spread beyond that."

Everything around me seems to sharpen and slow. I see Marjorie outside, twirling on the sand. Iris is standing by the window, the sun's last light resting on her shoulder. The North Star is punched into the deep blue sky like a white beacon.

"There has to be a mistake," I tell my mother. As if my refusal to believe this is powerful enough to turn reality around.

"There isn't a mistake, Isabelle," she answers, her voice muddy and somber.

"Did your shaman tell you this? Because if he did I hardly think he's qualified."

"No. I went to a regular doctor. I just felt something was very wrong. I've felt bad for a while."

"I'm coming over," I tell my mother. "I'm leaving in a few minutes."

Iris is staring at me when I hang up; I know the blood has drained from my face. "My mother has cancer," I tell her. "She says it's incurable." I nearly finish my wine in a single gulp. "God, Iris—my mother is dying?" It comes out like a question because it can't possibly be anything else. It's someone else's voice coming out of me— that incredulous tone, the words foreign and strange. It's someone else's story. There was a mix-up. I wandered into the wrong scene, the wrong dream. I'll wake up in a minute.

Iris comes over and puts her arms around me. "How can I help?" she asks, her mouth a warm pocket against my neck. "What can I do? Do you want me and Marjorie to go with you?"

"No. Let's not tell Marjorie yet."

But we have to tell her something because at that moment she runs through the door and stops abruptly when she figures out that our embrace is not just a casually affectionate one. With all that she's gone through, Marjorie has a well-honed instinct for bad news.

"What?" she says, the glass door leading out to the deck still open behind her, as if offering an easy escape to the wide shore just below the deck.

Iris takes this one, for which I am extremely grateful. She leaves me, goes to Marjorie, swinging the door shut with one hand and slipping the other around Marjorie's waist. "Grandma isn't feeling well, so Isabelle's going to drive into town and see her. We'll order some pizza, okay?"

"Can I go?" Marjorie asks, her eyes boring into me.

I shake my head no, trying to pull some soothing words out of the air around me. "It's better if I go by myself. She doesn't have a lot of energy—she's just feeling sick. You know? Like when you're sick and you just want to sleep?"

Marjorie says okay but I have a feeling she doesn't believe me.

Less than an hour later, I pull up to my mother's house and notice the front door ajar. The yellow porch light is on as well as several lamps in the living room. But as I walk up the path I feel emptiness in front of me, the silence of no one there.

"Mother?"

I get no answer and I suddenly have a glimpse of what the world will feel like without her in it. Her absence is vast, terrifying.

"Mother?" I call out again, louder this time. I'm standing beneath the yellow wash of the porch light, training my eyes into the darkness.

"Over here, Isabelle." Her voice comes out of the shadows along the side of the house.

I go down the wooden steps and find her crouched alongside the fence, stroking a large tabby cat who is eating from a tin of cat food—I assume, courtesy of my mother. "I don't know his name," she says in a soft voice when I crouch down beside her. "He started showing up a couple of weeks ago and he has no collar. I've asked around and no one seems to know anything. So I feed him and let him stay as long as he wants."

My mother's hair is pulled back into a single braid that falls down her back. She's wearing sweat pants and a baggy blue sweater that must be as old as I am. Light spilling from the neighbors' windows makes the lines in her face look deeper. I find myself memorizing details, imprinting images in my mind—the veins in her hand as she pets the cat, the careful way she's rolled her sleeves so they just graze her wrists. There is the shiver of another presence in these shadows. Something dark, attached to her heels. This presence will slow her steps, shorten her stride, and eventually consume her.

She stands up and leaves the cat to his feast, walks slowly around to the steps knowing I'll be right behind her. I've followed my mother over dozens of thresholds, often into houses we had no business entering. She used to stop at open houses and pretend that we were actually in the market for a new home—that we could afford one. Incorporating me into her game of make-believe, she'd lead me through elegant, large rooms, marble-floored bathrooms, sometimes with the real-estate agent close behind. She'd invent other family members—one time I had twin brothers who had just turned two, so of course we needed a larger home.

As I got older, I realized she was wandering through the rooms of a life she thought she might have had…if she had chosen differently…if she hadn't settled on my father, who stole so much more than merchandise.

When we step through the front door into a pool of lamplight, she stops and looks around her house as if she's seeing it for the first time.

"I've lived in this house most of my adult life. And now it's nearly over." She says this softly, as if for a moment she's forgotten I'm there and is only talking to herself.

"Mother -"

"Isabelle, I know this is hard for you to accept. Especially so soon after Nathan," she tells me gently. "But this is what life has dealt us. We'll make the best of the time we have. It's all we can do."

My legs suddenly feel weak. I go over to the couch and sink down into it. My mother comes over and sits down beside me, delicately putting a hand over mine—as if I'm the one who is sick. But she's the one in the crosshairs of a disease that's used to conquering its victims.

"I want to find a specialist to send you to," I tell her, trying to regain control, to switch the roles back to their rightful place. I'm feverish, desperate and she's a cool stream. It's supposed to be the other way around.

"I don't want anyone else surveying my organs," she says. "They did a whole picture of my insides. I guess it's amazing they have all that machinery to look inside a person, but I find it slightly disturbing. It is an invasion, you know. Anyway, I have cancer in several places including my liver and pancreas. I'm not going to finish out my life pumped full of poisons and hooked up to tubes. And I won't go into a hospital under any circumstances. I'm afraid you're going to have to respect my wishes, dear."

"So that's it? You're going to give up, just like that? Without a fight?"

"Isabelle, this isn't a war. I'm dying—I have no choice about that. The only choice I have is how I die. I won't be a guinea pig for doctors and I won't go into one of those horrible white places where death is just another day at work."

I can't argue with that, even though tears are pushing at the back of my eyes. My mother looks serene, almost relieved. I wonder if for all these years, without me knowing it, she's been growing tired of life. Not too long ago, she had a reason to wake up every day—to be delighted with life—when Nathan was still here. When he died, something died in all of us, but maybe it was even more pronounced in her. This small, empty house, the whisper of memories that, after a while, stop caressing and just haunt. The bed that's so big around her thin shape. The toys she bought for her grandchild, now just sad reminders scattered on a floor he will never run across again. I imagine her in the evenings turning on lights in rooms no one will go into. Has she wondered: Why am I doing this—I could get by with one lamp in a single room? Did the loneliness just wear and wear over time until the threads couldn't hold anymore?

Many things can end a life—some have nothing to do with the body.

My mother goes into the kitchen to make tea for us. It's her remedy for everything. Cancer, death, a bad day at work…tea.

I look around this room, this house—my history. I remember a day so long ago I'm not even sure how old I was—around ten I think—when, despite the gray threat of a storm, or perhaps because of it, my mother decided we should go to the beach. All of us. My father was actually there that Sunday morning, sitting at the kitchen table with his coffee and the newspaper. As if this were a normal thing.

My mother was making French toast. As she lifted the pieces with a spatula and placed them on a platter, she cast a dreamy look out the window at the gray drizzly day and said, "We should go to the beach today."

"Have you lost your marbles, woman?" my father asked, peering over the top of his newspaper. "It's going to rain cats and dogs out there."

"It will be an adventure, Frank," my mother said, pointing a look at him that suggested they had once shared adventures—in another time. "We'll have the whole beach to ourselves. We can sit under a beach umbrella to stay dry."

"And then drive to the hospital with pneumonia," my father grumbled, slapping down the paper for emphasis and looking at me.

"I swear, no one comes up with these hair-brained ideas except your mother, Isabelle. I think some gypsy tribe must have messed with her mind when she was a kid."

My mother put some pieces of French toast onto my father's plate. "Is it too much to ask that we can just have some fun?" There was a serrated edge to her voice that made me nervous.

"If your idea of fun is to get soaked down to your knickers, you need a head doctor, woman."

We went to the beach. My mother and I danced in the sand on that stormy day, twirling like gypsies as rain slanted against us and seagulls swooped down to peer at us with curious black eyes. My father sat huddled under the beach umbrella, which did little to keep him dry—the rain just angled its way beneath the cheerful blue and white striped canvas. Glowering, he finally tossed his soggy paper aside. But my mother didn't seem to notice or care about his surliness.

She and I held hands, swung each other around on the damp sand and laughed at the rain. I thought she was the most beautiful woman I had ever seen, and I wondered why my father wasn't enchanted. She released my hands, picked up a long trail of seaweed and flung it around her shoulders like a shawl. With her face tilted up to the low gray sky, and rain plastering her hair to her head, she looked so elated I believed for a moment that she could fly if she wanted—just lift off the sand and circle around with the gulls.

"We're so lucky to live in a world with seasons!" she exclaimed to the sky and the rain.

Now time has left us on a new shore. We're older, we've accumulated years and memories, and she's told me she's dying. Yet she still looks lovely, her eyes wide and calm. Her face reminds me of that day on the beach.

"How could this happen so suddenly?" I ask her. "One day all you have is some discomfort in your stomach and then just like that you're given a fatal diagnosis?"

"I know what you're thinking, Isabelle. You're thinking if I'd gone to doctors earlier they might have found something, treated it, and we wouldn't be here like this. But I've lived my life as I wanted to live it. And I'm going to die the same way. I don't regret my choices."

"Mother, I want to talk to your doctor—the doctor you went to. There are things I'm going to need to know."

She nods slowly. "I understand. I'll give you his name. But I don't intend on seeing him anymore. There's no reason—although I guess I'll need something for the pain. Eventually." She says the word eventually with a wave of her hand, as though she can push the inevitable away, into some fogbank up ahead that may never reach us.

We both know better. Our eyes meet, linger, then drift away. I reach for her, hold onto her tightly, memorizing the feel of her bones, the knob of vertebra that sticks out just below her neck. Everything feels so fragile to me, even the air around us and the way her back expands with each inhale.

"Everything will be all right," she tells me, pulling back and looking at me with faraway, shiny eyes.

It strikes me as a strange thing to say, and I have no answer.

There is a business to dying, I think, as I drive back to the sea, having left my mother in her small lamp-lit house with the tabby cat who raced in the minute I opened the front door to leave. There are things to organize, settle, plan for. I scramble through lists of worries, plans, contingencies—my mind keeping itself busy so I won't fall apart. I need to learn about pain medication. She can't be alone—not through this. She can't be sick, weak, crippled in that little house by the freeway. As the Pacific Ocean spreads out in front of me, black and satiny, my brain is a loud chattering thing while my heart is a small red fist, trying to uncurl itself away from the pain.

Marjorie is asleep by the time I get home, which is a relief because I don't know how to tell her. But I know I'll have to. I finally let go of my tears with Iris, but I'm keeping a secret from her. I don't tell her about the thought that bloomed in my mind tonight and is now taking up space there—that my mother's cancer has something to do with me. This is my punishment for causing my child's death. If I could know for certain that it wasn't my fault, would she be miraculously healed? Or if I am guilty, and if I cut off the offending hand— the careless appendage that neglected to lock the screen door—would that be penance enough? There is no rationale to my thoughts, just a dark spiral in the night.

13.

I wake up long before dawn. The air outside is quiet—the winds have died down, shifted direction, no longer blowing furiously off the desert. They'll be back, they're persistent this time of year. But for now we get a reprieve. Through the open window in our bedroom, I breathe in the moisture that's finally drifting in from the sea. Too restless to lie there and wait for morning to arrive, I slip out of bed, put on some clothes and go downstairs. The sky is just getting light when I go out to sit on the sand with a cup of tea.

Just me and the seagulls out here, I think, watching stars get swallowed by the sky. But then I see a lone figure near the water's edge—a man doing tai-chi. It takes me a minute to realize that it's Harlan. He looks graceful, lithe; his arms move in slow arches and his legs look longer than they actually are. I decide to move closer and when the sun starts pushing into the sky he notices me. He continues on for another few minutes and then comes over and sits down beside me.

"Do you do this every morning?" I ask him.

"Not every morning, although that's what I aim for. I like to start in the dark and watch the day arrive. What about you? What brings you out to the beach at this early hour?"

"My mother's dying," I blurt out. It seems like an explanation for everything right now.

Harlan squeezes my shoulder. "I'm sorry. Can I ask what from?"

"Cancer. Of…basically everything."

"So it's past the point of trying anything." He says this as a statement, not a question.

"Yes."

"That's rough," he says softly.

"I don't know how to do this," I tell him. "Lose my mother. I'm still crumbling under the weight of Nathan dying. Sometimes I see his face so clearly—I look up at the sky or out across the water and it's like he's there. The pain that crashes in is so huge…even the air hurts."

I look at Harlan to see if he's going to say anything but he seems to be waiting for me to continue. So I do. "I know there are people who have even bigger losses than this to deal with. People lose entire families in a single minute. How do they get through it? Where do they put all that grief?"

"They don't know how they're going to get through another day either," Harlan says slowly. "No one ever knows how to handle death, Isabelle. Even if you've done it before, you still don't know how to do it the next time it comes around. But the amazing thing is that we do find our way—badly sometimes—but we do. Before Bruce, I was in a relationship for six years. Larry was HIV positive when I met him, already having some health scares. I loved him more than I ever thought possible. I knew AIDS was going to kill him sooner rather than later and I tried to prepare myself for it, especially when he really began getting sick. But there's no way to prepare. You just wake up each day and try to do the best you can. I'll tell you what I realized, though, after he died—all that sadness, all that breaking apart inside made me able to love more. When Bruce came along, I was shocked by how much more room there was in my heart. Maybe I shouldn't ask you this—I haven't known you that long—but do you think you'd have been able to love Iris without going through a tragedy like Nathan's death?"

I've thought about this, but have never talked to anyone about it before, not even Iris. "No. Probably not. But doesn't that seem kind of diabolical on the part of God, or fate, or the universe, or whatever you want to call it? Shattering us with tragedy so there's more room in us to be loving and vulnerable?"

"I don't think of it as cruelty. I think of it as the laws of nature. As balance. Remember how we learned in Science class that nature abhors a vacuum? I think that's true on a lot of levels. It's not like there's an agenda against us. Challenges come that we don't think we'll ever get through. But just when we feel there's nothing left inside us—we've been hollowed out and left by the side of the highway like roadkill—something moves in to fill up the empty space inside us." He looks away from me then, squints toward the sun that's now angled above us in a cloudless blue sky. "What do I know, though? I'm hardly a philosopher. In fact, being a movie producer probably disqualifies me from even trying to philosophize. At least in some people's minds."

"I won't tell anyone that you crossed the line," I say teasingly.

I think he's about to tell me something else, but I turn at the sound of footsteps on the sand behind us and see Iris walking out with a mug of coffee.

"I wondered where you went," she tells me, plopping down on the sand beside me. She's still wearing pajama bottoms and has pulled on a sweatshirt. Even in that outfit, Iris looks effortlessly sexy and elegant.

"I couldn't sleep. And now I've discovered Harlan's early morning ritual—tai-chi."

"Ah," Iris says, smiling at Harlan. "Secrets revealed. Well, Marjorie has a sore throat. I told her she could stay home from school today."

"Did you take her temperature?"

"Uh-huh. It's normal."

Harlan stands up, brushes sand off himself. "I'm going to leave you two to your parental duties." He starts to walk away, but then turns back to us. "Isabelle, I was about to tell you—I hope this doesn't ruin our friendship—but I was invited to Thomas' Halloween party.

He's doing his usual huge bash, costumes required. Bruce will divorce me if we don't go, I'm sure of it. So I think I pretty much have to say yes."

"It's fine, Harlan," I assure him. "Can I give you some arsenic to drop into Thomas' drink?"

"Too obvious. But I can smuggle in my camera phone and try to catch him rubbing up against the caterer, or the bartender. Or maybe the parking attendant. Or passing an envelope to pay for illegal drugs…actually, that would be too plebian for him."

"'Bye Harlan," Iris says, waving sweetly.

"I wonder what he'll dress up as?" I ask Iris after Harlan has gone.

"Who? Harlan or Thomas?"

"I was thinking of Harlan. It's too early in the morning to mull over Thomas' Halloween costume."

We make our way back inside, peek in on Marjorie who has gone back to sleep, and go into the kitchen to make some breakfast. There is something soothingly normal about this morning—a child home from school, voices lowered so as not to wake her, the morning smells of coffee and toast filling the house—I wish time would stall for a while and leave us here for hours and hours. I wish Marjorie's sore throat were the only ailment within the orbit of our lives.

"Iris, can you stay home today with Marjorie? I need to go see my mother."

"Sure," she tells me. "I figured you'd go into town and check on her." She sits at the kitchen table with her re-filled coffee mug and a plate of jam-slathered toast. "I had a weird dream last night. I don't know if I should tell you about it, though."

"I think you have to now. You don't want my imagination to be set loose on that one."

"Right, of course," she says, nodding slowly. "Well, I dreamed that my mother died. I'm sure I dreamed it because of your mother, which is why I wasn't sure I should say something, but…my experience in the dream was a little different." She pauses, studies her coffee cup as though she's looking for signs in tea leaves.

"Go on."

"A tree fell on her. It was very Wizard of Oz."

I can't help it—I laugh. "I'm sorry," I tell her, biting down on my laughter. "How did you feel? In your dream…and when you woke up?"

Iris looks at me with eyes clear as water. "Well, Dr. Freud…in my dream I felt very light. Relieved I guess. Like her death was my birth. It's sad, you know, because that's probably how I will feel when she dies. I envy the sadness you feel about your mother, the wrench of it all. It's the way it should be. But it won't be like that for me."

"You don't know that, Iris."

"Yes, I do," she says matter-of-factly. "A lot of my restlessness, my travels to remote places with nothing but a backpack, have been because I was determined to be nothing like her. I didn't want her rigid, controlled life to rub off on me. I didn't want to eat dinner at the same time every night, no matter what night or what season, just because that's the schedule. I didn't want to see the world from behind car windows or look down on it from the fourteenth floor of a luxury hotel. My parents have traveled through Europe, they've been to Hong Kong, Tokyo…my mother couldn't tell you what any of those cities smell like, or what it's like walking along the sidewalks. She can't tell you what sunsets look like in any of those places, or how it sounds at dawn. Is it noisy or quiet? But she can tell you about the restaurants, the five star hotels, and the shopping. When I went to Darjeeling, in the Indian Himalayas, I sat with strangers—who within minutes were no longer strangers—and ate dinner off banana leaves. The people were so real and peaceful and giving, so glad to share their meal with me…" Iris gets a faraway look in her eyes that suddenly makes me nervous.

"Iris, please tell me you don't have a suitcase packed and stashed somewhere, and that I'm going to wake up one morning to a note on the pillow saying you've gone to Nepal or Greenland or something."

She laughs, reaches across the table and squeezes my arm with both hands. "I don't. Scout's honor. Actually, for the first time in my life I don't want to go anywhere. It's the first time I've felt like I had a home—someplace I'm really excited to come back to every day. I've had beautiful houses that were the envy of other people, but I had no idea what a home felt like until now."

We hear the toilet flush upstairs and I go up to check on Marjorie. The sound of my own footsteps on the stairs makes me think of my mother's footsteps coming down the hallway of our small house to check on me when I was sick. I remember the cool reassurance of her hand on my forehead, the gentle way she coaxed the thermometer into my mouth. Homes are assembled from small moments— whispers in the night and soft hands on feverish skin. If you've never known that, you're always running, searching, hunting for what you sense is missing.

Marjorie now has a slight fever. She doesn't want to eat, but I coax her into having some applesauce; she isn't thirsty, but she agrees to drink some water. She doesn't want to go to her father's house on Saturday, which makes me wonder if she's convinced her body to get ill.

"This is only Thursday," I tell her. "You might be better by Saturday."

"I might not be, too." She tugs the covers up under her chin and rolls onto her side. "I know where Daddy keep his diary," she says in a soft, secretive voice. "You know—where he writes about Nathan? Should I read it and tell you what it says?"

My arms reach gently to turn her over and give her a serious look, but there is nothing gentle about the avarice that surges inside me—of course I want to know what Thomas is writing. "Marjorie, you don't go into people's things and spy on them. You hear me? That's not right."

"Okay."

"Iris is going to stay home with you today. I want to go into town and check on Grandma."

Marjorie looks at me with what I think is suspicion in her eyes. "What's wrong with her?"

I'm not prepared to tell her yet. "Her stomach is bothering her," I say, trying to lighten my voice. "You get some rest now, okay? Sleep's the best medicine."

I leave her to her nap and start downstairs but end up sitting down on the top step, listening to the sounds of our home. I hear Iris in the kitchen, loading dishes into the dishwasher; I hear the faint sound of the hot water heater filling up. I think of what Harlan said earlier—hearts breaking to get bigger, roomier—and what Iris said about finally having a home. People find each other in this life—sometimes in the most ragged and desolate times. You look up from heartbreak and another person is there; it's who you were waiting for but you had no idea before that moment.

Iris and I ran down different roads, but for the same purpose—to escape the lives we were born into. I didn't want to be the convict's daughter, scraping by in our shabby little neighborhood; she didn't want to be just another rich girl, shiny on the surface but with only vapor beneath her skin. All that time we were heading toward each other without knowing it. Maybe that's always the way it is. People think they're running away from something, but really they're being pulled toward an unexpected meeting with the one other person who will see past the running, the desperation…straight through to their soul.

Sitting on the stairs, I'm aware of how still I feel inside. Even though in a little while I'll look at my mother's face and probably think it's paler than yesterday—that's what happens when you know death has moved into the doorway—at this moment everything in me is quiet, calm. Even my heartbeat seems muted.

There is a place beyond tears. You can't look for it, or try to swim out to it. You just have to wait for it. It's like you've drifted out past the swirl of currents into calmer waters. You know it when you're there, and you know it probably won't last, but for a while you float.

That's where I am as I listen to the now-familiar sounds of family that fate and love have assembled between these walls. I think about Nathan and my mother, about Iris and Marjorie. And I know all these endings and beginnings are the stitches holding my life together. I'm not through crying over Nathan—I may never be—and I haven't even begun weeping over my mother. But right now I'm miles past crying.

In every body of water there is a calm spot. A pool beyond drowning, far away from the undertow. You memorize the feeling, chart the meridians, and hope you'll be able to find it again.

14.

I arrive at my mother's house late in the morning. The door is unlocked and she's asleep in the armchair, the tabby cat curled in her lap. Beside her on a small wood end table, scuffed with time and use, is a delicate tea cup and saucer flocked with red roses. I stand just inside the doorway and watch her, her chest lifting and falling with each breath. The cat opens one eye, glances at me, and closes it again. After Thomas and I were married, my mother came to the house one afternoon and admired the rose-patterned china. I bought her four of the cup and saucer sets and I still remember the way her eyes lit up, how her hand traced the thin gold band along the rim. It's strange how people look at things differently. To me, Thomas' fine, elegant possessions were evidence that I had fooled the world and entered a place that was hardly my birthright. My mother just saw a lovely cup and saucer for tea.

"Hello, dear," she says quietly, her eyes fluttering open. The cat lifts his head and yawns.

I kneel down beside her. "How are you feeling?"

She smiles at me. "Just a little drowsy. Isabelle, you don't need to ask me that every day."

My face flushes. I'm on my knees beside her, as if I'm begging for something—which I am. I lower my head onto her knee, competing with the cat for space. "I do have to," I manage to say. "I'm scared.

And I think if I keep asking, maybe you'll keep telling me it's okay. Or maybe one day you'll say it was all a mistake and you're actually fine."

She strokes my hair. "It's not a mistake, sweetheart. This is how I'm going to leave the world. But you know what? It's strange— knowing you're going to die is a great way to get on with life."

"I want you to come live with us. You can't be alone here." The thought has come to me suddenly, and I'm surprised it didn't occur to me before.

She gets a faraway look in her eyes. "Remember when you moved into Campbell's house and you wanted me to move in there too? You felt bad living in luxury in Malibu Colony while I was here." She laughs a soft whispery laugh, waves her hand vaguely through the air as if my concern was just whimsy.

"I do remember. I did feel bad. There was room there, you could have moved in..." I find myself feeling annoyed at her for shifting the subject and then guilty for my irritation. "Mother, why are we talking about Campbell? It's completely different. You're sick and I need to take care of you. Iris and I need to take care of you. It's just...different."

My mother visited Campbell's beach house frequently once I had taken up residence there. She loved being by the sea. I hated watching her drive away in the yellow Volvo, back to a house with empty corners and what remained of my father's scent. But she would just smile and say, "That's my home, dear."

She looks away from me, her eyes wandering around the room. "I guess at some point I'll have to think about needing help. But you need to speak to Iris about it."

"I will, of course. But she'll say yes."

The cat stares at me with steady green eyes. I already know what the outcome will be. Iris, Marjorie and I will have two new room-mates—my mother and the fat tabby cat who has no intention of leaving her side.

As I drive back to Malibu, I suddenly remember a seagull Iris and I saw weeks earlier when we walked on the beach. The bird had a badly broken wing; it was dragging on the sand right at the water's edge. We thought maybe we could scoop him up, take him to the wildlife station. But, frightened and hurt, the bird headed for the water and was carried out on the next wave. We stood and watched helplessly as the seagull slid down the backs of waves, being carried farther and farther out to sea. We knew he would drown and there was nothing we could do.

My mother has a broken wing and there is nothing I can do. The tide will carry her out and I'll be left on dry sand, watching.

Marjorie is feeling better by the time I get home, but I can tell she's trying not to let on. Devious girl, she's still aiming for a reprieve on Saturday. Hunger has betrayed her efforts, though.

"Can I have a sandwich?" she asks me when I go in to check on her. She's wide awake, sitting up in bed looking at a photo book of dolphins.

"A sandwich? Sure. So, you're feeling better, huh?"

I see her realize her mistake. "No. But it isn't my stomach that's sick." She looks at me with a deliberate attempt at authority. "I have to keep up my strength."

"Uh-huh. Good point. Sustenance."

Iris comes into the kitchen as I'm making Marjorie her favorite sandwich—peanut butter and honey with raisins squished in.

"How's your mother?" Iris asks me.

"Stoic and serene…at the moment anyway. I don't know, Iris, I wonder if it hasn't hit her yet. But then I think maybe it has and this really is how she's responding."

Iris slips an arm around my waist. "And what about you?"

"I might be able to muster up the stoic part but I think serenity is totally out of my reach. Iris, I asked her to move in with us. I know I should have talked to you about it first, but seeing her sitting there in that little house…I just…what about when the pain starts, when it gets bad? She can't cope with this all alone. She's dying. I can't let her die alone."

Iris turns me into her and hugs me tightly. "Of course she can stay here. We'll take care of her. If we need a nurse down the line, we'll find one. Whatever she needs, Isabelle. But we're going to have to tell Marjorie the truth...before Catherine comes. She has to have time to process this."

"Right. Yes, of course. There's just one more thing. She's sort of adopted a cat."

"Great. We won't have to worry about mice. And Marjorie will be ecstatic about having a pet. She's been asking for one."

Right now, my love for Iris is a physical sensation that starts deep inside me. It's like coming in from a cold day, drawing a warm bath, peeling off clothes and stepping naked into steamy water—that first rush of warmth seeping through skin, into bones and sinews. Those times when you didn't even realize how chilled you were.

I take Marjorie her sandwich and go back down to the kitchen where Iris is making another pot of coffee.

"I never thought it would be like this," I tell her.

Iris' brow knits a little, as it always does when she's trying to decipher something. "You mean your mother?"

"In part. But actually I meant all of this—this life we have now. The fact that I'm not alone. If I ever allowed myself to think about my mother dying, about adjusting to the world without her here, I always just assumed I'd be going through the whole experience by myself."

Iris kisses me. "Banish that thought forever, okay?"

When we mount the stairs again to tell Marjorie the sad news about my mother and the happier news that she'll be moving in with us, our footsteps sound so heavy to me. As if we've gained weight in the last twenty minutes.

"We just have to be completely truthful with her," Iris says. "No euphemisms. No sidestepping the facts."

"I know. But this is one of those times when I feel strongly attracted to a good old fashioned lie."

As Iris once pointed out, we are condemned to tell the truth.

Marjorie has finished most of her sandwich and is lying on her back with the crumb-filled plate on her stomach. She looks at us when we come into the room and I suspect she knows we have an agenda. We sit on either side of her; Iris removes the plate and puts it on the nightstand.

"What?" Marjorie asks, looking from Iris to me. Yes, she definitely knows.

"We need to tell you something about your grandmother," I say to her. I feel myself being pulled back into Thomas' living room the day Nathan died. I tighten my rib cage, willing myself to stay right here in this room, with Laura Ashley bed sheets, the pale pink lampshades, the child who's going to have to shake hands with death again.

"She's really sick isn't she?" Marjorie says.

I realize she didn't believe a word of what I said before about my mother just having stomach trouble. I inhale and get ready to answer her, but only breath comes out of my mouth. Thankfully, Iris takes over.

"She is, yes. She has cancer, sweetheart. And there isn't anything they can do for her because it's spread. Medicine won't help at this point."

"Is she going to die?"

"Yes, Marjorie. She is. I'm afraid she is." Iris says this smoothly, and then looks at me. I know I have to say something.

I put my hands on Marjorie's forearms, trying to ground myself with the heat of her skin, the syllables of her name. "Marjorie...I didn't want to lie to you the last couple of days. I just needed some time to deal with this myself. It was a shock and I had to figure out how to talk about it...she's my mother..."

"I know," she says.

I believe her. This sweet girl who rescues stranded starfish and scans the sea for dolphins has had more sorrow in her life than any child should. Her eyes can sparkle and dance like the little girl she is, but they can quickly settle into an older, more watchful gaze.

The older eyes are the ones looking at me now and I'm hoping the rest of our news will make them turn young again.

"Iris and I decided that we want your grandma to come live here with us so we can take care of her. How do you feel about that?"

Marjorie's face bends into a smile. "Yeah."

"She won't be coming by herself though," Iris adds. "She has a cat now."

"Really? Can the cat sleep with me sometimes? In my bed?"

"I'm sure we can work that out," I assure her. "I don't know exactly when this is going to happen—her moving in—but probably soon. Marjorie, is there anything you want to know or ask about this? About your grandmother? About her being sick like this? I mean, there'll be lots of questions along the way, but right now?"

Marjorie's smile narrows. "Will she have to stay in bed all the time?"

"No, Not yet. Eventually, I guess she will. But at the moment she's doing okay. I'm not really sure what to expect. I'm going to go talk to her doctor soon and then I'll know more."

Marjorie nods slowly. "Okay," she says to us, almost under her breath, and then she slides down in the bed, pulling the covers up to her chin. "I'm going to take a nap now."

She sleeps on and off for most of the day. I remember being able to do that—to quickly escape from life by diving into sleep. I wonder if medical science has isolated some mysterious ingredient in children's blood that allows sleep to flood in whenever the world is too much for them. At what age do we lose that ability? Does something just blink off in us? Does a hormone die and condemn us to long sleepless nights, minds racing with inescapable fears?

At sunset, Marjorie comes downstairs in bare feet, still in her pajamas. Iris has gone to the store and I'm stretched out on the couch in the living room looking at a magazine, although I have no idea what's on its pages. My mind is miles away—with my mother, with the questions I plan to ask her doctor. I have an appointment with him tomorrow, I look at my own fear and think this is nothing compared to what my mother must have felt walking into his office. She went through so much alone—the tests, the waiting, the horrible phone call and the finale of the sit-down visit. The you're-going-to-die visit.

"Hey, sleepy-head. How're you feeling?" I ask Marjorie.

"Better," she says as she drifts past me.

She goes to the window seat that gives her a panoramic view of the ocean—her favorite spot in the house. She sits facing the window, her back to me, looking out across the water as a deep orange sun falls into the sea. I don't know if I should go to her or leave her alone with her inner wanderings. There's a balance point somewhere—between allowing Marjorie room to process my mother's dying and steering her into a dialogue about it.

I decide to leave her with her thoughts, to not intrude. There will be plenty of time for talk. We will probably run out of words long before my mother runs out of life.

By nine o'clock, after Iris and I have put Marjorie to bed, with her agreeing to go to school the following day, I'm struck by how long this day has seemed. I've been waiting for the refuge of night all day without knowing it. My mother once said, many years ago, "Some days feel so much longer than others." I think I was about Marjorie's age when she said it and she was waiting for my father to come home—always a waiting game and an unpredictable one at that. But she was anxious on that day, I can't recall why. I remember looking at her when she said that and understanding, perhaps for the first time, that she had lived so much more life than I had. She looked older to me at that moment, with a tiredness that can only come from years. It might have been the first time I let myself admit that she would, in all probability, leave the world before me.

With Marjorie tucked in and the lights in the house turned off, I uncurl against Iris in the dark, shiver a little at the cool smoothness of the sheets and the warmth of her skin. This bed is our island, our sanctuary. I start to wonder how I would cope with losing my mother if I didn't know that night would bring me here...but I stop myself from thinking too much. If we can turn our faces from death, even for a short while, and slide into love, we shouldn't dwell too much on the miracle of that journey, we should just tumble into it.

Iris has a single slender hair just above the nipple on her right breast. My mouth found it early on, when we were first exploring each other. My tongue touched it, memorized it. It's not that long, it's thin as spun silk. So blonde that in daylight I can barely see it—only if the sun is slanting at just the right angle while we're making love. Sometimes it's gone; she's plucked it out. My tongue looks for it and can't find it. Then, days later, I feel it poking through the skin. I've never mentioned it to her because I like the adventure of discovering whether she has remembered it, taken tweezers to it when she's alone in the bathroom. I like how specific it is—that one ritual of grooming, so much more personal than shaving one's legs or underarms, which just becomes habit after a while. She does this for me, I think—her lover. For my mouth, my tongue. Looking for it, noticing how long it takes to grow back and how many days pass before it's removed again is my secret in the dark.

Tonight it's still there, as it has been for nearly a week. So, I guess for days she hasn't thought about it. She hasn't paused in front of the mirror, damp from her shower, and imagined my mouth on her breast in the dark. But she will. In the days ahead, she will.

I slide down Iris' body to where she is open and wet for me. My eyes are closed but I don't need them to see. I know the bars of her ribcage, the slope of her stomach, her pale skin. I know the shape of her thighs and the white tracing of a scar above her left kneecap. If I were struck blind, I would still be able to see Iris.

I wake up a little after three A.M. jittery from dreams I can't remember. Iris is sleeping on her side, the pillow squished in the crook of her arm, wedged under her head. I roll onto my back carefully, slowly, not wanting my restlessness to wake her. I think about the delicate thread that separates life from death. We all walk along it. We can go years without thinking about it, pretending it's not there. But then something happens and we look down and see the thread is actually a tightrope. It's always beneath us. It always has been.

When I was about fourteen, I found my mother out in the back-yard early one morning; she was kneeling on the grass with something cradled in her hands.

"Look, Isabelle. I think it must have fallen from that nest up there. Come look before I put it back."

It was a baby hummingbird, no bigger than an acorn.

"If you look carefully you might be able to see its heart beating," she told me.

It was barely dawn. The sky was lilac colored and the breeze was gentle and lazy. She put the tiny creature in my hands and went around the side of the house for the ladder. I felt so clumsy and huge, holding in my human paws a small, eager throb of new life. My mother took the bird back from me when she had the ladder set up. Carefully, she climbed the rungs and placed it back in the nest.

"There are two babies there," she reported when she came down. And then scanning the sky, she added, "I hope the mother hasn't been killed."

For days we watched the nest, waiting to see a feeding ritual, a mother bird racing toward her young, some sign they hadn't been abandoned. My mother climbed the ladder several times and said the birds seemed to be doing all right. Then she called a vet's office and was told that the mother must be coming back—we just weren't watching at those moments.

She decided we should learn about hummingbirds and checked a book out of the library. Hummingbirds' hearts can beat more than a thousand times a second when they're excited. Their wing beat is so fast it makes a humming sound, which is how they got their name. And they are unique in their ability to fly backwards.

An afternoon came when we were rewarded for our patience and our diligent studies. We were sitting on a blanket in the yard, keeping our eyes on the tree when two tiny birds ventured into the sky for their first uncertain flight. We knew that soon they would be able to show off and fly backwards—but on this day, they were pushing into the wind, learning about all that sky around them.

We had been hoping for flight, for life, sending prayers up into that one small nest, all the while knowing death might be the end of the story. Life and flight won out; my mother and I smiled about it for days, glancing often at the sky, hoping the birds would make our garden their home. Maybe life and flight always win out, one way or another, even when it doesn't seem like that. Even when all you can see in front of you is the fall to earth. Maybe my mother already knows this, and that's why she has such a light, faraway look in her eyes.

I used to imagine teaching Nathan about hummingbirds by telling him that story. Stories need to be passed on—from older hands into younger ones. I know how this one should be handed down—from my mother to Marjorie.

15.

Dr. Ken Butler's office is in a Century City medical building. As I approach the door, my eyes linger on the word "oncology" and I find myself missing the quaint new-age feeling of Savasa's house—the scent of incense, trickling water from the carefully placed fountain. My mother must have been terrified to walk down the halls of this tall, formal building with its rows of doors, all with doctors behind them. The glacial world of American health care.

The waiting room is the temperature of a refrigerator. The walls are painted a pale lavender color; I can't help but think this was a deliberate choice, an attempt to offer something soothing, even if it's just the color of the room.

"I'm Isabelle Berendon," I tell the receptionist. "I have a nine o'clock appointment."

"You're here for a consultation?" the girl says. She looks to be in her late twenties, with perfectly done eye makeup and shiny black hair.

"Yes…I mean, no…not for myself. I'm here about my mother, Catherine Haller."

"It'll be just a few minutes," she tells me, smiling warmly.

I sit stiffly in an upholstered armchair and eye the stack of magazines, too distracted to be interested in any of them. Does anyone come in here and pick up Us magazine? Or the latest issue of Vogue? Who could possibly be that calm in an office like this?

A man walks out of the inner area and into the waiting room. He is perhaps sixty, with white hair, a square jaw and an athletic build. He stops briefly in front of the receptionist. "See you Tuesday," he says, and then leaves. I wonder...but then I don't let myself. People come in here for only one reason.

After a few minutes, I'm shown into a wood-paneled office where a slight, dark-haired man in wire-rimmed glasses is sitting behind an enormous mahogany desk. He stands when I come in and reaches to shake my hand.

"Mrs. Berendon, I'm Dr. Butler. Please, sit down."

I sink into the fine leather of a large armchair and wish I were here to discuss anything but this. "My mother came to you..." I begin, and pause when he nods. There is a thin file on his desk—I'm sure it's my mother's—and I think how sad it is that a human being can be reduced to a few sheets of paper.

"Yes. Catherine Haller." His fingers touch the edge of the file. "I'm sorry I couldn't give her more hope, Mrs. Berendon. It's the hardest part of what I do—cases like your mother's. Medical science has made a lot of progress in treating cancer, but when it's spread so much... well, there just wasn't anything I could do. If she had insisted on trying chemo, I would have gone along with her wishes, but frankly it would have been pointless and would have increased her suffering. And she was quite resolute in living out her days without medical intervention."

I shiver violently, either from the cranked up air conditioning or the rustle of death in the elegantly decorated office. "You could have tried having her sit here for a while—see if the cancer cells froze," I offer.

Dr. Butler frowns slightly, trying to figure out if I'm serious.

"That was a joke, Doctor. The thermostat seems to be stuck at forty. I have a bad habit of making jokes when life has handed me something horrifically un-funny. I try to joke away the terror, you know? It usually doesn't work, though, and no one else seems to get on board with it…Anyway, I've never been through anything like this before. I don't know what to expect. What happens when the pain gets worse? I assume it will."

He nods slowly, solemnly, glances at her thin file beside him as if answers might be hidden inside there. "I'll prescribe whatever she needs, Mrs. Berendon. Ultimately, morphine is going to be about the only thing that will alleviate her pain. Is she allergic to morphine?"

"I don't know. I don't think she knows."

It strikes me that no one really knows the answer to this until something terrible happens and you're crying out for the pain to stop. Until a diagnosis slams the door on any future you thought you'd have. Then it becomes desperately important to know if your body will accept the relief morphine can bring.

"Well, we have some time to determine that," he tells me. "You might want to look into private nursing care as the disease progresses."

"She's going to live with us. With my daughter and me. And my partner."

He nods again. I'm sure he's familiar with all aspects of our family scandal. "Are you prepared for this, Mrs. Berendon? For what will happen to your mother?"

"Is that possible? To be prepared?"

"No," Dr. Butler says, without hesitation. "My father died seven months ago from inoperable lung cancer. I owed him so much. He put me through medical school. He was so proud of me…and I couldn't help him. I'm a very good doctor. I can predict clinically what will happen when cancer spreads. I can list the physical symptoms, the pattern of decline. But I wasn't prepared to lose him. Not emotionally—no one is. The people who worry me are the ones who think they are. You might need some help down the line—home care. We can discuss that whenever you want."

I've stopped shivering because I'm so intent on what he is saying, and on his calm brown eyes staring at me through his glasses. Or maybe I'm frostbitten.

"My mother must have been really frightened of how she felt, and really certain that something bad was happening to come here. She doesn't particularly like your profession, but I'm sure it's nothing personal."

He smiles then, and it's startling to see how his face is transformed; he has one of those smiles that spreads beyond his mouth, all the way up to his forehead. "She mentioned that. And I don't take it personally. People have a right to make their own choices about health care."

"I'm sure she appreciated you telling her the truth, though. Even if it was an unwelcome truth."

"Actually, she did thank me for being honest," he says. "It's not something I generally get thanked for."

I stand up to leave, grateful that he didn't say something like, 'Too bad she didn't come in sooner.' I have to concentrate on uncurling my fingers to shake his hand goodbye; I swear my hand is bluish from the cold.

"Please feel free to call me whenever you have questions, or need anything." He shakes my hand gently, but firmly. I have to look away from the sad edges of his eyes.

When I arrive at my mother's house a little before eleven, I walk in to find complete chaos. She's emptied every closet, nearly every drawer and cabinet, and is sitting in the middle of the floor surrounded by everything she owns. The tabby cat is curled up beside her, sleeping contentedly in an open suitcase.

"Mother, what are you doing?"

"Cleaning things out. I just can't figure out what to do with everything, though. A yard sale is a silly waste of time. There's nothing of value here—money-wise."

I sit down beside her on a stack of blankets and comforters. "Iris said it's absolutely fine that you move in with us. And Marjorie is really excited."

My mother nods. "I thought the answer would be yes. But it's always good to ask. Did you discuss Aristotle?"

Oh God, she's becoming delusional already, I think. Isn't that supposed to come later?

"Uh…we didn't get around to Greek philosophers," I say gently, carefully. "We were discussing fixing up the guest room for you."

My mother reaches out to stroke the cat's back. "Aristotle the cat, dear. I decided it was a good name for him. He's very wise. I thought I'd mentioned that to you. Oh well, I guess not."

The tightness in my stomach relaxes. "It's fine that he comes along. Marjorie's been asking for a pet. Are you sure he doesn't belong to anyone?"

She keeps stroking him and he purrs loudly. "I put up signs a while ago and I asked most of the neighbors. No one knew anything. I think after all these weeks he's officially mine."

"And you're sure he's a he?"

My mother leans over the cat, starts to turn him on his back and part his hind legs. Aristotle offers no resistance. "People think it's hard to tell the sex of a cat, but if you look in the logical place…"

"That's okay, I'll take your word for it." Studying cat genitalia isn't that appealing to me.

"You might need to know this sometime, Isabelle," my mother says in her teacher-voice.

"Well, if I need to know I can always ask you."

It's the small things, the quick utterances that trip you up—words that seem casual until they bounce back at you with a weight you didn't realize they had. As soon as I said it, I thought I won't always be able to ask my mother about cats or anything else. One day I'll turn to say something to her, expecting to hear the jingling of her earrings or see her hand brush her hair back from her face. And there will be nothing there but blank space. Empty air will tumble over the places where she once stood; the silence will wound me. It still happens with Nathan. I still find myself reaching back to lead him across a street. I expect to feel his hand, cushiony with baby fat. But there's only air.

Who will I be without my mother? She's been the mountain my voice has bounced off of. I always knew, whether I cried, laughed, whispered, or lashed out in anger, she would return my voice to me. She stood between me and the abyss. How will I find myself without that echo?

"Isabelle?" Her voice snatches me out of my thought, returns me to the cluttered living room.

"Sorry. I was daydreaming."

She pushes herself up to her knees and stands—with some difficulty, I notice. My mother once moved like a swan. When I was younger, I'd close myself in my bedroom and try to imitate the smooth circle she made when she turned around.

"I have to get back to this," she tells me, sweeping her arm through the air, indicating the disarray surrounding us.

"I'll help you."

Aristotle opens his eyes and gives me a half-lidded look that warns me I'd better not consider removing him from his suitcase.

For more than an hour we scoop up the possessions of a lifetime and separate them into piles. We even find my old roller-blades buried in the hall closet. She's saved the jackets my father once wore. I hold one of them to my face when my mother goes into the kitchen to get us some coffee. It's a faded blue parka with plaid flannel lining. After all this time, it still smells like him. My father, whose life of larceny stole so much from my childhood, now makes my heart hurt with an unfamiliar sting of missing him. Maybe I'm not really missing him, I tell myself quickly. Maybe I just long for another family member to be going through this with us. It feels so lonely here. Even the pounding of my father's footsteps would be better than this.

My mother is going through a bundle of shawls. She used to wear them often, flinging them around her dramatically, like Isadora Duncan. There are the heavier ones she wore in winter and the light, cool ones she brought out for summers that seemed like they'd never end.

"I guess there's no point in saving these, is there?" she says, lifting up the corner of a silk shawl—a pale rose color like the sky at dawn.

"You might want to wear them again. Let's keep them." I can't bear the thought of my mother abandoning her gypsy wardrobe, it's been so much a part of who she is.

She looks out the window at the muted day—the sun hasn't been able to burn through the film of fog and haze. "I don't think I'll be getting dressed up too often anymore," she says softly and then gets up and moves toward the den.

I follow her and find her standing in front of a pine trunk, placed as an end table beside the armchair, but used also as storage space for photo albums and other mementos.

"Do you want to go through that?" I ask her, knowing it's a redundant question.

She nods and I think I see her eyes starting to mist. Maybe she wants to be alone, or maybe I just want to step back from her emotions for a bit. Whichever it is, I seize on an excuse to leave the premises.

"Why don't I run out and get us some lunch? You must be hungry."

"All right," she says, still staring at the trunk. "Get something with chicken or tuna in it so Aristotle can join us. I don't want him to feel left out."

I go to Subway, pulling my silver Jag into a parking lot with beaten up Corollas and aging Volvos taking up most of the spots. How spoiled I've become, I realize. I'm used to getting to-go orders that have arugula and endive, crumbles of Feta cheese, dressing on the side and heated slices of French bread.

"Two tuna fish sandwiches, please," I tell the acne-faced boy behind the counter.

"Six inch or ten inch?"

"Huh?" For a second, I wonder if he's making some obscene joke—I have no idea what he's talking about.

"The sandwiches?" he says in an are-you-stupid tone. "Six inch or ten inch?"

"Oh…uh…six."

I feel eyes crawling over me. I look terribly out of place in my cashmere sweater, with diamond stud earrings glinting through my hair.

As I walk back across the parking lot carrying my white-bagged lunch, I pass two men who have just gotten out of a Ford Explorer. They appear to both be in their thirties and are dressed in jeans and T-shirts.

"Ma'am?" one of them says. "You dropped something back there on the sidewalk." I turn reflexively, see nothing, and then he says, with a loud guffaw, "Your smile!"

Ignoring him, I take a few more steps toward my car, but the anger bubbling up in me gets the best of me. I wheel around and go after them.

"Excuse me!" I call out. Two surprised faces turn toward me. "Before you go making smart-ass comments to strangers, maybe you should consider that you have no idea what's going on in other people's lives. My mother is dying of cancer and if I don't feel like smiling, that's my business. Not yours! Take care of your own life—leave other people alone."

The man's eyes pull back, his mouth tightens. His friend takes a couple of steps back, leaving his buddy alone on the battlefield. I stand there seething for a few seconds, wondering if this fool will apologize, or even say a word. He doesn't, so I say, "Asshole," under my breath but loud enough for them to hear me clearly. And then I walk back to my car.

I hate them, these two arrogant punks with their bratty mouths. But I know it's really cancer I hate. They were just stand-ins for the moment.

When I return to my mother's house, she's sitting cross-legged on the floor in front of the pine trunk.

"I got tuna sandwiches from Subway," I call out on my way to the kitchen.

Aristotle promptly climbs out of his suitcase and follows me, rubbing against my leg while I get plates down from the cupboard and napkins from the wooden holder that has sat on this pale yellow countertop for as long as I can remember. The chipped remains of a painted rooster can still be seen on the front of the holder. Other remnants of my mother's attraction to kitsch are scattered around— the spice rack stenciled with leaves and lavender blossoms, the wall-mounted clock with a happy rabbit squatting behind the numbers, the bread box painted with daisies. As I look around the kitchen my eyes become portals to memory.

My mother used to pad around here in the gray light just before daybreak, her blue terrycloth slippers scuffing across the linoleum. She squeezed fresh orange juice every morning, filling the house with the smell of orchards. She stood right here at the sink, where she could look out the window at the large pepper tree that Mrs. Middlington said was a mere sapling many years earlier when she bought her house. What did my mother dream of on those mornings with the nectar of oranges running over her fingers? Did she dream of forests, wider spaces, acres of green? Things that would always be out of reach while she was married to my father? Did she watch the sky lighten and imagine that this day would be different from the last? That my father would come home with something other than stolen goods and a clenched-up face? A job perhaps?

Aristotle and I go into the den where my mother is now sitting on the loveseat with a photo album open in her lap.

"Look at this, Isabelle," she says as I sit down beside her with our sandwiches. She points to a photograph turned golden-brown with age. It's of my parents—so much younger it's startling—standing on the Santa Monica Pier, their faces bright with wide-open smiles. A sailboat can be seen behind them, tilted between white-caps; cotton puff clouds float in the sky. "The fortune teller took this of us," my mother tells me. "She had just told us that we belonged together, that we'd have a long, happy life. We weren't even engaged yet."

"Mother, I don't mean to sound overly cynical but I think fortune tellers are required to give sunny, uplifting predictions. In fact, I would wager that it's chapter one in the fortune teller's handbook. Otherwise, why would people hand them money?"

"Nonetheless, your father proposed to me that night."

She eats a small bite of the sandwich, scoops some tuna onto her finger, then onto a napkin, and puts it on the floor for Aristotle. "Isabelle," she says softly. "I was happy with your father. I know you think I wasn't. I know you blame him for what he couldn't give us, and for his shortcomings. But I was happy—most of the time."

"What he couldn't give us? Don't you mean what he didn't give us? You make it sound like he was incapable. He wasn't disabled, Mother. He was dishonest."

"He did the best he could. I knew him better than you did, dear. And I'm going to be seeing him soon, so I'd like to be able to tell him that you've forgiven him."

Aristotle is now on the loveseat between us, begging dollops of tuna from my mother, who willingly obliges. I want to tell her that I don't forgive my father and never will, so please don't float through the pearly gates and tell him I have. But I'm quite sure I should stay silent on this point, so I do.

Between bites of a truly awful sandwich—more mayonnaise than tuna—I look down at the photo of my parents—so long ago, more than a year before I was born. Photographs freeze-frame time. My mother's head is tilted back, she is laughing, her long hair is blowing in the ocean breeze, sweeping across my father's chest. He is staring directly into the camera lens as if he's asking a question of it. On this page of the leather-bound album, they will always be young. The crisp afternoon wind will always be curling around them; they will always have tomorrow.

"We took you to the Pier once when you were a baby," my mother tells me. "We were looking for that fortune teller. We wanted to show her how right she was. But she was gone—no one knew where."

She leans her head back against the faded green velvet of the loveseat, one of the rare things in the house that we actually purchased when I was younger. It's the color of tired leaves. "I need to close my eyes for a few minutes, dear," she says.

I nod even though her eyes are already closed. She's put her plate on the floor and Aristotle is methodically mutilating the sandwich, foraging for every morsel of tuna. I can hear cars passing outside on the street. Behind that sound is the constant noise of the freeway. If I use my imagination, I can almost pretend it's the ocean. Even with all that background noise, it seems frighteningly quiet in the house where I grew up. Left alone with the photo albums, with my mother asleep and Aristotle intent on his pilfered meal, I lift one of the other volumes of our life from inside the pine trunk.

When do we finally look at our parents as mere humans—with hopes, mistakes, joys, fears? Maybe it only happens in unplanned moments—when memories sneak up on us, unearthed by a scent or a familiar landmark. Or a photograph.

My younger face stares back at me from some of these photographs—angry at my father's thievery, his absence, the nights my mother scraped his dinner into the sink because once again he didn't show up. There's a faded color shot of me holding an orange kite my father stole for me. I'm glaring into the camera lens—why can't he ever buy his kid a toy like other fathers? He's standing behind me, smiling, but I see something in his smile now that I didn't then—an uncertainty, a self-consciousness that in the right light might even look like guilt.

I turn the page and there is a picture taken on a picnic at a city park. My mother and I are sitting on a blanket with scraggly grass all around and sandwiches in front of us. She's smiling sweetly at my father who is behind the camera. I'm doing my best to arrange my ten-year-old face into an accusatory mask. This was the best he could do for a family picnic, and I suspected he stole the camera, too.

But my mother still dreamed beyond her life. I see it in every photograph. It was she who danced with me on the beach in the rain, who lifted her face to the gray sky and pointed happily at pelicans flying above us. It was she who planted bulbs outside our front door in Spring and introduced me to the delicate life of irises. How strange that I would end up falling in love with a woman named after the flower my mother tended to so patiently.

As my mother sleeps soundly in the chair, I keep rummaging through the trunk. I find my high school diploma, a couple of report cards. A cheap drugstore photo album is at the bottom and I open it to find my father as a young boy, staring at me with impatient eyes. A basketball is at his feet. In my imagination a world takes shape around that picture—he wants to go back and play, but someone is telling him to stand there and smile for the camera. He's gangly and freckled, his jeans are cuffed at the ankles, and he isn't smiling because his fun has been interrupted.

My mother stirs in the chair but doesn't wake up. As I put my father's photo album back, a pale blue envelope falls from it and drifts down into the trunk, light as a petal. My hands dive for it, retrieve it, and I see my mother's penmanship on the envelope. "Frank" is all it says. My fingers feel clumsy and large as I slide out a folded piece of stationery and start to read the letter my mother wrote to my father years ago.

"My dearest Frank,

I wish you hadn't left like that. Now there's this echo of angry words. I don't know where you are, maybe in a bar somewhere. I'm sitting here alone with the moon hanging in the sky so clean and white like it hasn't a care in the world. I wish I could be like the moon.

You leave me with so much absence—that's what I was trying to tell you. How can you blame me for thinking of leaving you? Making a clean break and starting over, just me and Isabelle? You couldn't have been shocked at my feelings. Maybe you were just shocked that I finally spoke up.

I reach for you at night and you aren't there. I watch the moon fade at dawn and you aren't there. I feel like the victim of one of your thefts—the life I thought I'd share with you has been stolen.

I love you,

Catherine."

So my mother once thought seriously about divorcing my father. But when? There was no date on the letter. Was I still a baby? Or had I already grown into a girl who aimed knife-blade looks at her father with cunning accuracy? My mother's penmanship was precise, her spelling perfect—an indication that she had taken her time, given it careful thought. Not her usual hasty writing full of errors and misspellings. I stand up slowly, trying not to disturb the air. Tip-toeing across the floor to my purse—on a table by the front door—I slip the letter inside it. Only Aristotle is watching. But as soon as I notice that, I wonder if the cat is only one who sees.

My father rarely came through the front door. He was a back door guy—curling in through the shadows when the moon was bright, slipping in with the blackness on other nights. But on this day, with my mother asleep in the den, he enters through the front door like the ghost he is. I feel him so strongly I might as well be seeing him.

"Is that your business?" he whispers to me. "Does that belong to you? Who's the thief now?"

"You should know," I whisper back.

"People have a right to their privacy."

"People have a right to be loved."

"Isabelle?" my mother calls out, "Who are you talking to?"

I didn't realize I'd whispered aloud.

"No one, Mother. Just talking to myself."

I've taken a piece of her history, something private between her and her husband. Will I ever confess what I've done? Ask her about the letter? When she wrote it?

My mother and I, along with Aristotle planted firmly in his suit-case, drive back to Malibu as the afternoon air is turning wispy with thin tendrils of fog. Iris smiles delightedly at the strange sight of me carrying the large tabby as if he's some oriental emperor whose feet shouldn't touch the ground; then she folds my mother into her arms.

"Catherine, I'm so sorry," Iris says. "But I'm glad you're going to be here with us. And Marjorie can't wait to get home from school today."

Olivia, our three-day-a week housekeeper, comes downstairs and reaches out her arms to take Aristotle from me. I hand him over in his suitcase and watch as Olivia carries him through the living room toward the kitchen and the laundry room where we have set up his personal necessities.

"Oh wait till you see the lovely litter box we got for you," she coos. "And your dishes for your food and water are so cute..."

Marjorie insisted on leaving early for school this morning so she and Iris could stop at the market and buy provisions for the cat. Olivia's voice is trailing out of the kitchen. "Good boy! You like your litter box! What a good boy!"

Olivia was part of Thomas' household staff, but when Iris and I fell in love and the household was thrown into turmoil, she slipped me a note and said she wanted to work for me.

I go back to the car and get the one suitcase my mother has packed—as if she is only going away for a week—I'll have to go back to the house and bring more of her clothes, even if she thinks she doesn't want them. Upstairs, in what will now be her room, I put the suitcase on the window seat and start to unzip it, but stop because I'm afraid I'll be intruding. I've done enough of that already. The stolen letter is probably singeing the lining of my purse.

Later, Iris leaves to pick Marjorie up from school and when they return Marjorie runs into the house like a small whirlwind.

"Where's Grandma?"

Trying to calm her is futile, but I attempt to lower the volume just a bit. "She's upstairs—she might be lying down." I say this in the deliberately muted tone parents use when they want to set an example of where they'd like the decibel level to be. "And she might be asleep too, Marjorie."

But Marjorie runs up the stairs in quick staccato beats after dropping her book bag loudly on the floor. Iris and I look at each other and shrug.

Voices travel down into the rest of the house—two excited voices, one young, one so much older and weaker than it used to be. Apparently Aristotle is also in the guest room because Marjorie is squealing, "Oh, he's so cute! Hi, Aristotle! Hi, I love you!"

Then I hear my mother's voice. "Dear, you need to talk to him more gently. Cats are very sensitive to noise." Ah yes, I think, the hummingbird lesson can't be far behind.

Iris and I make dinner as festive and as non-nutritious as we can. We order in pizza, open wine for the adults, let Marjorie drink 7-Up instead of milk. We light candles. We light a fire in the fireplace. We let Aristotle pace the length of the dining room table while we're eating. Discipline can come later; tonight we need some celebratory anarchy.

My mother tells us stories about her early years dancing, directing most of them at Marjorie, the budding ballerina who might try to combine that career with one in marine biology. "You must strengthen your ankles," my mother says, her earnestness cutting through the veil of candlelight. "Otherwise you can injure yourself. I'll show you some exercises. We'll work on that."

"Will you come to my class sometime?" Marjorie asks her.

"Of course. I'd love to see you dance."

We are a new family now, I think, an expanded one. We will live under this roof, inhabit these rooms, and one of us will surrender to the onslaught already going on inside her. But on this night we are golden, we are laughing, we are in sweet denial of everything the future has in store. I feel like I'm training the muscles of my memory to curl around this one night, these few hours. As if it can protect what's here right now.

Sometime after nine, after Marjorie has been put to bed and my mother has walked slowly upstairs—followed by her faithful shadow, Aristotle—Iris and I walk out to the deck and look out at the dark sea.

"That was fun tonight," Iris says.

"Yeah. I guess the best we can do is try to keep things light and fun for as long as we can."

Iris nods slowly, slides her arm around my waist and pulls us tightly together. "We'll figure it out as we go along," she says.

16.

Thomas and I were married at the Bel Air Hotel in early January. The protocol of the bride's family paying for the wedding was set aside for obvious reasons, but Thomas was gracious enough to ask for my mother's input. I think it's supposed to be good luck for rain to fall on your wedding day. Rain did not fall on mine, although the sky was thick with low gray clouds. Maybe I should have read more into that—as if the clouds themselves were saying, Sorry, we just aren't going to bless this union.

What I remember most about that day is white—the white of my dress, the white swans drifting in the narrow waterways that surround the front of the hotel. Early in the day, hours before I was to become Mrs. Thomas Berendon, I stood outside in the wintry air, leaning on the railing of the bridge and watching the swans. Swans mate for life—I'd read about that. Was that why I was drawn to them on my wedding day? Was I trying to figure out how they do it? Did I sense a looming failure in my own life? White is the color of a blank page, a hopeful start, a clean future. The truth is I didn't feel like I belonged in white.

I'd continued to work for Campbell until a week before my wedding day. I guess I was unwilling to release my grip on my former life. Even though Campbell had, for months, grown increasingly petulant as my relationship with Thomas became more serious. I slept most nights at Thomas' house, but returned each morning to attend to my employer's life. I was often greeted with grumpiness—a clear message that in Campbell Lockett's mind, I'd abandoned him.

One morning when I returned, I smelled the lingering scent of a woman's perfume in the living room. Then I spotted a pair of Manolo Blahniks tossed in the hall near Campbell's room. I guess I shouldn't have been surprised, but I was...sort of. Surprise abruptly twisted into irritation when a slender blonde woman with flawless skin, long tapered fingers and a perfect French manicure came into the kitchen where I was making coffee. She was wearing my robe.

"Oh, I was going to do that," she said, indicating the coffee maker. "You must be Isabelle."

My brow was squeezing into a frown and I did nothing to unstitch it. "And you would be?"

She ran a hand through her shoulder length hair. I was sure her pubic hair was brown, just like the roots I spotted on her head. "I'm Pasha," she said, yawning. "Pasha Peterson."

Pasha Peterson? What is that, I thought—a combination of Russian and Plymouth Rock? I reminded myself that since this was Campbell's house, not mine, I should rein in my sarcasm. But he was definitely trying to throw this woman in my face, after first throwing her in my robe.

"Uh, you know that's my robe," I told her in as even a tone as I could muster.

She was getting bread out of the breadbox and heading for the toaster. "Yeah—Campbell said you wouldn't mind."

I let it drop. But I showed him how much I did mind by charging a three hundred dollar robe to his credit card later that day.

Campbell brought Pasha to my wedding and she arrived in a tight, low-cut red dress with a flouncy skirt. She looked like a Salsa dancer who'd wandered into the wrong event. But she displayed impressive athletic prowess when it came time for me to toss the bouquet. She dove past several women who stood with their arms pathetically outstretched and caught the bouquet like it was a football and she was a star running back. Never underestimate determination. I knew even before that day about her agenda. This was a woman on the prowl for a husband—a rich one. One hint was the fact that she kept leaving home decorating magazines around the house.

I've thought back to my wedding on this Saturday morning because I'm driving Marjorie to Thomas' house for her weekly visit and we've passed a church where wedding guests are just starting to arrive. Marjorie is slumped against the window, sulking, refusing to look at me or engage in conversation. So my mind has traveled back in time—not to the most nurturing memory, but that can't always be controlled.

As we turn off Sunset Boulevard into the exclusive Brentwood neighborhood I once called home, I decide it's finally time to interrupt Marjorie's defiant silence.

"Earth to Marjorie. We're almost there."

"I know," she mumbles into the window.

"Is this going to get worse every week? Because so far that's been the trend."

She turns her face to me then—the corners of her mouth pulled in tight, her eyebrows flat and low. "Grandma just got there. I shouldn't have had to go today."

"She'll be there when you get back. She's living with us, remember? This is one day out of every seven. Can we just try to not turn it into a Biblical disaster every time?"

"What does that mean?" Marjorie asks, her face still pinched and unhappy. "Biblical disaster."

"I have no idea. I think locusts are involved somehow, and plagues. But it's open to interpretation." I turn into Thomas' driveway and stop at the intercom. "It means I don't have the energy to argue with you every weekend."

The elm and alder trees lining Thomas' long driveway are emblems of the only autumn Los Angeles gets; their leaves are turning gold, drifting down onto jasmine vines and white cement. Coins of sunlight are scattered on the drive ahead of us.

Thomas answers the door, greets Marjorie warmly, pretending to ignore her sullenness. She steps resolutely into the foyer, adjusting her backpack and looking around as if she couldn't possibly be more bored. He's dressed in khakis and a blue oxford shirt. Apparently tennis isn't on the schedule today.

He looks away from her to me. "Isabelle, could you come in for a moment? There are some things I want Marjorie to have and I'd like you to take them back with you for safe-keeping."

I look down at the threshold Marjorie has just crossed and realize I'm going to have to enter the house I once lived in, the place where my son died and my marriage followed. "Okay," I tell him in a small voice. I command my feet to move forward.

Once in the cool interior of the foyer, with the large portrait of Virgil Berendon, Thomas' father, staring down at me like he did throughout our relationship, I have a panicked feeling that Thomas is going to lead me into the den, point at the screen door and some recently uncovered evidence of my guilt. Maybe having something for Marjorie is a ruse. But instead he goes to the foot of the stairs and turns back to me, impatience tugging at his features.

"Are you coming?"

I follow him upstairs to the library, Marjorie trudging unhappily behind. The library is the color of a forest—deeply-hued green walls, dark wood floor-to-ceiling bookcases with a sliding ladder. The French windows are framed by heavy drapes, the same color green as the walls. The sofa is a lighter shade of brown, more the color of pale oak. The first time Thomas and I made love was in this room, on that couch. Later, when I was Mrs. Berendon and pregnant with Nathan, I would sneak into the library late at night while Thomas slept and choose books from these shelves to educate myself in ways my years at public school failed to do.

He goes over to the corner where his massive antique desk is stacked neatly with papers and files, all arranged like satellites around his computer. He picks up three leather-bound books and brings them first to Marjorie.

"These are first editions," he tells her. "Alice in Wonderland, Leaves of Grass, and Peter Pan. I want you to have them. They're extremely valuable, so I'm going to have Isabelle take them back and put them somewhere safe."

"Okay," Marjorie says graciously, losing some of her grumpiness. "Thank you."

"You're very welcome," Thomas tells her and then hands the books to me. "I trust you'll find a suitably protected place for them," he says to me. "Out of harm's way."

"Yes, of course."

I glance past him to the desk and remember that Marjorie told me Thomas writes out his account of the day Nathan died. Is this where he does it? Does he fill pages with longhand or just compose it over and over on his computer?

"Isabelle?" Thomas says, a splinter of irritation in his voice. "Is there something on your mind?"

"No. Nothing. See you later, Marjorie."

When I leave the estate and the wide metal gates close behind me, my thoughts return to the library. A room full of history and secrets. I'm making an assumption about the secrets, but where else would Thomas go to write about that day?

I have my own history in that room. Some parts involve Thomas; many don't.

I'd been dating Thomas for a couple of weeks when he invited me to have dinner at his house. It was the second time I'd been there, the first being an afternoon pool party at which I met Iris and Peter. Marjorie was still a toddler and being cared for by her Scottish nanny, Myra. I'd seen Marjorie , but had little sense of who this child was.

On the night of my second visit, Thomas and I were served dinner in his elegant dining room. Candlelight danced across crystal wine goblets, classical music played softly through concealed speakers, and the butler who served us had the practiced air of someone who knew part of his job was to seem invisible. Over dinner, Thomas made several references to authors I didn't know and books I'd never read. I believe at one point I said something lame like, "You read a lot, don't you?" It might have been that comment that resulted in him taking me upstairs to show me the library. Or he could always have been planning on seducing me in that room, with Yeats and Faulkner peering down from the bookshelves.

I had never seen so many books in someone's home. I craned my neck to look up at the shelves going clear up to the ceiling. Then I noticed a book by William F. Buckley on an end table near the couch. I picked it up and turned it over to look at the author photo. I remembered seeing this man, Mr. Buckley, on television sometimes when I was in high school.

"Have you read any of his books?" Thomas asked me.

I wanted to say something snippy like, Sure, they were required reading at my public high school. But instead I answered. "No, but I know a little bit about William Buckley. I know he's a Republican."

"True. But politics aside, he's a man of acute perspicacity."

Moments later, when Thomas excused himself to go to the restroom I looked up the word perspicacity in the huge dictionary that was open on a wooden stand. 'Keenness of mental perception' it said. Okay, at least I know that much now, I thought. But I felt hopelessly out of my league, and I think that's why I so readily made love with Thomas on the couch in the library that night. It was the only thing I knew how to do in that imposing room.

Months after we were married and I found out I was pregnant, the library became my secret refuge. I was tired during the day and tended to nap, but nights found me restless, unable to sleep. In the still hours after midnight, I'd pad softly across the Aubusson rug in the hallway and curl up in that forest green room with a lifetime of knowledge around me. I read some books all the way through, others only in part. I absorbed odd facts and literary references. I began speaking differently, choosing words I hadn't known before. Language became my paint box and I was enthralled with what I could do. I'd had no idea words could be so colorful, so expressive.

Thomas soon noticed. He had no idea how I spent my nights, nor was I about to tell him. I enjoyed my secret life. And I enjoyed seeing him puzzled.

One evening at a cocktail party, one of his golf buddies whose wife was also pregnant, said they were considering the name Ishmael if it was a boy.

"Inspired by Herman Melville or the son of Abraham and Hagar?" I asked.

Thomas looked at me with a dumbstruck expression.

"Melville," his friend answered. "Moby Dick is one of my favorite novels."

Another time, Thomas was watching a dog competition on television and a Jack Russell terrier jumped nearly six feet to catch a frisbee.

"He jumps like a jerboa," I commented.

"A what?"

"A jerboa. Oh, you know what that is, Thomas. It's a mouse-like rodent from North Africa with long hind legs. It can jump very high."

"Yes, of course," he said, turning up the volume on the television. He hadn't a clue about jerboas.

As I began to feel my baby in me—the small person growing inside me, pushing against my organs, pressing against the wall of my body—those hours spent alone in the library became more precious. I was doing it for my child—my son, I found out in the fourth month. At that time I was leafing through a book on Greek mythology.

"I want to name our son Lethe," I announced to Thomas one morning over breakfast in the dining room.

Thomas slapped down his newspaper, making cups rattle in their saucers. "Isabelle, do you *try* to be difficult? Contrary? Is this your intention?"

"I'm not being difficult. I'd like to name him Lethe."

"What the hell kind of name is that?"

"It's from a Greek myth. Purified souls on their way back to earth line up to drink from the river Lethe. It's the river of forgetfulness."

He picked up his newspaper again, but he wasn't focusing on it. "We're not naming our son after a fucking river," he snapped. "Is this some hippie idea you got from your mother?"

"No, Thomas. And don't insult my mother. She isn't a hippie, she's a dancer. I got it from a book on Greek mythology. Apparently you're not as perspicacious as you think you are."

There are victories in life that seem small on the surface, but those are often the huge ones. I walked ungracefully out of the dining room, since I was a bit hefty right then, but I felt like I was soaring— high above my history, high above the woman my husband believed he owned.

After Nathan died, when Thomas and I lived like strangers in the same house, I would bring my dinner upstairs into the library. I guess Thomas ate alone in the dining room—I don't even know.

I would crank open the window nearest the armchair and twist around so I could look out at the sky. I'd feel breeze drift across my face, I'd eat food methodically from the plate on my lap. And I'd wonder why I was bothering with any of it. I never tasted the food, and the evening breeze hurt my skin. I sat in that room and I thought about dying. Somewhere in all those hours I decided to live, but I'm not sure when or how.

By the time I get back to Malibu, I've exhausted my memories of Thomas' house and all I can think of is the secret that might be hiding in the library I once felt so comfortable in. Is my freedom there? My reprieve? Is my innocence written down somewhere and shoved into a drawer?

I convicted myself in Nathan's death with no clear evidence. I decided my hand must have been the last one on the screen door even though I don't remember touching it that morning. These are my snapshot memories: the screen was open when I returned to the den. I raced through the empty room, through the ominous yawn of the doo. I plunged into water and death and the rest of my life without my son. But I don't really know who left the screen door unlatched.

Iris and my mother are sitting out on the deck with Harlan and Bruce. A tray full of coffee cups and a plate dusted with crumbs is on the table.

"Good morning," Harlan says. "Wait, is it still morning? I don't have my watch on. Anyway, I told everyone to leave some scones for you, but do they listen? Of course not."

Bruce smiles at me like a mischievous kid. "They were blueberry. Delicious."

"That's okay. I forgive you," I tell them.

I look at my mother, bundled in a sweater and jeans even though the sun is warm. Everyone else is in t-shirts and shorts. "How are you this morning?" I ask her.

"Fine, dear." She's wearing sunglasses, so I can't see what her eyes are saying.

I'm still holding the three books that Thomas handed me. Iris squints at the titles. "Interesting choices," she says.

"Thomas wants Marjorie to have these. They're first editions. He sent them back with me so I can put them out of everyone's reach and make sure no one tries to read them with peanut butter on their fingers. I'm surprised he didn't send me home with latex gloves as well."

"He'll probably send the gloves back with Marjorie," Harlan says.

He and Bruce move simultaneously to stand up, some invisible communication having passed between them. "We'll leave you all to your day," Bruce says. "Thanks for the coffee and …sorry about the scones, Isabelle."

A thought had blinked into my mind when I came home and saw Harlan and Bruce there. I suddenly decide to follow them…out onto the sand and out of hearing range of everyone else.

"Harlan?"

When he and Bruce turn around I walk close to them and lower my voice.

"Are you still going to Thomas' Halloween party?

"Absolutely," Bruce says. "I won't let him out of it."

I know what I'm about to ask is crazy, but I go for it anyway. "I want to go with you. In disguise, of course. I mean, it's a costume party so I should be able to get away with it. I know this sounds weird, but I can explain… I think."

Both men stare at me with absolutely no expression on their faces. Finally, Harlan speaks. "Not that it's any of my business, but I do feel I should ask why."

"I want to spy on him. Marjorie hates going there, I don't really know what that house is like now that I'm not living there. Maybe there are new people hanging out there, you know a different crowd. I might get an idea from the party. I'm just curious."

I'm not a very good liar, a small voice inside me whispers. And Harlan's eyes are boring into me. He knows there's something more. Eventually I'll have to tell him.

"You're not going to be armed, are you?" Bruce asks.

"No. Promise. I'll even let you search me."

"I guess we can do it," Harlan answers slowly. "But we have to make sure your costume is absolutely foolproof."

"I can do that," I assure him. "I'll be…uh…I don't know who I'll be but I promise you it will be a really good disguise."

"We'll be the judges of that," Bruce says as they turn and walk away, making sand clouds with their feet.

I'm the daughter of a thief and a liar. That background should help me in this dishonest venture, but I'm not sure it will.

17.

It's early Monday morning. Already the sunlight has a coppery look to it—a forecast of more Santa Ana winds. Marjorie is dressed for school; she and Iris are making pancakes in the kitchen.

"Your mother is still sleeping," Iris tells me when I come downstairs into the warm smells of coffee and butter melting in the skillet.

"We'll let her sleep as long as she wants."

"Can we put raisins in the pancakes?" Marjorie asks.

Iris is about to pour some of the batter into the skillet. "Raisins? I guess so," she says, putting the bowl down and going to the cupboard. "I've never heard of raisin pancakes..."

"And chocolate?"

"No. No chocolate."

"And brown sugar?"

I scoop Marjorie up in my arms. "Who plugged you in this morning?"

"No one. I don't know," she giggles and squirms out of my arms.

As the reassuring sound of batter being poured into the skillet fills the room, a less reassuring sound intrudes. The phone rings.

"Who could be calling this early?" Iris asks.

I answer the phone and hear Libby Fenimore's curt hello. Iris' mother has a grating voice that sounds like it's caught in the back of her throat. Once we moved out to Malibu, she apparently decided that, despite how mortified she was at Iris' behavior, political correctness dictated she should be civil to her newly-gay daughter.

"Good morning, Libby. Just a second." I hand the phone to Iris, who has just lost her smile.

I take over the job of cooking pancakes, with Marjorie glued to my side, and listen as Iris says, "Okay," and "Uh-huh," about five times. The she lets out an exhale.   "Well, it's a school night so Marjorie can't come. We'll have to get a sitter. But it will be three of us. Isabelle's mother is living with us now."

I turn to look at Iris after she has said this, trying to decipher what she's hearing on the other end, but I can't interpret anything from her expression.

"Just a second," she says and swivels around to face me with her hand over the phone. "My mother would like us to come to dinner tomorrow night. Apparently, the couple who were scheduled to come have fallen ill and she's left with all this food, so..." She shrugs her shoulders dramatically.

"Okay," I tell her. I would rather have my big toe amputated than sit at the dinner table with the Fenimores, but I can't send Iris there alone—she'd never forgive me.

"Do I have to go?" Marjorie whispers, pouring maple syrup over two large raisin pancakes that I've put onto a plate.

"No," I whisper back. "School night. Homework. Watching Finding Nemo for the sixty-seventh time."

Iris says goodbye to her mother after sealing our fate for six-thirty the following evening.

I put pancakes on two more plates and the three of us sit at the table to eat more than we should. I'm waiting for Iris to fill me in on the details of her conversation, but she seems completely engrossed in her pancakes.

"Iris..."

"What?"

"What did she say about my mother living here?"

"Nothing. I think she said, 'Oh.' I couldn't really interpret the meaning behind it, or maybe I wasn't trying. Thanks for saying yes, Isabelle. I know it's not how you'd like to spend the evening."

"Is Kim going to baby-sit me?" Marjorie asks. Her lips are shiny with maple syrup.

"That's the plan," Iris tells her. "I'll call her this morning."

Marjorie gives me a mischievous look. "Why don't you want to go over there?"

"Well, for probably the same reasons you don't. It's not fun. And, to be honest, I'm afraid if I say the wrong thing they might lock me in the tower until they locate the guillotine."

Winking at Marjorie, Iris says, "Oh, they haven't used the tower in ages. And guillotines are so last year."

"That's a relief. What do they use now?"

"Longer dinners," Iris answers through a mouthful of pancakes.

The next day, as the sky is turning orange, we leave the ocean and maneuver through rush hour traffic. Dry winds scrape the air and I have the uneasy thought that a wildfire could start while we're gone and we wouldn't be allowed back into Malibu. I've heard of that happening, but I push the thought out of my mind. The evening will probably be tense enough without adding rampant paranoia to the mix.

We've taken Iris' Mercedes and my mother has insisted on sitting in the back seat. She looks so tiny to me in her ankle-length black dress with the rose-colored shawl wrapped around her shoulders.

As we turn off Sunset Boulevard into the lush hills of Bel Air, my mother leans toward the window and looks out at the huge trees, their canopy of branches shading the streets.

"Evening has such a different feel to it through all these trees," she says wistfully. "Do you girls ever miss trees living at the beach?"

I twist around to answer her and have a sudden image of her younger self turning just that way to talk to me as I sprawled restlessly in the back seat of our yellow Volvo.

"Sometimes," I tell her. "Sometimes there's too much sky and too much relentless blue. But everything's a trade-off. They don't have dolphins in Bel Air."

Iris turns into a wide driveway and stops the car at the imposing metal gates. She pushes the buzzer on the intercom.

"May I help you?" an accented male voice asks.

"It's Iris."

The gates slowly open and we start down a long drive bordered by rose bushes and azaleas.

"Oh my," my mother says. "Is this where you grew up, Iris?"

"It is. Me, my parents, and a small army of servants, gardeners, and the occasional caterer and party planner. My best friend in grade school used to hate coming here. She'd always get lost, either in the house or on the grounds and she'd end up crying and calling her parents to come get her."

The Fenimore house would probably look fine on a hundred-acre parcel of land in Connecticut. Here, the brick exterior and square stone columns, the massive balconies on the second floor, look oddly out of place. Even on several acres, with lawns and oak trees around it, the house overpowers the property.

A butler is holding the front door open as we get out of the car and start toward the wide bleached stone steps. My mother composes her dancer's body. She lengthens her stride, pulls her spine up, making herself appear taller—it's instinct, second nature to her. Dancers inhabit the air around them. They can expand like they have wings, stretch toward the clouds, spin against the wind. They make you believe in the miracle of the human body, while at the same time transporting you beyond the physical. My mother was never a star; people won't recall her name or list her credits. But I believe she could have sailed across the grandest stages, bowed to standing ovations, if her life had taken different turns.

We step through the front door into the marble foyer. The ceiling is so high that the massive chandelier—at least four feet in diameter—actually makes sense. There is a curved staircase with polished mahogany banisters, Chinese urns that could be bathtubs for small eco-systems and two David Hockney originals hung conspicuously, so you can't miss them when you cross the threshold.

Libby Fenimore descends the staircase gracefully, giving us a restricted smile on her way down. A bit too Norma Desmond for me, but Iris is probably used to it and my mother is too distracted by all the extravagance around us to notice.

I've always thought Libby Fenimore would be a lovely woman if she could thaw to room temperature. It's obvious that Iris got her chiseled features, her high cheekbones and blond hair from her mother, although I'm sure her mother's hair now has some chemical help. This evening she is dressed in loose black pants and a blue satin blouse that brings out the blue of her eyes. Her hair is, as usual, secured in a bun at the back of her head. I have no idea how long her hair is; probably only her husband and her hairdresser know for sure. It's always said so much to me, this concealment.

"Maybe her hair is really long," I once said to Iris. "And she lets it down at night, lets it fall all around your father's face while she climbs on top of him and fucks his brains out."

We were in bed when I made this unlikely suggestion. Iris turned on the bedside lamp and scrutinized my face.

"Isabelle, are you on crack?"

I probably seemed like I was because I started giggling and couldn't stop.

Mrs. Fenimore crosses the floor to her daughter first and kisses her delicately on the cheek. "Hello, dear."

I get a similar greeting, although her lips make a point of not touching my flesh. She only started doing this after Iris and I became lovers. When I was married to Thomas she'd leave lipstick marks on my cheek. Now, it's like she fears catching something—gayness, perhaps.

Extending her hand to my mother she says, "Hello, I'm Libby Fenimore." As if they've never met before. Which they have.

"Yes, we met at Isabelle's wedding," my mother says graciously. "Catherine Haller—don't you remember? We had a long conversation that evening."

"Oh, of course," Mrs. Fenimore says. I know she has no memory of their exchange. People in my mother's tax bracket are disposable to this woman.

She is saved by her husband's entrance. He slips in as if he'd prefer to not be noticed, which is how I think he's gone through life. The Fenimores are wealthy because of Libby's inheritance. She was born Libby Weyburn and grew up in Texas where her father turned whole sections of the state into gushing oil wells. Somewhere along the course of her life she decided to lose her Texas twang, but she talks in that studied way that people do who have adopted a new way of speaking. Words don't seem comfortable in her mouth. When she married Arthur Fenimore—an entrepreneur who knew nothing about the oil business—she asked Daddy to give him a job. Mr. Fenimore has, for years, drawn a salary for sitting on the corporate board of a company he doesn't really understand.

He greets us without making eye contact and we move into the living room where cocktails are to be served. The Fenimores divide their evenings into designated segments: cocktail hour, dinner hour, coffee and brandy hour. Another predictable thing is that Mrs. Fenimore uses the first wedge of time to talk about herself and the people who inhabit her world. By dinner time she's usually run out of gossip and seems to suddenly realize that someone else might have something to say.

"Iris, do you remember Doris Kensington?" she asks as soon as drinks are poured and we are seated on less than comfortable furniture that has been artfully arranged to discourage intimacy.

I give Iris a here-we-go-again look, which she acknowledges with a wink. "The name sounds familiar," she tells her mother.

My mother is sitting straight as a new green shoot, occasionally glancing at the walls where a Jackson Pollock hangs across from a Norman Rockwell.

"You used to go to swimming parties at their house when you were young," Mrs. Fenimore continues. "Well. Doris went in for a routine face-lift and the doctor apparently cut a nerve in her neck or someplace because a week later, her shoulder just fell right down. She's suing, of course, but there doesn't seem to be anything they can do to fix her shoulder. She doesn't even want to go out of the house, poor thing. Her face looks fabulous, but with her left shoulder drooping like that..."

"What a nightmare," Iris says in an exaggerated tone, which her mother doesn't pick up on. "But at least she isn't showing a wrinkled face to the world. We can be grateful for that."

"This is definitely going to be a lawsuit. And this so-called plastic surgeon will be sorry he ever had the audacity to call himself a doctor."

As Libby Fenimore chats on, I notice Iris staring at the bookshelf. She is scrutinizing it, squinting as if to catalogue every book title and art object on the shelves. Then she gets up, walks over to it—slowly, deliberately—and turns back around to give her mother a cold, accusatory look. I have no idea what's going on, but clearly something it. Iris attacks her mother's eyes, forcing them to meet hers. As if it's a jousting match, Libby Fenimore gets snagged for a second, then leaps away. Her arm lunges for her wine glass and she takes a long un-ladylike swallow. But Iris continues boring into her with eyes like blue fire.

"Dinner is served," their uniformed maid announces delicately from just outside the room. She is tiny, Hispanic, and I wonder if either Libby or her husband bother to remember her name from one day to the next.

As we file into the dining room, I whisper to my mother, "Welcome to another planet. Where face-lifts are routine."

I look at Iris for clues as to what's going on and find none. But there is an uneasy chill hovering over us as we take our seats—not that this room could ever be warm and inviting. It's as stiff and formal as the rest of the house—the long, polished table, perfectly appointed place settings, heavy Waterford goblets, an elaborate flower arrangement as centerpiece and tall silver candlesticks that look like they will fall if anyone breathes too hard.

Midway through the salad course, Mrs. Fenimore comes to her usual realization that her guests also have lives. "Catherine, Iris tells me you're living at the beach house now."

My mother puts her fork down carefully and gives her hostess a direct, hard-to-read look. "Yes. I just moved in. Isabelle thought it would be better and Iris agreed. You see, I have cancer."

The air suddenly seems sucked from the room. Except, apparently, where my mother is sitting. She's breathing just fine.

"I'm sorry to hear that," Libby Fenimore says after a few seconds of jittery silence. "So, you're going through treatment, I assume?"

"No. I'm dying. I have ovarian cancer, although it's spread beyond that. There really isn't any treatment at this point."

A different maid has begun circling the table with a large silver platter of chicken, cooked carrots and what looks like rice pilaf. The same jagged silence closes in as plates are filled, everyone concentrating more than they need to on the food. When the maid has left the dining room, Mr. Fenimore clears his throat and looks at my mother. "If there's anything we can do," he says, but doesn't finish the sentence.

Like what? I think. Sue God?

"Thank you," my mother answers.

"You know, I heard that Sophia Loren had cancer and she took some experimental treatment involving urine from some animal, I can't recall which, and now she's fine." Libby Fenimore suddenly says. "Except of course her hair never grew back. That's why she's always wearing wigs."

Iris laughs—one of those laughs that cuts like glass. "Oh, for God's sake. What are you talking about, Mother?"

"I hear things, Iris. People talk, you know." her mother answers defensively.

"Libby finds out all sorts of things at the nail salon," Mr. Fenimore interjects. "What was it you told me about Raquel Welch?"

"Oh, yes. Her elbow lift. The elbows are a dead give-away of age. So she had hers lifted."

Iris laughs again—a short, sharp sound, meant to be derisive. "Well, none of this really has anything to do with Catherine, now does it?' she says. "God, you two will say anything to avoid authentic human interaction."

"That's very rude, Iris," Mr. Fenimore says. "We were quite clear in expressing our sympathy."

I glance at my mother and see that she is trying not to laugh. And, right in the midst of all this absurdity and unpleasantness, I think she has never looked lovelier. Her long hair, peppered with gray now, is pinned back from her face with two shiny clips. Her skin looks papery and thin, but it's smooth and flushed tonight from the red wine she's been sipping.

After tip-toeing through the rest of the dinner, we are finally ready to leave, having begged off the Brandy and coffee segment of the evening. We file into the foyer and see that a large cardboard box has been placed conspicuously beside the front door. Iris' name has been written across the top in black magic marker. She edges past me, bends down over the box and opens it. I can't see the contents, but I know this can't be good.

Slowly, with anger spreading out across her back, Iris stands up and turns to face her parents. She's holding several framed photographs in her hands. I can glimpse one of them—a young teenage Iris, smiling in that wide-open way we used to before we learned how treacherous the road ahead can be.

"Am I dead now?" Iris asks, aiming her question and her defiance at her mother. "You take all my pictures off the shelf, put them in a box and leave them at the door? Is this your way of telling me I'm no longer part of this family?" She pulls some more things out of the box. Notebooks, a white garment that looks like a baby's christening dress. "Cleared out all the mementos from my old room, too, huh?"

Libby Fenimore straightens her spine, clenches her mouth and seems to will herself to meet her daughter's angry eyes. "I just thought you'd like to have these things," she says. "And, we need to make room. We're adopting a child."

The only sound is that of Mr. Fenimore's footsteps padding across the marble floor and ascending the stairs. Perhaps he has a refuge up there, I think—a secret hideaway. A man-cave. Or he might be heading for a second floor window to jump to his death.

"Excuse me?" Iris finally says.

"You heard me. We're adopting a daughter. From Romania."

"A daughter," Iris repeats softly.

I see her chest cave in. I want to run to her but I know I can't. Shouldn't. She has to tackle this one herself.

"How wonderfully convenient for you, Mother," she continues. "I just didn't follow the script you wrote for me, so presto! Get a new daughter. A new, improved model. God, it's too bad there isn't some genetic test you could do on the kid to determine if she's heterosexual through and through. So, good luck with this. I hope she turns out to be the perfect little daughter. Not the colossal disappointment I've been."

I notice Mrs. Fenimore shudder as if seams are coming loose inside her. I suddenly see her as I never thought I would—human, with warm blood in her veins and wounds opening beneath the skin.

"We had dreams for you!" she shouts at her daughter. "Hopes for the future, for grandchildren! This...this life you've chosen has closed the door on everything. You'll never have a marriage with children, a life that goes on for generations after you. You've stolen that from your father and me. You've taken everything from us!"

Iris' fury pauses. I wonder if it's because she's heard her mother say something so true and heartfelt, that she has to catch her breath before retaliating.

"I'm a human being, Mother, not an oven for your grandchildren. But then to you, everyone is just there for your benefit, right?"

"That's not true," he mother answers, but her tone is defeated. She's too tired to fight on.

Iris picks up the box, swings the front door open with her other hand and leaves the house she grew up in without looking back. My mother and I scurry after her, climb in the car as Iris is tossing the box into the trunk. When she gets behind the wheel, she screeches down the driveway and starts driving at suicidal speed through the winding streets of Bel Air.

"Iris, pull over," I tell her.

"What?"

"Pull over now. I'm going to drive."

She does, and we trade places. No one says a word for several miles. Finally, my mother breaks the silence.

"Is that a typical dinner at your family's home, dear?"

Iris' laughter is real and rich; her whole body changes, relaxes. "Yes and no," she manages to say. "The first part of the evening, yes— typical. The last part was a whole new chapter."

After a few seconds of winding-down laughter, she says, "Isabelle, pull over up here."

"What? Why?"

"Just do it, please."

She opens the car door as soon as I stop and I think maybe she's going to be sick. But instead she tells me to pop the trunk, which I do. She walks around to the rear of the car, removes the cardboard box, and carries it resolutely to a trashcan waiting at the curb for morning pick-up.

"Are you sure about this?" I ask her through the open window.

"Absolutely."

With her photographic history disposed of, Iris gets back in the car, scrunches down in the seat and closes her eyes. I don't really think she's sleeping, but I know I'm supposed to, so we drive home in silence.

Aristotle greets us at the door when we arrive home, followed by Kim who has cat hair stuck to her clothes.

"He's the most incredible animal," she gushes. "I swear we had some really deep conversations."

My mother sits down on the lowest stair and strokes him. "Well, of course," she coos, and he meows contentedly in return.

"And Marjorie?" I ask her, hoping she didn't get so involved with Aristotle that she forgot the child.

"Sound asleep. I put my foot down about the sugary foods."

Iris pays Kim, walks her out to her car and I turn to say something to my mother but suddenly feel I'm intruding. She's still stroking Aristotle and she seems far away, exhausted.

"Another day gone," she says softly, either to the cat or to herself—definitely not to me.

This is how it's going to be, I think—days flicked aside like so many burned matches. The truth is it's like that for all of us. But when you know death is closing in, the flame of each day must look brighter, warmer; something in the heart bruises each night when it's extinguished.

Iris and I move about our room, quietly getting ready for bed as if an agreement has been reached that no talking will be allowed. It is a sort of agreement, really—an intuitive one between lovers who know each other well—an understanding that sometimes people need to crawl into cocoons and they'll emerge when they're ready, not before.

I didn't know about this before Iris. Thomas and I used silence as a weapon, just as my parents did. My mother could fill the house with loud sounds of cooking, setting the table, cleaning up…without ever parting her lips to say a single word. My father's response was to stomp from room to room as if declaring that he belonged there. I got used to the absence of voices for long stretches of time; I learned that much can be communicated with noise. No wonder I married a man who could make shaving sound like a screaming fit.

Iris gets into bed with her back to me and pushes the pillow under her head. I stare into the darkness, study a splinter of moonlight falling through the shades we never close. I wonder if she's really going to sleep. I monitor her breathing.

"Isabelle," she whispers. "Are you awake?"

"Uh-huh." I don't whisper.

"I'm really glad you were with me tonight. I don't know what I would have done if you hadn't been."

I turn on my side and bend around her. We are two question marks curved against each other in the dark space of our bed. There is a world brushing past the windows; there is the sound of waves lapping, tides changing. Cars on the highway, either going somewhere or coming home. And we are lying here in the home we have made on smooth white sheets, skin to skin. Sometimes that's all a person needs.

18.

On Saturday morning, there's an unexpected occurrence: Marjorie doesn't launch into her usual rebellion at the idea of going to her father's house. She sits quietly at the breakfast table, contentedly eating a bowl of granola topped with blueberries. I stand at the counter drinking a cup of coffee, trying not to stare at her, but I'm wondering if she's ill. It's become so predictable, our Saturday morning scuffle that I find myself concerned by this sudden truce. Ironic actually, since I've said to Iris, "I wish she'd stop this routine every Saturday. She knows it isn't going to work." Well, now she has stopped and it's worrying me.

Iris left just after dawn for the women's shelter. She got an emergency call a little after six about a woman who was just beaten again by her husband. This is a woman Iris has been trying to help for months. I give Marjorie only the barest facts.

"Aunt Iris had to go to the shelter. There was an emergency." I'm still not sure how many details to give her.

Marjorie nods and reaches for the honey bear; she drizzles a thin pattern of honey over her cereal.

"How are you doing this morning?" I ask her, taking a seat at the table, trying my best to sound casual.

"I'm okay." She says this while blending the honey into her cereal with the spoon.

"You should probably wear shorts to your Dad's house. It's pretty warm out."

I've always wished that October in Los Angeles could bear some resemblance to autumn. But instead it turns hot and dry; the air over the ocean looks sooty.

Marjorie nods again, chews, and then says, "Okay."

I know I can't push this; I certainly can't say, So why aren't you arguing with me this morning? I consider the possibility that she might be waiting until we get in the car. But then she looks at me and says, "Grandma said she'd help me with my ballet when I get home tonight."

"Oh, good. That's great. You know, she was a beautiful dancer. I'll show you some pictures of her."

So that's what happened. My mother gave Marjorie something to look forward to. The day she doesn't want to spend at her father's is now just a passage, hours to count and get through, with excitement waiting for her at the other end. I don't know why I'd never thought of that. It's such a simple, tender way of easing a child through the day.

When I was a little older than Marjorie, my father insisted that we all go to a miniature golf course one Saturday. It was a sweltering hot summer day and I didn't want to go, but he was adamant. Someone had given him free passes, or else he'd won them in a card game—I'm not exactly sure which.

"We're going to do something together as a family!" he said, raising his voice in answer to my protests.

"Frank, can't we think of something else to do that's cooler?" my mother asked.

"I have these passes and we're going to use them, goddamn it! Why can't you ever appreciate anything I do for you?"

With that he stomped out of the kitchen, which was probably a good thing because I had a few answers on the tip of my tongue about what he did for us. My mother came over to me, smoothed the frown off my forehead with her hand and whispered, "I'll tell you what. After we go there, we'll go to the public pool and go swimming. You go put your swim suit on under your clothes."

"But what if he says no?" I asked her.

"Leave that to me."

All through the blazing hot hours at the miniature golf course, which I hated more than I'd ever hated anything, I thought about blue water, about diving in and feeling my hair pulled back like a stream behind me. When the sun was beating down on my shoulders, turning them red, and my father was barking orders at me, in my mind I sank under water and felt the bubbles of my breath as they left my mouth.

I don't know what my mother said to my father, but she kept her promise. We ended the day at a public swimming pool. Only my mother and I swam, which was fine with me. My father sat in a plastic chair beside the pool eating a Popsicle he got from a vending machine. I imagined splashing him with water like they did to the wicked witch in The Wizard of Oz, seeing him evaporate, but I knew I wasn't supposed to think such bad thoughts. So I pushed him out of my thoughts entirely and swam the length of the pool alongside my mother. I shut my ears to the other children splashing near us, angled my eyes away from the fat legs of adults standing in the shallow end, and I pretended my mother and I were swimming the length of a river. At the end of the river we'd climb out into a new town, a new life. Someplace pretty without my father.

Marjorie has finished her breakfast and is going upstairs to get dressed. The plan is that my mother will come with me to drop her off at Thomas' and then the two of us will go back to her house and clean out more things. I bought some boxes and have them stacked in the trunk of my car. But when I go upstairs to check on her, she's still in bed. Her eyes open sleepily when I come in.

"Hi, did you still want to come with me?" I ask her, keeping my voice low since she still looks caught up in sleep.

"I don't think so, dear. I'm awfully tired. I'd like to rest some more."

I bend over her, kiss her forehead the way she used to do when she put me to bed at night. Something heavy moves into my chest, starts to settle there, until I go out in the hall and see Marjorie dressed in pink and blue flowered shorts with a green checked shirt. The sorrow that had parked itself over my heart ruptures into a smile.

"Well, that's a colorful outfit," I tell her.

"I like it." The set of her mouth dares me to contradict her choice and I have no intention of doing so.

"You ready to go?"

"Isn't Grandma coming with us?"

I put my hand on Marjorie's shoulder and steer her toward the stairs. "She's a little tired this morning. But she'll be full of energy for your dance lesson tonight."

I want to ask Marjorie more about Thomas' diary writings about Nathan, but every time I plan a question my conscience clamps down on it. It's such a disquieting feeling having an agenda with a child—molding your questions to pry out information. I tell myself that maybe she'll volunteer something. After all, she has before. But so far she's silent on the subject.

After I drop Marjorie at Thomas' I drive back to the neighborhood that always embarrassed me. When I park in front of the house, I notice a young woman sitting in the yard next door—what was once Mrs. Middlington's property. I've never met my mother's neighbors before, so I wave to the woman to let her know I belong on this faded brick pathway. I make sure the key is visible in my hand. She nods her head in acknowledgement, but she looks exhausted, like she just woke up.

I suddenly miss Mrs. Middlington and her intrusive nosiness. She used to knock on our door sometimes and tell us that the mailman was looking a little too closely at our mail as he put the letters though the slot. He probably wasn't, but we always assured her we would speak to him about it.

I unlock the front door and then go back to my car for the boxes in my trunk. The wailing cries of a baby fill the air and I see the woman's husband carrying a tiny infant outside to her. I can't tell if it's a boy or girl because the child is wrapped in a white blanket—no telltale blue or pink. Her husband's expression, though, is easy to read—the ragged desperation of a man who's been trying in vain to calm a red-faced crying baby.

I offer them a sympathetic smile, but they don't notice. I miss that—the resolute focus when your baby is crying—how the whole world falls away. I feel it in my breasts, my womb. Missing Nathan crawls across the cartilage of every bone in my body.

When I carry a stack of collapsed boxes into the house, I suddenly find myself walking softly across the floor even though there is obviously no one there. But that's not really true. The house is crowded with ghosts. My father is sitting hunched over his coffee at the kitchen table, his eyes cloudy from too little sleep and too much Johnny Walker the night before. A young girl, her brown hair spilt into two braids, sits cross-legged on the floor with a new pair of black patent-leather shoes, scoring the soles with scissors so she won't slip the first time she wears them. I hated my father for his thievery, but I loved those shoes. My mother is drifting through the rooms too, graceful as the dancer she was, light as the wind but purposeful as a tiger. She marked her territory in our home, and my father knew it.

I assemble a few of the boxes in the living room and start filling them with things my mother has already removed from closets—towels, throw pillows, blankets, sheets. Some of my father's clothes. I notice how my eyes turn away from his jackets, his shirts—the things that might still hold his scent—as I toss them into a box. I have a ripple of irritation at my mother for not getting rid of his things years ago.

I'm avoiding going to my mother's closet because I know it's her scent that will wash over me and remind me that one day soon that will be the one that starts fading. I'm like an animal with scent in this house, sniffing out the residue of who used to be here, memorizing the smells I'm drawn to. All of it tears at me.

So I stick with safe things—house-wares, linens, tablecloths. My plan is to take all of that to Goodwill on my way home, and then bring back to my mother a few things I know she'll still want.

It's not so dependable though, these lines between what will wound us and what won't. Things are never just things. In the kitchen I find the platter she always used for the Thanksgiving turkey, cups with Christmas wreaths on them that only came out in December for eggnog or mulled wine. She's even saved my cereal bowl from when I was a child; Winnie the Pooh and Eyore grin up at me timelessly from their smooth ceramic home. I leave the kitchen with nothing in my hands and tell myself I'll tackle that on another day. Kitchens are where childhoods echo for many long years. I'm not strong enough yet for the echoes that this kitchen holds.

I do finally go into my mother's bedroom and find some of her shawls, her old navy blue sweater that she used to wear on cold winter mornings. I want her to still want that. I scoop up some silver jewelry and some jangly beaded earrings. I pick up a jade tree my father stole for her, which she always kept by the window because of the way the light filtered through the jade. A few books—old volumes of Anaïs Nin's diaries and a biography of Isadora Duncan—she might want to turn the pages again.

I'm on my second trip out to the car with filled-up boxes when the woman from next door comes out and walks over to the chain link fence separating the two properties.

"Need some help?"

She's brushed her hair, has changed into a short denim skirt and blue tank top. She looks shiny and blonde, where a little while ago she looked like a faded photograph.

"Sure, if you want."

She comes around and walks through the gate, extends her hand. "I'm Marilyn Dunlop. I'm guessing you're Catherine's daughter. She's talked about you a lot."

"Isabelle. Nice to meet you."

We walk into the house, each of us picking up a box. "Is she okay? Your mother?" Marilyn asks as we go back out to my car.

I wait until we've put the boxes we're carrying into the car. "No, actually, she isn't. She has cancer. We're going to be selling the house. She's moved in with me and my partner and daughter."

"I'm so sorry. We were worried about her a couple of weeks ago when the paramedics came."

"The paramedics?"

Marilyn Dunlop runs a hand through her hair. "Oh dear," she says. "I assumed you knew. They weren't here long. Your mother had apparently gotten dizzy and felt faint. So she called 911. She seemed fine the next day. My husband went over to see if she needed anything and she said it was really nothing—she'd just gotten a little light-headed is all."

I nod and we go back into the house for more boxes. A blue jay calls from the pepper tree. Marilyn Dunlop has no idea what the history of this tree is, how much it's towered over in its time here.

"I think that's it for today," I tell her after we've filled my Jaguar with boxes.

"Well, if there's anything we can do," Marilyn tells me. "With the house, or whatever…"

"Thanks, I'll let you know. And thanks for helping me."

As I drive away, I glance in the rear view mirror and see Marilyn turning on a sprinkler in front of her house and then walking back inside. I imagine her reaching for her baby, peeling up her shirt and putting the child's mouth to her breast. I could tell she's still nursing. "Mrs. Haller next door has cancer," she might say to her husband as the baby draws food from her body. "The house is going to be sold." Maybe she'll think about the cries of birth and the silence of death and how life is embroidered with both. Maybe the blue jay will screech again in the tree that was once a sapling, long ago when Mrs. Middlington was a young woman and had just moved in. Maybe her husband will turn away, shake his head in that stiff, cut-off way that some men do.

Then I think, No—that's what Thomas would do. Not all men are like that.

19.

As I head back home I notice Halloween decorations in store-front windows. Halloween—my brilliant or perhaps not so brilliant idea of infiltrating Thomas' party and snooping around for his confessional writings. Marjorie hasn't yet decided what she wants to be for Halloween, but she has decided where she wants to shop for her costume: a shop in Santa Monica along Wilshire Boulevard.

As I take short-cuts through residential streets, I call the house from my cell-phone. Olivia should have gotten there at ten. Iris and I decided we should increase her days because of my mother. She answers on the second ring.

"Yes, hello?" she says. When she worked for Thomas she was instructed to say, "Berendon residence." Iris and I didn't give her any instructions so 'Yes, hello' has become Olivia's phone greeting.

"Hey, Olivia, it's me. Is my mother up yet?"

"Oh yes, ma'am. She's out on the deck. Should I get her for you?"

"No, that's okay. Just tell her I'll be home soon. I have an errand to run on the way."

"Yes, ma'am."

I've asked Olivia a few times to simply call me Isabelle, but it's never worked. She just likes ma'am better. She calls Iris Mrs. Iris, for reasons I don't understand, but we can't both be ma'am so it's fine.

As soon as I walk into the costume store, a small boy who is trying on a turtle suit runs into my legs. I'm guessing from his size that he's about five. How Nathan would have looked at that age is something I'll never know.

"I'm sorry," his mother says to me, reaching for his fuzzy green arm. She's young, with wavy black hair and blue eyes. Her son has inherited her coloring.

"No problem."

I stand in the center of the store and look around at the costumes on display, the masks dotting the walls. I could easily get distracted by the children in the store, but I remind myself I'm here on an important mission. Then I see what I came here for, although I didn't know it before I looked at the wall behind the cash register. Staring down at me are Bill and Hillary masks. I wait for the store clerk to finish helping a pregnant mother put a Superman cape on her toddler and then I catch his eye.

"I'd like to get that Hillary Clinton mask," I tell him. He looks like he should be in college. I wonder if this is a part time job or a substitute for college.

"Sure. You want Bill too?"

"No. I don't think so."

He disappears into the back and returns a moment later with Hillary's face looped over one hand. "Sure you don't want the whole package? You might want to go as a couple—I mean, you and whoever."

"Don't think so. I'm kind of rooting for Hillary on her own. You know, I am woman, hear me roar."

He rings up the mask. "That was a song, right? The hear me roar thing?"

I hand him my credit card, feeling much older than I did three seconds ago. "Yeah—a long time ago," I tell him.

It's late afternoon when I get home and the day is finally cooling off. I find my mother and Iris sitting outside on the deck with

Aristotle curled up in my mother's lap. He is intently watching pelicans swooping and diving into the waves.

"Must be a lot of fish today," I comment, leaning down to kiss my mother's cheek. A breeze is blowing off the water, lifting her hair.

As I slip an arm around Iris and kiss her neck, my mother says, "I don't think Aristotle has ever seen pelicans before."

Iris laughs. "Not unless he has a beach house in his past."

"Iris was telling me about her work," my mother says. "The poor women who come to this shelter. Today, this woman came who'd been punched in the face..."

"I think she's finally ready to let us protect her," Iris says softly. "But then you never know."

I wonder if my mother is thinking that, all in all, her marriage wasn't so bad. At least my father never used his fists. She shifts her weight beneath Aristotle and looks out at the pelicans again.

I have Hillary Clinton's face wadded up and tucked into the back of my jeans, concealed beneath my shirt. I want to show it to Harlan and Bruce before Marjorie comes home. I can hear their voices next door.

"I'll be right back," I tell Iris and my mother, in what I hope is a casual manner. "I just want to talk to Harlan for a moment. Then I'll unload the stuff from the car."

Before I go up Harlan's steps, I put on my Halloween face. Bruce is at the far end of the deck, tending to a potted fern he's carried out from the house. He glances up at the sound of my footsteps and keeps one of the best poker faces I've ever seen.

"Harlan!" he calls out. "Hillary's here to see you."

From somewhere inside the house I hear, "Who the fuck is Hillary?"

"Clinton, honey. Don't keep her waiting."

Harlan comes out as if he's going to get mad at Bruce, and he almost does. But then he sees me and starts laughing. "That's good, Isabelle, only your legs beat hers by a country mile."

I take off the mask. "How did you know it was me?"

"Because your legs beat hers by a country mile," Bruce says. "And because you forgot the wig."

"I didn't forget the wig. I don't have one yet. So, what do you think? Will it work?"

"For Halloween?" Harlan asks.

"No, Harlan, for Christmas. Of course for Halloween. Did you forget what I asked you?"

"No. I just wasn't sure if you were serious. I guess you are." He looks at Bruce and some kind of silent communication passes between them.

"I'll help her," Bruce says. "We'll work on the wig and the pants suit. Isabelle, do you have a pants suit?"

"No."

"Well, you will."

For a second I consider telling them my real reason for infiltrating Thomas' party, but I'm afraid if I say Nathan's name, tears will come. There will be time for the truth, I decide. Instead I ask, "What are you two going as?"

"Harlan's going as Puff Daddy," Bruce tells me.

"P. Diddy," Harlan snaps.

"Whatever. I haven't decided on my disguise yet," Bruce says.

I try to imagine Harlan as Sean Combs and the obvious question pops up. "How are you going to make it clear that you're P. Diddy when…you know…you're white?"

Bruce laughs and Harlan frowns. "I've been mulling that over," Harlan says. "Bruce is dead set against me going in black face. He pointed out that it could be interpreted as racial insensitivity and there is nothing worse than an insensitive gay man."

"Yeah, that's a good point," I tell him, giggling. "Well, you'll figure it out, I'm sure."

That evening we move some furniture in the living room so Marjorie and my mother can have a wider space for their dance lesson. My mother's voice is crisp and strong. "Pull up from your center, dear. That's where your strength is." And she applauds when Marjorie does everything right—turns perfectly, extends her arms to the ceiling. It's clear my mother has missed teaching and this private session in our living room is invigorating her. In the coming months my mother will teach all of us about leaving this world. We never plan to teach others about dying; sometimes it just works out that way.

After we've put Marjorie to bed and my mother has closed the door to her room, when Iris and I are alone and going through the usual bedtime rituals of teeth brushing and face washing, I slip into the closet, put on my Hilary mask, and walk back into the bathroom. Iris is flossing her teeth and starts laughing, a piece of floss dangling from her teeth.

"The hair isn't right," she says through her laughter.

"I know. I'm going to work on that. You have floss hanging out of your mouth."

She removes it, studies me now more carefully. "So, is this what you're going to wear to take Marjorie trick-or-treating? I think that's great that you're getting into the whole spirit of Halloween and donning a costume along with the kids."

"Actually, I was going to ask you to take her trick-or-treating." I remove Hillary from my face and give Iris an I-need-to-tell-you-something look. "I'm going to go to Thomas' Halloween party with Harlan and Bruce. In disguise, of course. As Hillary. He won't know it's me. At least, that's the plan."

Iris moves into the bedroom and plops down on the bed. "Uh-huh. And is there more to this plan, or do you just want to see if you can get away with it?"

Hillary goes back into the closet and I join Iris on the bed. We're sitting cross-legged, facing each other like two girls having a slumber party.

"Marjorie told me that Thomas has been seeing a therapist about Nathan, and he's been writing down what he remembers about that day," I tell Iris. "I want to read what he's written. I want to know what he remembers. I want to know if it was me who left the screen unlocked."

Iris puts her hands on my knees, leans in. "And what if you find out it was? I mean, you've already been blaming yourself. But what if you don't find any other version in what Thomas has written? What if your guilt is confirmed?"

"I'm not sure."

"What if you don't even find this journal or diary or whatever it is?"

"Don't know that either."

Iris sighs and backs up a little from me. I know I have to try and make sense of this for her, but I don't know if I can.

"Iris, I just need to do this. You know how when there's a disaster, people want to find the bodies of their relatives who've died? Or even just a part of them? They already know those people have died—having proof isn't going to change anything really. But somehow it matters. Just knowing what happened—whatever it is—just finding a piece of them—matters. It's not closure, because there isn't any such thing. But it's something irrefutable, sitting in front of you, and it's a whole lot better than questions. It's the not-knowing that keeps pulling you under."

Iris nods slowly. "I'm not going to try to stop you. I just want you to really think it through."

"I have and I am. Thomas is never going to tell me what he remembers. Or if he's remembered anything. I need to know. I deserve to know."

We get into bed and as I reach to switch off the lamp, Iris says, "I definitely want you to work on this Hillary costume. The mask alone is not going to work. You'll be discovered and sent home in a police cruiser."

"Bruce is going to help me."

"Good choice."

In the middle of the night my mother screams. Iris and I both leap out of bed and race into the guest room. She's lying on her side in a fetal position, moaning. Aristotle has retreated into the corner and is cowering behind the drapes.

"It hurts," she says in a voice that seems to come from somewhere other than her throat.

Iris and I get on the bed, on either side of her, and I ask, "Where?" Which is so stupid. It isn't as if she's injured her ankle or something. My mother waves her hand over her torso as if to say 'Everywhere.'

Marjorie comes in, her eyes blinking sleepily. "What happened?" she asks, reaching past me to touch her grandmother.

Iris gets off the bed, scoops Marjorie into her arms, which is getting more challenging the bigger she gets—I see Iris almost lose her balance. "Let's go get Grandma some medicine. I have some pills in the bathroom."

She and Marjorie go into our room and I look at my mother, her eyes shut tight against the pain, her mouth a thin line.

"I should have thought of this. I should have insisted we get medicine for you," I whisper to her. "I'm going to take care of it tomorrow."

She nods but doesn't say anything. Iris comes back with some pain medication she was prescribed after dental surgery many months ago. Marjorie is walking carefully with a glass of water. I manage to slide my mother into sort of a sitting position—upright enough for her to swallow two of the pills with water. And then we stay hovered around her, waiting patiently for the chemical relief we hope will come. When her brow finally relaxes, she opens her eyes halfway and says, "Okay."

"Better?" I ask her.

"Uh-huh."

"Do you want to stay in here with her tonight?" Iris asks me.

I do, and Iris leads Marjorie out to put her back to bed, but the scared look on Marjorie's face tells me she's going to end up sleeping next to Iris.

I spend the night curved around my mother's back, the knobs of her spine more pronounced than they once were. Once—long ago—I was a tiny crescent shape inside her. Now I'm bigger than her—taller, younger—and I curve around her like a green leaf so she won't blow away too soon.

20.

"Can I go to Crista's house after school today?" Marjorie asks me in the car as we're driving to school.

"If her mother says it's okay. Did you and Crista already talk about it?"

"No," Marjorie says, more to the window than to me. "But it'll be okay."

I wonder if this is because of what happened during the night. I wonder if Marjorie was more scared than she let on. But we're approaching the school and there isn't time to talk about it. As I kiss her goodbye and watch her trudge up the walk, I scan the cars around me for a gray Lexus SUV and Crista's mother behind the wheel.

Stephanie Haskell is the only mother I've gotten to know so far since Iris and I enrolled Marjorie in this exclusive Malibu school. That's because Crista Haskell is, so far, Marjorie's only friend. I've watched Marjorie in her ballet class, the way she holds back from the other girls, keeps her eyes focused elsewhere, never on them. I haven't asked her about it because I think I understand. She's still trying to breathe into everything that's happened—Nathan dying, our new family structure. All that she knew and trusted to remain has been dismantled, re-shaped. It takes time to find your place in all that newness.

At least she's made one friend, I've said to Iris.

She and Crista have exchanged play dates. What I know of Stephanie is that her husband Raines is a film director and is almost always away shooting. She sat on the beach with Iris and me one Sunday while the girls played and told us she feels like a single parent most of the time. Stephanie has a long mane of reddish-brown hair, which Crista has inherited. She has a splash of freckles across her nose except when she remembers to cover the freckles with makeup, and a wide dimpled smile that makes her look, on first glance, like a college girl. There are diamond studs glinting in her ears and an impressive diamond on her ring finger, but there is a sad shadow in her eyes. Maybe there are other reasons her husband is away so much, I've thought.

I don't see Stephanie outside the school—maybe Crista is already inside. I imagine Marjorie rushing over to her, saying I have to go home with you today, things are kind of upsetting at home.

I feel suddenly helpless—how do you help a child through an adult's slow dying?

"Of course Marjorie can come over," Stephanie tells me on the phone. "She can stay for dinner if you guys have plans."

"No, we don't…" I hesitate for a second but decide to be honest with her. "My mother has cancer, Stephanie, and she's living with us now. She woke up in pain last night and I think it scared Marjorie. I'm going to get pain medication for her today, but…"

"I understand. Why don't you let her stay here for dinner and I'll bring her back after."

"Okay. Thanks, I appreciate it. Things will be easier once my mother gets some medicine. Well, easier for a while is what I mean."

When we say goodbye and hang up I have the selfish worry that maybe Stephanie won't want Crista to come over here anymore. Then Marjorie will feel marked, shunned. I tell myself what my mother would say: "Don't worry yourself about things that haven't happened yet."

I find my mother in the living room sitting by the window wrapped in a beige sweater that I brought for her from the house.

She's wearing black sweatpants and, even sitting down, I can tell her legs are thinner. A heavy book is resting in her lap and her head is bent low toward the pages.

"What are you reading?" I ask, sitting down beside her.

"Tale of Two Cities. I always wanted to read it again and I found it in your bookshelf."

"Ah yes. The best of times and the worst of times."

She smiles at me and tilts her head. A thin ray of sun falls over her shoulder and rests on her hand. Her veins are blue and raised.

"Mother, I'm going to go see Doctor Butler today and get you some pain medication."

She nods and lowers her eyes for a moment. "As long as I don't have to go and get poked and prodded anymore."

"No. Of course not. But there is something else. I think we're going to need help here. A caregiver. A nurse maybe. What if you need injections? I can't do that and neither can Iris."

My mother straightens her posture then, pushes her shoulders back and expands her chest—as if she's trying to inhabit more of her body. The body that's failing her.

"I suppose that's best," she says and looks down at her book again. "I don't want to be a burden."

"Mother, don't do that. You are not a burden. I'm trying to be responsible here. I'm trying to think of as many things in advance as I can."

She turns back to me again and her eyes are softer. "I know, dear. And I'm so grateful, really. It's just hard—this business of dying. I resent it sometimes. I didn't want it to be like this."

"You get back to Charles Dickens," I tell her—a little too brightly to be convincing. "I'm going to get ready to go."

I'm almost out of the room when she says, "Isabelle, did you call a realtor about the house?"

I wasn't sure, the day before, if she had really heard me when I mentioned listing her house. Apparently she did. "Yes, I called late yesterday."

"Okay," she says and starts reading her book again. I wonder if it really is, but I have to go on what she tells me.

I never imagined myself as a woman who would sit in a doctor's office weeping. It seems so stereotypical. Yet here I am, in Dr. Butler's office, crying into the tissues he has generously handed me. I came in as my usual self, asking him how the polar bears are doing since it's still the temperature of Greenland. But as soon as he shut the door and I opened my mouth to speak, sobs came out instead.

"Sorry. Sorry," I manage to say, struggling to gain control as he waits patiently. He probably does this a lot. After all, his job is cancer and all that comes along with it—which means dying people, or people who aren't dying but who will never be the same. Not after his scalpel slices them, not after the radiation burns and the strip-mining of chemo.

"It's okay, I understand," he says gently.

I have the most absurd thought in the midst of this. I suddenly think that, if I weren't in love with Iris, I would want him. I bet a lot of his patients fall in love with him.

"I wish I could tell you this is going to get easier, Mrs. Berendon," he continues. "But it's going to get harder first."

I take a few deep breaths, push my weeping down, compose my face, which now feels puffy as a down pillow. "I need some drugs, Doctor. For my mother, I mean. Well, I guess I could use some, too, but I don't do drugs. Which is a choice I'm seriously re-thinking at the moment. She woke up in pain last night, screaming, and we had some pills—Iris did, from…"

"Mrs. Berendon?"

"Yes?"

"May I call you Isabelle? I think we're going to get to know each other pretty well over the next few weeks. Maybe less formality is better."

"Weeks?" The word had hold of my jugular.

"Maybe longer. Anyway, I just thought…"

"Yes, fine. Of course. Call me Isabelle. Or call me Ishmael."

He doesn't smile.

"Never mind. Stupid joke. Isabelle is fine."

"I'm going to give you a prescription for Morphine tablets. At some point your mother might want to try a patch, and ultimately we might have to go to injections." Dr. Butler's voice is now crisp and professional.

"They make morphine in a patch now? God, pretty soon we'll be able to get our morning coffee in a patch. Save on water."

Again he doesn't laugh, which is probably for the best. It's about time someone refused to let me spin out dumb jokes when all I really want to do is curl up in like a baby and cry.

I wonder what he does when he walks through his front door at night. He has a thin gold band on his left hand. Does his wife have a stiff drink prepared for him? A bottle of wine uncorked? God, he must need something to dull the edges of the day. Does he ever come home and say, Wow, great day at work?

"Dr. Butler, I also think I need someone to help us. I know my mother's pain is going to get worse, and I think maybe it's best to deal with getting someone now."

He leans over his desk and writes something down on his note pad. "I'll give you the name of a woman I think you might like. Her name is Delba Morrison. She's a registered nurse, and she primarily does private work with people who are dying." He peels off the slip of paper and hands it to me. "Give her a call. If it doesn't work out, I'll think of someone else." I look at the paper he's handed me. Her name is printed neatly; the number beneath it is in perfectly slanted numbers.

"Are you sure you're a doctor?" I ask him.

"Excuse me?" his eyes widen, pull back.

"Your handwriting. It's so legible."

He lets out a relieved laugh. "Oh. I guess I buck the trend on that one. One of my professors in med school suggested I try calligraphy instead of medicine."

We're quiet for a few seconds. Between us is a slip of paper with a name on it of someone who might ease my mother out of this life. Between us is also the unwieldy shape of death.

"Doctor, I don't know how to see my mother as someone who is dying. It sounds so idiotic to say I thought she'd always be here—I mean, our parents usually die before us. But I don't know how to do this. I don't know how to lose her."

"Do you know what hysteresis is?"

"No. Do I have it? It sounds serious."

Dr. Butler smiles a sad bend of a smile. "Most of us have it at one time or another. Hysteresis is the tendency of a system to cling to its present state, to resist the imposition of change. It's why, often, when a sudden trauma has occurred, a person will go make coffee or sweep the floor—do something ordinary. But in a larger sense, in our psyches, we also cling to what's familiar, ordinary. We want to protect ourselves from change we aren't yet ready to absorb. You're still a daughter. You can't separate yourself from that yet and see your mother as a woman with cancer who isn't going to live much longer. Because it steals from you part of your identity. You won't be anyone's daughter anymore. That's what you've always known, depended on as a definition of who you are."

I nod slowly, understanding more than I want to. "I guess there isn't a drug for that, is there?" I ask him dryly.

"Time," he answers. "Time is the only medication. As unsatisfying as that is."

I put Delba Morrison's name and number in my purse and watch while he writes out a prescription for Morphine. "Time is what's in short supply right now," I tell him.

I wait until afternoon to tell my mother that I'm going to call a woman named Delba and see if she'll be the right person to help us. I wait until we've returned from an afternoon walk on the beach. Iris and I let my mother set the pace—we didn't go very far and she was winded when we got back. She sits down heavily on the couch, not even bothering to take off her sweatshirt. Aristotle immediately jumps into her lap.

"Mother, I got medicine for you today. Dr. Butler said you can take one pill before you go to bed at night, even if you don't have any pain yet. To prevent it coming."

"All right, dear," she says softly, her hand stroking Aristotle's neck.

"And he gave me the name of a woman he thinks I should call. A nurse who does...this sort of thing. Her name is Delba Morrison."

"That's a pretty name."

Just then Bruce comes onto the deck and taps on the glass door. I motion for him to come in and he politely dips his feet in the pan of water we keep by the door—our feeble attempt to keep sand out of the house.

"Hey, Catherine—how are you?" he says when he comes in.

"Fine. A little tired. We went for a walk on the beach," my mother answers. She's smiling at him in a way that looks more girlish than tired, which amuses me. Bruce is an extremely handsome man. In his white tank top and jeans he looks like the latest Calvin Klein model, and I suddenly wonder why he isn't.

He gives me a pointed look. "Did you want to show me that... thing in the kitchen?"

"Oh. Uh-huh."

God, are we fooling her or do we just sound ridiculous? Bruce follows me into the kitchen and lowers his voice when the door closes. "I didn't think you wanted me to talk about Halloween in front of your mother."

"No, I don't. Not yet anyway. I haven't said anything to her. I did tell Iris, though."

"And?"

"She thinks I'm insane, but she didn't threaten to hog-tie me and throw me in the closet, so I think we're good."

Bruce nods and frowns a little, as if we are in a very important stage of strategizing. "Harlan wants me to take you wig shopping. How's tomorrow?"

"Okay…late morning maybe?"

"Good. We have to get you a good Hillary wig. You have to look authentic."

"I understand. Trust me, I'm very committed to authenticity," I assure him.

A brilliant sunset is streaking the sky when Marjorie calls and asks if she can stay at Crista's for dinner. I already told Stephanie it was fine, but I think Marjorie wanted to hear my voice, make sure that it really was all right with me. When I hang up with her, I realize that all afternoon. I've been avoiding calling Delba Morrison. It's as if that one call, that one step, will plant me permanently in a reality I still want to believe is some awful mistake. How does one do this, anyway? Hi, are you equipped to help my mother die? My stomach is in knots when I pull out the slip of paper with Dr. Butler's perfect penmanship.

She answers on the third ring. When I identify myself, she says in a light British accent, "Yes, Mrs. Berendon. Dr. Butler rang me earlier and said you'd likely be phoning." Her voice is soothing, warm, almost ageless although I have a feeling she's in her forties.

"I don't know how much he told you, but my mother has cancer—advanced cancer."

"He explained it to me. I'm very sorry."

"Thank you. I just—I think I have to look ahead at what's coming, not that I really know what's coming. But I know we won't be able to handle everything without help…"

I'm grateful when she interrupts me. "Mrs. Berendon, no one knows what to expect in these situations. I've been tending to patients—most of them dying—for years now and every situation is unique."

"Yes. Well, I guess we should meet." I feel calmer, comforted. Her voice is like flannel.

We make an appointment for the next afternoon. She wants to come to us, meet my mother, and I readily agree. What a strange day I've arranged for myself—wig shopping to look like a convincing Hillary Clinton on Halloween and then meeting a woman whom I hope will be fluent in the language of death and dying, able to row my mother across the river into the shadowland on the other side.

21.

"Do you have something mousier?" Bruce asks the salesgirl in what seems to me an inappropriately loud voice.

We're in a small, cramped wig shop on Santa Monica Boulevard. I'm sitting in a chair, in front of a mirror, with Bruce behind me as if he is my traveling hairdresser. He picked out a short blond wig cut in a style that vaguely resembles Hillary's current do, but it's way too shiny and blond.

"You want a mousy color?" the salesgirl repeats, flipping her henna-red hair over her shoulder and giving him a what's-up-with-you-dude look.

"This is for Halloween," Bruce tells her. "We have a particular look in mind. A *mousy* look." He crosses his arms and stares at her. I'm almost expecting him to start tapping his foot.

Sheepishly, I hand the blond wig back to her and watch her walk briskly into the back of the store. She's flipping her hips the same way she flipped her hair. Everything this girl does radiates a message of fuck you.

"Bruce, it doesn't have to be the exact color, does it?" Sitting in the swiveling chair with him hovering over me I feel tiny, whittled down.

"Of course it does. We're going for verisimilitude here."

Two women with scarves around their heads come into the shop. They appear to be in their forties, maybe early fifties, and I can tell they're bald beneath the scarves. Seconds later, they prove me right, unwinding the brightly colored scarves from heads smooth as grapes. As they begin looking at different wigs, I think of my mother's long red hair—how hard it would have been for her to lose it, watch it come out in fistfuls and drop to the floor. Maybe in some strange way it's a blessing that her cancer is incurable, a non-negotiable verdict. I don't think she could have endured the treatment—endless visits to doctors, the scary white-coated world she wants nothing to do with, the sickness, going bald.

The two women are laughing and chatting like friends out on a festive shopping spree for shoes or dresses. Where do people get this kind of courage? I wonder as the salesgirl returns with a wig that is indeed mousy. It's longer, cut in a chin-length pageboy style, but Bruce's face brightens.

"This is good. I can cut it in the right style," he says, turning the wig around in his hands. "Of course, Hillary's style these days is really no style at all. Whack and walk."

"Whack and walk?" I repeat, laughing even though I'm not sure what it means.

Bruce grins at me. "Uh-huh. Whack it off with whatever's handy—gardening shears it looks like—and walk out the door. It's sort of Peter Pan meets I-don't-care."

The salesgirl, who has left us for a few moments, returns. "So, you want this one?"

Bruce squints at her, like he's trying to bring her into focus. "Yes. Do you gift wrap?"

"What?"

"Never mind. Just put it in a bag."

I pay for my disguise and as we walk out to Bruce's car, the sound of a ringing cell phone sends both of us fumbling for ours.

"It's me," I tell him.

Iris' voice is uncharacteristically nervous. "Isabelle—thank God I caught you."

I stop walking and lean against a parking meter. My legs feel paralyzed. "What happened?"

"Your mother left…"

"Left?" I repeat. I flash back to a sunny afternoon, coming up the walk to see black decorations and my mother saying my father had left. "Left the house?' I ask Iris. "Left this life? What do you mean?"

"Oh God, no—no, I didn't mean …She left the house while I was at the market. She wrote a note and said the realtor called about an offer on her house and she had to go over there."

"But she has no car."

"She called a cab. Isabelle, she said she was going to stop the sale."

"Okay. Okay. We'll go over there right now."

Bruce is staring at me when I hang up, waiting for me to fill him in. "I'm so sorry, but we have to make a detour," I tell him. "My mother took a cab to her house. Apparently she's changed her mind about selling it. Do you mind?"

"Of course not." He opens the car door for me and hurries around to the driver's side.

As I direct Bruce to my childhood neighborhood, I think how strange it is that some people get swept into your life at moments that have nothing to do with them. Bruce is about to witness…what? My mother's tears? Anger? Will we find her blocking the property like Annie Oakley, yelling Get off my land?

We've just turned off Pico Boulevard onto a narrow residential street. Bruce's white BMW looks seriously out of place.

"I didn't grow up in a very fashionable area," I tell him, as if that weren't already obvious.

"Honey, I grew up in a trailer in the wilds of Montana. My baby cradle was a drawer."

"You slept in a drawer?"

"Yep. Right under the stuffed moose head. When I was in high school I figured out that gay men in Montana might very well end up like the moose—dead as a door nail, stuffed and mounted…on the wall, I mean. Right after they've been mounted in other ways, all under the radar of course."

"I know what you meant, Bruce. Turn right at this stop sign. How old were you when you left Big Sky Country?"

He laughs. "Seventeen. I fucked my way out. There are a lot of moose with secret lives in Montana. But this is hardly the time for that story. Remind me to tell you someday about the wealthy rancher who joined the sheriff's department on weekends because he liked the uniform."

"I will definitely remind you."

We pull up to the house and find a tense triangle—my mother, Alice Silvano—the realtor, a friend of Iris' who agreed to list the house after a phone call—and a lanky, middle-aged man in a rumpled black suit. They are standing on the dried up front lawn. It's my mother's face that grabs me—it looks like heartbreak. I feel guilty, as if I betrayed her by listing the house, but then I remind myself that she said it was okay.

She comes toward me quickly. "Isabelle, I can't do this. I just can't."

"Okay...that's okay." I slide my hand across her back. Her spine feels so delicate now. I keep the pressure of my hand light, as if too much weight might break her.

I extend my other hand to Alice Silvano. "I'm Isabelle. We spoke on the phone."

Alice looks like she's about thirty-five. She has black, shiny hair that falls straight and thick to the top of her shoulders. She's dressed in a camel-colored jacket and stylish black slacks; her face has that curious blend of sensuality and disinterest. It's the look of a woman who appears to not need a man, but who is never without one. She returns my handshake with a firm, lightly perfumed grip.

"I thought everyone would be happy with this," she says to me, her brown eyes carving their way into me. "Mr. Carlton drove past, saw the sign and called. He's ready to make an offer today."

Mr. Carlton, the poor man who innocently stumbled into so much more than a real-estate transaction, smiles sheepishly at me.

"I apologize for the confusion," I tell them both. "Let me try to sort this out." I tighten my arm around my mother. "Mother, let's walk over here and talk."

I lead her over to the shade of the huge pepper tree. Bruce walks slowly over to Alice and Mr. Carlton; I'm hoping it's to distract them with entertaining small talk.

"What's going on, Mother? I thought you wanted to sell the house. Remember we talked about it?"

"Of course I remember. I have cancer, not dementia." Her eyes are blazing at me, but suddenly they soften, retreat. "When I picked up the phone at your house and heard that it could all be done so quickly, I just wasn't prepared. I'm not prepared. What if I want to visit? I still have time left."

"We don't have to sell it now. You can come visit whenever you want."

She jabs her finger in the direction of the house. "I still hear your father's footsteps on that floor in there. It was our home…"

I nod and brush her hair back from her face. I hear him, too, I think to myself. Only his footsteps echo differently for me. They are the soundtrack of years of bad nights. If he was drunk, his footsteps were hard and decisive. Sober, his footsteps were softer, almost shuffling. He got authority from a bottle, which is why he was so rarely sober, and so unhappy when he was.

My mother and I walk back to the others. "Alice, Mr. Carlton," I begin as if I'm in a courtroom. "I'm sorry, but it's just too soon to part with the house. We made a mistake by rushing it."

Mr. Carlton nods quickly and hurries off. I'm sure he feels relieved to be escaping. Alice remains professional, but she's obviously irritated.

"I'll have someone take the sign down right away," she says, flipping open her cell phone. I know she's thinking she wasted her time, and all because she did a favor for a friend.

My mother slides into the back seat of Bruce's car and for a few blocks none of us speak. Then, while we're stopped at a red light, a scruffy man with long hair and a beard crosses in front of us; he's walking an equally scruffy dog.

"Oh look," Bruce says. "Charles Manson is out of prison. And he has a dog."

The sound of my mother's laughter ripples through the car. I listen more carefully to it now, memorize its rhythms. A time will come when I desperately need to hear her laughter and all I will have is my memory of it.

When Bruce drops us off, my mother and I walk into the house and into the murmur of voices from the living room. I'm late for my meeting with Delba Morrison, and I'm carrying Hillary's hair in a wrinkled paper bag.

"I need to go upstairs," my mother says softly and starts up, her hand holding the railing. I wonder if she's going to lie down and fall asleep. Should I wake her up to meet Delba? I put the bag behind a large planter, just in case someone sees strands of hair protruding from it.

In the living room, Iris is sitting with a tall black woman whose face is handsome in bone structure and gentle in the curve of her mouth and the faint webbing of lines at the corners of her eyes. Her hair is swept back in a French braid and as we shake hands I notice her manicure, her gold bracelet, and her clothes. She's wearing a gray pants suit that I think is Calvin Klein, strappy sandals that I know were costly, and her Prada handbag is on the couch beside her. Iris has fixed tea for them.

"I'm sorry I'm late," I tell Delba, sitting down across from her. "We had an unexpected detour."

"Iris told me," she says. "Your mother doesn't want to sell her house just yet. That's normal—this is overwhelming. There's a need to hang onto things for a while."

Iris glances at her watch. "I'm going to have to go pick up Marjorie in a few minutes. Delba was telling me that she grew up in London,

Isabelle. Her father was a doctor, and she took up medicine too, but she got sort of disenchanted with the profession as a whole."

"My mother will like that—the disenchantment with medicine I mean," I tell Delba.

Having set me on my way, Iris leaves, but I still feel hopelessly lost. What should I ask her? Delba smiles warmly at my hesitation and plunges in. I think I decide to hire her right then.

"I came to America in my twenties and worked in a couple of hospitals. But I found myself quite disturbed at how terminally ill patients were treated. I decided my calling was outside the hospital system. More along the lines of hospice work, really."

"Right. Well, that's...that's what we need here...unfortunately. What if—down the line—I wanted you to stay here? Move in for—you know—however long it takes."

"I do that sometimes," she tells me. "And I am free at the moment—that's why Dr. Butler suggested me. He knows I generally only take one patient at a time."

I know I want this woman here and I also know I have to be professional—discuss her schedule, her fee. Her wardrobe is making me nervous, though.

"Delba, I apologize for being blunt, but I'm wondering of we can afford you. I'm looking at your clothes and -"

She interrupts me with a kind laugh. "Oh, I could never have afforded these," she says. "Some of the women I've worked for were extremely generous with me, giving me things they wouldn't be needing anymore."

"Your clothes belonged to women who are dead now?" I blurt out.

"Yes," she answers calmly. "I realize that must seem strange to you. But I deal with death all the time. I guess you could say I've made friends with it. It will come for all of us eventually. And I treasure the gifts I've been given by women I hope I helped."

My mother says, "I think that's lovely," from the doorway where she's been standing.

I didn't hear her footsteps. Has she become so light that she drifts across the floor silent as dust motes? She comes in, shakes Delba's hand and sits down next to her. Delba holds onto her hand a bit longer than one usually does in a first meeting. I imagine her reading the Braille of my mother's palm, tracing her lifeline. An insistent meow lets us know Aristotle has also made an entrance and will not be ignored.

"This is Aristotle," my mother tells Delba, who immediately reaches down to stroke the cat's back.

This is going well, I think, as I excuse myself so Delba and my mother can get acquainted. It occurs to me that my mother could end up giving her more than clothes –the house, perhaps—but I suppose I'll have to let her do what she wants.

Marjorie is about to come home to yet another change—someone else joining our household. But maybe that's what death is supposed to do—pull in more life.

22.

Delba slides into the creases of our life so effortlessly I wonder if she was born with some mysterious gift or if she acquired it along the way. She comes four days a week, and we're now at the end of the second week. Marjorie has been excited about having someone else here. It's as if, even with sadness at the center of it all, there is an ever-expanding party going on. She's already roped Delba into watching Finding Nemo with her, and I suspect has also gotten her to sneak more sweets to her than Iris and I allow her to have.

I sense that my mother misses Delba when she isn't here. At moments I feel a sting of jealously when I see the two of them walk slowly out to the water's edge, or putter in the kitchen, preparing some recipe they found in the pages of a cook book. I've seen them sitting together in a pool of coppery afternoon light, the trail of their voices drifting through the house. Sometimes I linger outside doorways or in the hall, trying to pick up breadcrumbs of their conversation, knowing my spying is petty and immature.

I've figured something out, though: Because Delba has no history with my mother, she's better able to help her in the awesome challenge of walking toward her own mortality. I have too many memories, too many emotions. They have weight; they tumble me back down the years. I will always be a daughter losing her mother.

Delba is gentle and calm; she wears her authority easily, comfortably. She's the kind of person you'd like to have with you in a lifeboat.

And she's the gatekeeper of my mother's morphine. When she's here, she keeps the tablets in her pocket and before leaving in the evening she transfers them to me, telling me precisely when the next one can be given. Iris and I have told Marjorie that sometime soon Delba will move in and be here all the time. It's given her something to look forward to, which was our intention. But none of us know how to look farther down the road than that.

Marjorie is sitting at the breakfast table eating cereal with her ballet costume tucked into her book bag beside her. It's Friday and she has a performance this afternoon, which my mother has promised to come to. Iris is on her second cup of coffee—she's going to the women's shelter and she wants to beat the worst of the traffic. My mother is still in her bathrobe, eating a piece of toast with little mouse bites. I notice details like this now; I wonder if she wants to eat at all.

"Have you decided what you want to be for Halloween, Marjorie?" Iris asks.

Marjorie wipes a dribble of milk from her chin and nods. "A princess. And Delba said I should have a tiara."

"Absolutely," Iris tells her. "We'll have to get your costume together."

"And a kingdom," Marjorie says.

"I told her that," my mother admits. "Every princess should have a kingdom."

"This is true," I tell Marjorie. "But not before you're eighteen. Kingdoms are never dispensed before that. Tiara first, kingdom much later."

"What kind of kingdom would you like?" Iris asks her.

"I want Canada."

I give my mother a questioning look and she shrugs innocently. "Why Canada, dear?" she asks Marjorie, emphasizing that she had nothing to do with this choice.

"They have geese there."

Iris comes over and sits down next to Marjorie. "Listen, Your Highness. I'm going to be taking you trick-or-treating this year, okay?"

Marjorie looks from Iris to me. "Why can't you go too?" she asks me, her eyes narrowing a little.

I wish Iris had warned me that she was going to bring this up today; my story is only partially composed. "Well, Bruce and Harlan really wanted me to go with them to a party. It's a surprise for the person giving the party—someone I used to know and lost touch with. But you and Iris will have a great time."

I can't look at Iris. I can't look at my mother either because I'm sure she knows I'm lying, although she doesn't yet know what the lie is concealing. Marjorie doesn't say anything for a few seconds and my heart starts speeding up. Then she turns to Iris and says matter-of-factly, "Well, you'll have to wear a costume."

"I'm going to get to work on that right away."

The phone rings and Iris reaches behind her to the counter to answer it. She hangs up two seconds after she says hello.

I ask the obvious before anyone else can. "Who was that?"

"A telemarketer," she says and gets up. She stands at the sink and pours the rest of her coffee down the drain.

I don't believe her. I've taken three messages from her mother and Iris has mentioned nothing about returning the calls. The third time I answered a call from Libby Fenimore, I heard a baby crying in the background. I didn't pass along that detail to Iris—just the message—but I'm sure Iris hasn't called back. I suspect Libby has made other attempts to reach her daughter—like this call before eight in the morning.

I think about this on the way to school, as Marjorie chats on and on about how she wants to be a pink princess with a fluffy skirt and glittery jewels. My lie seems to have passed inspection because she doesn't say another word about my not taking her trick-or-treating.

"I'm sure Grandma will let you use one of her shawls," I tell her, eager to keep things on her wardrobe.

"Okay. A pink one?"

"Maybe. We'll make sure you're color-coordinated."

The sun is already beating down hard and there is no moisture in the air. Santa Ana winds are predicted but at the moment it's deathly still.

"We'll see you later at your ballet performance," I say to Marjorie as I let her off in front of the school.

"Grandma, too."

"Absolutely."

"And Delba."

"Okay. Anyone else? I don't think they'll let Aristotle come."

She laughs at me and wheels around toward the school. I wait until she goes inside, as I always do. And I suddenly wonder if Libby Fenimore ever did the same for Iris when she was a child. What happens to a child who never finds her mother's eyes reaching for her, brimming with love? A child who always turns around to absence?

The night we drove away from the Fenimore house, too fast down hilly streets before pulling over to dump Iris' photographic history into a stranger's trash can, I prayed for access to the deepest recesses of my partner's emotions. She didn't give that to me, and I don't take it personally, but I still wish for it.

People have twilit places inside them where they go to work things out in private. In time they emerge with a sharper eye and a more resolute step. I've long known this. But never before has my heart reached so hard, wanted so desperately to follow someone into that place. There are couples who swear they know everything about each other, that nothing is concealed or in shadow. But I'm not sure that can ever be true. Don't we all need to slip away sometimes, hide our faces, our thoughts, our messiest quandries?

Maybe I'll try to bring up the subject of Iris' mother to her, and just be willing to drop it if she doesn't want to go there.

When I walk into the house I'm confronted by my mother and Delba standing near the front door, apparently on their way somewhere. My mother is dressed in a loose peasant skirt and a white blouse; she has her purse looped over her arm.

"I was just going to write you a note," Delba says to me.

"Oh. Where are you off to?"

"Home," my mother tells me. "I want to go home for a while."

Since I'm well acquainted with my mother's habit of speaking in abbreviated terms, as if she's composing Cliff Notes, I hold my alarm at bay. Does she mean go home for good? For a few days or weeks? I glance at Delba but get no hint from her.

"What do you mean, a while?" I ask my mother carefully.

"For a visit. I need to visit one last time and then I think I can let it go. Let it be sold."

"Oh. Okay." Relief floods through me. Maybe I was more alarmed than I admitted. "Well, I can drive you. We'll all go."

Aristotle is winding around my mother's legs. She bends down and gently strokes his head. "Except for you," she says to the cat. "It would confuse you." He purrs insistently. "Oh, I know. You don't want to be left alone."

"Carla will be here soon," I remind her. "We can write her a note telling her we're out and to give Aristotle a lot of attention."

We turn onto our old street in the swelter of late morning. Smog coats the sky and not a leaf is moving. But the wind is just holding its breath—it's coming and it will be fierce. This is fire weather. The plants around the front yard are already dying from lack of water and the lawn looks like scabs of cardboard. Delba helps my mother out of the car and we walk slowly up the path. Close to the house, bits of prismed light glint up at us; someone has broken the living room window and the shards are scattered on the ground. My mother shakes her head sadly.

"This neighborhood used to be nicer," she says softly.

"Not by much, Mother."

There are more pieces of glass inside, beneath the window, but there is no sign that anyone came in and took anything. The vandals probably saw the disarray and decided it wasn't worth the risk. My mother goes directly to the kitchen and returns with a broom and dustpan. Both Delba and I let her sweep up the debris, carry it into the kitchen and dump it into a wastebasket. It seems important to her, this simple task of cleaning. She returns to the living room and stands in the middle of the floor, looking around.

"Your father used to love the way the sun came through this room," she tells us.

I can't imagine my father taking the time to appreciate something as poetic as sunlight across a floor, but I say nothing. Delba is standing back near the wall, as if she's afraid of intruding.

My mother walks into the hall and suddenly leans toward the wall, steadying herself with her hand. Delba moves in then, protectively taking her arm and helping her walk the length of the hallway to the bedrooms. Now it's my turn to hang back. Delba and I have evolved into our roles—we each step back when it's our turn to do so.

I lean against the wall at one end of the hall. The walls are the color of café-au-lait; the scuffs and scrapes along them are the scars of the family who once lived here. I look at the heating vent just above the floor and it takes me back to a rainy afternoon, days after my ninth birthday. I was sitting on the floor by the heater reading A Child's Garden of Verses, which my mother had given me for my birthday. That day, she had gone to teach a dance class and had told me not to wake my father. "He's taking a nap, he doesn't feel well," she said as she left the house. That was code for, he's hung over.

It felt strange sitting in the hall with him in the bedroom just yards away. I wasn't used to being in the house alone with him. I could have gone into my own room, but I liked the way the heater blew across me, warming my skin and ruffling the pages of the book. The sound of rain on the roof was strong and steady.

I heard him moving around in the bedroom; then the doorknob turned and his footsteps filled the hallway. I stared stubbornly at the page I was reading, but his footsteps filled my ears and then his shadow swallowed me. Defiantly I punched a finger down onto the word I'd just read and looked up at him with hard eyes.

"Where's your mother?" he asked me.

"At dance class. You know—that job she has?"

"Don't smart-mouth me, Isabelle. I just asked a question." He looked as if he might walk away, but he didn't. He just kept standing there.

"What?" I asked him, jabbing my finger on the word like a thumb-tack.

"Why are you always so mad at me?"

"I'm not." My nose should have grown like Pinnochio with that one.

"Yes, you are. Look how you talk to me. I'm your father—you show no respect for that."

That was it. I could taste anger. My tongue curled around my hurtful words. "Fathers are supposed to take care of their families. You can't even keep a job."

"I put a roof over your head, don't I?" he said, his mouth a narrow bitter line. "You eat three meals a day and you got clothes on your back."

"Stolen ones."

"I don't see you turning down the clothes I get for you. If you're so high and mighty, then don't wear 'em."

He walked off then—shuffled really—and I returned to my book, trying to hide in safe gardens and childhoods sweeter than mine. But there is no hiding from the childhood you have. It scrawls itself on your body, your spirit. We end up scrimshawed and there's nothing we can do about it.

"Isabelle?" my mother says. "Are you day-dreaming?" She and Delba are coming out of what was once my parents' bedroom.

"Sort of," I tell her.

They walk up to me and my mother puts a hand on my arm. I notice how cold her skin is.

"We can sell the house now," she tells me.

"Are you sure? Because if you're not, then we should wait. You might want to come back again."

She shakes her head. "I don't think I'll be able to."

By the time we go to Marjorie's school later in the afternoon and file into the small ballet studio, winds like sandpaper are punishing the trees, hurling leaves and trash across streets and parking lots.

Iris has come back from the shelter in time to go with us. She and I sit with my mother and Delba as Marjorie performs with the rest of her class, smiling delightedly at us every time she does something well. My mother looks just as happy, her cheeks flushed with color and her smile transforming her face. I wish I could freeze-frame this piece of time, but time has become my harshest teacher. It moves on despite my prayers.

Marjorie's friend Crista also twirls and dances across the floor. She's a good dancer—light and lithe. If she grows up like her mother—Stephanie is small and delicate—she'll have a better chance at a ballet career than Marjorie, who is already growing tall like her father. When the performance ends, the crescendo of parental applause washes over the girls. Marjorie clasps Crista's hand and they bow dramatically in appreciation; I can't even remember who I held hands with when I was seven.

I don't know who the mother is who first opens the door to the parking lot—her pink-tutu'd daughter beside her—but I will never forget her. The smell of smoke washes in and she turns around to the rest of us, her face suddenly lacquered with fear. She is our messenger. There is a fire—near enough for us to smell it.

We pour into the parking lot—a suddenly united group of frightened people, looking up at the sky, the backdrop of hills, trying to determine just how frightened we should be. The sky is a deep blue everywhere except over the hills; in that direction, mushroom clouds of brown-gray smoke obscure every trace of the sky. Now we can hear sirens and it's hard to tell which way they're coming from at first. In less than a minute two fire trucks scream by on the highway, heading east.

"It looks like it's on the other side of Topanga," a little girl's father says.

We all hurry to our cars and I know everyone will follow the same script—we'll race into our houses, turn on the television, hang on every word and every image. What are the predictions? What's the wind doing? How likely is it that the fire will race through the canyon and down to the sea? After all, it's happened before.

"I'm scared," Marjorie says when we pile into my car and drive down the highway toward home.

"It'll be all right," my mother tells her soothingly.

The color of the late day is changing because of the smoke and we can smell it in the car even with the windows rolled up and the air-conditioner on.

As soon as we open the front door, Aristotle races toward us, meowing loudly. Carla left earlier, so he's been alone, although not for long. He must be frightened, too—the smell of smoke is in the house, drifting through the windows.

Iris goes into the living room and turns on the television. The fire is on the other side of Topanga Canyon, and on the other side of the freeway, but the fear is that it will jump across and then Malibu will be in danger.

"I think I should stay here tonight," Delba says. "Just in case."

"In case what?" Marjorie asks.

I bend down close to her and smooth her hair back. "If it gets bad and we have to evacuate. It'll be okay. We'll have plenty of time."

I focus hard on evening out my voice. "In fact, we'll put some stuff in the cars now just to set our minds at ease. But there are a lot of firemen out there, Marjorie." As I'm saying this, we can hear more sirens.

"We have to put cat food in the car," she tells me.

"Absolutely. We'll put that in first."

"And something for Aristotle to pee and poop in."

"Spare litter box. Good thinking. Maybe we'll line a cardboard box with plastic, put litter in that." My suggestion sends her racing toward the garage to fetch a box.

This is going to be a long night, and I've already decided that Marjorie can stay up with us as long as she wants. It would do no good to tuck her into bed frightened.

After she's gone upstairs to change out of her ballet clothes, Iris and I walk out to the beach to look up at the hills again. The wind is fierce; it lifts streams of sand that batter our legs. Harlan and Bruce are standing in front of their house, also looking at the massive wall of smoke.

"Oh, good—you're home," Harlan says. "I knew when I woke up this morning there was going to be a fire. I felt it."

"His left toe was aching," Bruce adds. "You know, like a farmer predicting rain? Only Harlan does fires."

"Shut up, Bruce. This is no time for jokes," Harlan snaps.

"I think we're going to put some stuff in the cars now in case the fire jumps the freeway," Iris tells them.

We all turn solemn then, stare silently at the hills—the buffer between us and an inferno. You always hear people in Malibu say it's such a lovely place to live, they don't mind living with the risk and the occasional reality of natural disasters. But you never hear them say that when disaster is bearing down. That's when everyone starts to wonder if it's worth it.

"We're going to be up all night," I tell Harlan and Bruce. "So come over any time if you want. We need to load the cars in case."

"Us too," Bruce says. "See you later."

Iris and I work calmly and efficiently, putting bottles of water, canned tuna fish, sweatshirts, cat food, and insurance papers into the cars. We haven't lived here very long, it's not like we have that many mementos lying around.

My mother and Delba are cooking pasta in the kitchen and the television is blaring constant news about the fire. Over a thousand acres so far, one house gone, people on the other side of the hills ordered to evacuate. Horses are being led out, taken to a football field at a high school. The last thing I carry out to the car is a scrapbook of Nathan. Only a quarter of the pages are filled with photos. It's all I have left of him...except the river of tears inside me.

I make up the bed in the other guest room for Delba, and all of us huddle around the television in the living room to eat pasta and salad. Iris opens a bottle of wine and I'm sure there will be another opened before the end of the night. The fire is the only story on all the major channels, and the reporters keep repeating that if flames jump the freeway, there will be no way to stop the fire from burning down to the beach.

We try to keep an ordinary rhythm to the evening—dinner, washing dishes, settling again in the living room. But the television screen and the smell of smoke is our reminder that nothing about tonight is ordinary.

Marjorie finally dozes off, curled on the sofa between my mother and Iris. I carry her upstairs and tuck her into bed with her clothes on in case we get word that we have to evacuate. When I come out of Marjorie's room, Delba is helping my mother up the stairs.

"I think we're going to try and get a little sleep," Delba tells me.

"Okay. But sleep in your clothes—both of you. Just in case."

Iris has opened another bottle of wine. We pour two full glasses and carry them out to the deck. The wind has quieted down a little and amazingly the sky over the ocean is still clear—black and dotted with stars. Tiny flakes of ash are floating all around us; they've coated everything. We brush them off the deck chairs before we sit down.

"Iris, where are we going to go if we have to evacuate?"

She looks behind us to the ominous glow over the mountains—thousands of acres on fire. "I was thinking about that. Your mother's house isn't sold yet. We could go there."

"Right. Good idea. We obviously can't go to your parents' house."

Iris laughs sharply and shakes her head. "No, we can't," she says.

"You haven't called her back, have you?"

"No."

I'm not sure how far I can go with this, but I take another tentative step. "So, are you going to?"

Iris looks at me for a moment before answering. "I know this is probably hard for you to understand given your relationship with your mother. But I never really had a mother, Isabelle. Ever. The all consuming, unconditional love that a mother's supposed to have for her child?" She shakes her head slowly. "Not in my family. I was a prop. Just like their adopted baby is. That kid will grow up the same way, knowing that she's disposable. I figured something out after our last horrible evening there. Something really important, I think."

She hesitates, looks over her shoulder at the smoke-filled sky, then out again at the black shiny sea. I can taste smoke in the back of my throat and my eyes sting, but I don't want to go inside. I want us to sit here between fire and water until we have no more secrets between us.

"It was like everything came into sharp focus," she continues. "How for all my life there was this little spark of hope. This fantasy that one day I'd walk through the door and see something in my mother's eyes that I'd never seen before. Maternal love. Devotion to her only child. I didn't really admit it to myself, of course, because it would have sounded idiotic. But I admitted it that night. I saw the fantasy I'd been clinging to. And I finally knew—absolutely, without question—she has none of that to give. Not a molecule. She hasn't a shred of love anywhere in her. It was liberating, actually. Now I feel like I can go on with the rest of my life and accept that there's a part of me that's kind of…disabled."

"Disabled?"

She leans toward me. "Isabelle, if you've never had a mother's love, there's a hole inside you that can't be filled. Ever. The rest of you can be filled up in other ways—by other people, other loves—but that empty place will always be there. It's like any other disability or affliction—it's just there. And it's okay. I know it now, I see it, and it's okay. I'll tell you a story that will reveal pretty much everything about my mother. For a long time—until I was about fourteen—I believed I was one of two twins, only my twin was born dead. I believed this because that's what my mother told me. And she didn't stop there. My sister, had she lived, would have been pretty and clever and feminine, not the tomboy I was, not the embarrassment I was. The wrong twin died was the point that was driven home to me with absolute precision. When I was fourteen, my father came into my room one night. He'd been drinking—actually, he was sloshed—and for some reason he chose that night to tell me the whole thing had been a lie. My mother had invented a fantasy child, a child who died at birth. He said she first made it up when she was angry with me and wanted to hurt me. But the story stuck and she kept repeating it. He said he suspected after a while she started believing it herself."

"God, Iris, that's the most diabolical thing I've ever heard."

Iris smiles a little and shakes her head. "There are worse things, but that's right up there. The strange thing is, that was something that brought Peter and me closer—when I finally told him about it. His father was cut from the same cloth as my mother, so he really understood. Peter does have a tad more insight than Thomas. I'll give him that."

"Well…I understand now, more than I did before. I can't identify, but I understand."

She slips her hand into mine and I brush a few flakes of ash from her shoulder. All up and down the beach, lights are on in houses.

People are watching the news, watching the winds, thinking about the homes their houses have become and what it would mean to lose them. We find our homes with other people—in the architecture of relationships, in the spaces of moments and years. So many things seep into walls and rooms and floors. The rug in front of the fireplace where you made love when the children weren't home. The scar on the kitchen floor where you threw down a sauce- pan in an argument instead of throwing it the one person who can bring you to the brink of love and rage all at the same time. The corner of the living room where the Christmas tree always stands. The spot by the window where you sat in a flea-market rocking chair nursing your baby in the dead of night when it seemed like the whole rest of the world was sleeping. The bathroom where you hid to cry, just because you were so tired—where you turned on the bathtub faucet to drown out the sound. The bedroom that was once painted with clouds and pale blue walls, where a crib held a tiny new life…and then had to be re-done to accommodate a child growing up way too fast.

Watch the faces of people who have lost homes—the well of their eyes is full of life's vanished pieces. Their loss has little to do with wood and plaster.

There are different kinds of loss, though. Some crash into your life and carve you up in an instant. The destruction of a home. The death of a child. Others are the ones you're born into, like the absence of a mother's love. Those losses take longer to recognize. And there are also the scars of betrayal and lies—carved into the softest tissues of the heart—brands that stay forever.

In the end it's always about tracing the shape of emptiness and deciding that you have to build a life around that shape.

23.

I wake up sprawled on the couch, my neck aching. The phone is ringing and I lunge for it. The only thought in my head is that we have to evacuate. But it's Marjorie's school saying that they aren't going to open today. The TV is still on—it's been on all night. Iris is slumped in the armchair and is just waking up. We both stare at the television, trying to get caught up on the fire. It's still only partially contained, but because the winds have died down they're no longer worried about it jumping the freeway. Three canyon houses have been destroyed, thousands of acres; hundreds of people are still in makeshift shelters. The sky outside is sooty and dull, and the deck is covered with a film of ash.

"Should I go tell Marjorie she doesn't have to go to school today?" I ask Iris, who looks as stiff and sore as I am.

"No. Let her sleep. We'll give her the good news when she wakes up." Iris rubs her neck, rotates her shoulders. "God, I feel like shit."

"Me too. We need a spa day."

Iris stands up, stretches her arms up. "Good idea. Let's wait until the flames die down though and we're officially out of danger. Have you ever actually gone for a spa day?"

"No. Have you?"

She shakes her head and laughs. "I've always assumed the reality would never live up to the fantasy." She stretched again, rubs her neck. "Caffeine. We need lots of caffeine. I'll go make coffee."

There is a loud thump from upstairs, followed by Aristotle's sharp meow. Iris and I bolt for the stairs simultaneously and take them two at a time. Delba has just come out of the guest room and is running toward my mother's room.

We find her sitting on the floor with a disoriented look on her face and Aristotle circling around her like a protective tiger.

"I fell out of bed," she says weakly.

Delba kneels down beside her, looks at her eyes, puts a hand on her wrist—I know she's checking her pulse. "Let's get you up."

She helps my mother to her feet, sits her on the bed and seems to still be checking her out, although subtly. Iris and I stand there helplessly, knowing that Delba can do far more than we can.

"Mommy?" Marjorie is standing in the doorway, the same frightened look in her eyes that she had the night my mother screamed out in pain.

I fold her against me and lead her back out into the hallway. "It's okay," I tell her. "Grandma fell, but she's fine."

"Why didn't you wake me up for school?"

"Because this is your lucky day. There's no school today."

Marjorie turns to me abruptly. "Is the fire still bad? Is that why I'm not going to school?"

"The fire is still bad, but not nearly as bad. They're getting control over it. We're going to be fine, sweetheart. Promise. They don't expect it to come this way. I think the school just felt that everyone had a long sleepless night so it was best to have a day off."

"Okay." She shuffles sleepily back to her room. Before she reaches the door she turns back to me. "Can I play with Crista today?"

"Sure. I'll call her mother." I have a feeling that whenever things get scary here, Marjorie is going to want to escape to Crista's house. It makes me wonder what will happen when my mother's cancer gets worse, when the ravages are not only on the inside but are visible to all of us. Will Marjorie ask to go live with Crista? Will we miraculously come up with the right words to thin out her fear? To make her feel it's safe to stay?

She closes her bedroom door and the house closes in around me. I need to ask Delba to start living here now. I need to get a hospital bed for my mother. I need to think past today. I've known this moment was coming, and it's the first of many. I'm frightened of all the unknowns in front of us, but I can't let myself give in to that.

Years before I met Thomas, when I was still Campbell's assistant, I drifted away from one of his summer night parties, left the crowded deck, and sat out on the beach with a glass of wine. A three-quarter moon was floating in the sky and its twin reflection shone in the sea. Shallow lazy waves lapped on the shore. I was thinking about all the people behind me in Campbell's house—most of them could care less about him. Campbell attacked the demon of his loneliness by arranging parties, assembling neighbors and assorted guests who only came because it was a party and they didn't want to be alone either. I think secretly he knew this, but for a night he could fool himself, feel like he was part of a pack. Of course I enabled this fantasy—I sent out the invitations, hired the caterer. I understood Campbell...probably better than he realized.

But I treated my own solitude differently. I liked my aloneness; I wanted to preserve it. It was the only place I felt truly safe. I was proud of the clever ways I'd found to protect it.

Footsteps were coming toward me on the sand; my precious solitude was about to be interrupted. But turning around and seeing who it was, I actually didn't mind.

Allen Corday was probably Campbell's only true friend. Like Campbell, he worked with vast amounts of money—investments, currency exchange—things I listened to them discuss but never understood. Allen had recently turned thirty-three, but he had a calm demeanor that made him seem older. I actually found him attractive. He was tall and lanky with messy brown hair and wide-set dark eyes. I had a strong feeling he was gay, though, so I never bothered to flirt with him.

He sat beside me on the sand and looked out at the moon float-ing in the sea. "Escaping the drunken revelers up there?" he asked me.

"Sort of. Welcome to my lifeboat. How are you? How's your father?"

Allen's father had been diagnosed with ALS more than a year earlier. Allen didn't talk about it much, but I knew he paid for his father's round-the-clock nursing care and had insisted the doctor make house calls, no matter what it cost.

"Getting worse. But that's what happens," he said. "The other day he started crying. Just weeping horribly. I didn't know what to do. Finally he said, 'You have no idea when you're walking through each day that something like this might happen and putting one foot in front of the other will be the biggest challenge of your life. All you want is to take a simple step. Or grab the milk in the fridge. Or turn the page of a newspaper. Why does it take some God-awful disease to make us appreciate what we have?'" Allen's voice was starting to break. "I had no answer for him," he said softly after pawing the sand for a few seconds. "I didn't want to insult him by trying to come up with an answer. I knew all I could do was just be there."

I think about that night a lot these days. I lost touch with Allen. His father is certainly gone by now. But I keep his words inside me, in a quiet warm-lit place. I don't want to forget them. Just be there—it's the best you can do.

This is what I'm thinking about as I stand in the hallway staring at Marjorie's closed door. But another thought intrudes—I wonder when it first dawns on a child to close the bedroom door as a state-ment to parents. When did I first turn away from my mother and put that barrier between us? I can't remember, although I bet it was early, maybe even at Marjorie's age. It's a rite of passage, encoded in our DNA. Our room is our empire and we reserve the right to seal it off. Iris has told me that many of the battered women she counsels grew up in homes where no boundaries were honored. They had no privacy, no walled-off space that was theirs alone. Everything was crashed through, invaded. Later it was fists that crashed through. Bad things happen when we aren't allowed sanctuaries.

I hear Delba behind me, saying something to my mother about a nice warm breakfast. She has her arm around my mother's shoulders and they're starting down the stairs. I don't say anything—I don't want to intrude—my mother is concentrating so hard on each step.

I stay where I am, staring at Marjorie's closed door. I hope she knows I will honor that door and all it means. Because we don't ever stop closing doors behind us. We grow up, grow older, and still turn and softly shut the door to say please leave me alone right now. Iris did it about her mother, and even though she let me in briefly, she's closed the door again. Lovers, partners, friends all do this when they need to, asking only that the sanctuary they've constructed be respected.

I do it the first night I finally dream about Nathan. I don't tell Iris. I don't tell anyone.

In the dream, he was three—the age at which he died, the age he's trapped in for eternity. We were walking across a green hilly landscape, his small hand clutching mine. He was barefoot. I asked him where his shoes were and he said he didn't need them. I accepted this, didn't think it odd at all. I looked away from him across the roll of green hills. How far are we going? I asked him. Far, he answered, and giggled. Then he started running, still holding my hand and laughing. I struggled to keep up. His small legs were fast and light, mine were heavy and cumbersome. The slope of the land suddenly seemed punishing. Then I woke up. I lay there breathing harder than normal, certain that I smelled grass and dirt and clean strong wind. Certain it wasn't just a dream. It was a visit.

It's been several days and I've still said nothing to Iris about the dream or about my efforts each night to return to it, recreate it. I think I may never tell her, only because some things are so fragile and precious they shouldn't be spoken of at all. It's the first time Nathan has come into my dreams as a bright alive little boy. It's the first time I wasn't in water, trying uselessly to get to him, wishing I could drown instead.

The thing about dreams is, they can seep into your days, alter the world as you experience it. It's probably that—just my own altered perception—but as days go by and Halloween gets closer, it seems like everyone in our house is moving more slowly, acting distracted, drifting rather than walking.

My mother now sleeps in a hospital bed in what was the den but is now her room. Delba is in the upstairs guest room, a full-fledged member of our household. Halloween is so close, it's occupying a lot of our time. Marjorie has come up with additions to her Halloween costume that either Iris or I have to get for her. She now has rhinestone bracelets for both wrists and a long string of pearls.

"I don't know," Iris said to me one night. "Do you think she's starting to look like one of those kids on Toddlers and Tiaras?"

"God, I hope not. We'll look like really bad parents if she's following in their footsteps."

Bruce came over with scissors and trimmed my Hillary wig—so authentically that I said, "Wow, it really looks like I could go to the Middle East and negotiate with terrorists."

Maybe I feel distracted because in a few nights, if I find what I'm looking for in Thomas' house, I'll have to step into the rest of my life without the question that's been following behind me for all these months. Iris asked me the other night if the answer might be worse than the question. No, I told her—I'm sure of one thing—Hell is paved with unanswered questions.

But what if I'm wrong? That's another thing I haven't confided to Iris—the thin whisper of doubt that finds its way in. What if I find Thomas' writings and he has absolutely remembered seeing me go in and out of the screen door earlier that morning? First of all, will I believe him? And if I do, what then? Will my grief flood every part of my life? Spill over all the boundaries until I'm engulfed and invisible?

What if I learn that Thomas' hand was the careless one, the one stained with his son's death? Will my guilt turn to a rage so fierce I won't be able to look at him? He is, after all, Marjorie's father. I can't banish him from my life.

The more questions I ask, the deeper into a hole I go, and maybe that's why I have to know. I'm looking for the place where this black fall ends. I can't wonder and ask anymore, or one day I'll be down so deep I won't be able to claw my way out. I have no idea if the truth sets us free—maybe not. But I think it can stop the fall.

24.

Iris has refused to show any of us her Halloween costume before the actual day of October 31st.

"It isn't a wedding, Iris," I've said to her. "Brides are supposed to keep their dresses secret, not trick-or-treaters."

"I don't care. This is the way it is," she's said, and there has been no persuading her.

Finally the day has come. As the early dark moves in, I'm putting on my black pants suit, preparing to become Hillary, and my mother is helping Marjorie with her transformation into the Princess of Canada, which is what she wants to be called.

I'm in the bedroom when I hear Iris behind me in the doorway say, "Meow." At first I think she's talking to Aristotle but when I turn around she's standing there in a complete cat suit, head and all. A gray cat with white whiskers.

"Oh my God! Where did you get that?"

She takes off the head and pushes her hair out of her eyes. "It wasn't hard. Costume stores have them. You know those people who stand out on sidewalks and advertise for businesses? I figured there had to be costumes like this around."

"Has Marjorie seen you yet?"

"Nope. You're the first."

I suddenly remember that Iris is driving Marjorie to Crista's neighborhood in Point Dume to go trick-or-treating there.

"Iris, promise me you aren't going to drive with your cat head on."

She gives me a narrow-eyed look. "I haven't lost my mind, Isabelle. Even if I am wearing a costume that most sane adults wouldn't consider wearing."

She puts her head back on, walks down the hall into Marjorie's room and I hear both my mother and Marjorie scream with delight. Aristotle is apparently not so delighted by the sight of a giant feline. He races in to me and dives under the bed. Male egos are so fragile.

I leave first, my transformation complete. My mother and Delba stand in the doorway beside the Princess of Canada and a five-foot-eight cat, all of them cheerfully waving. Harlan has ordered a limo and Bruce is standing at the open car door so I can sit between them. He'd said he was going as a soldier, but when I see him in his army fatigue pants, combat boots, wife-beater T-shirt, and a pin that says, 'Don't ask, don't tell,' I'm not so sure.

"Bruce, are you a soldier or a member of the Village People?"

"Very funny, Hillary. Get in the car."

I slide in next to Harlan, a Caucasian P-Diddy in a fancy white suit and maroon shirt. Thank God he didn't try going in black-face. As the limo pulls out onto the Coast Highway, a wave of nervousness goes through my stomach. I'm really on my way. I'm really doing this. I take a deep breath and try to distract myself. I notice the crescent moon in the sky, dangling over the roofs of houses. I spot jack-o-lanterns on the deck of an ocean-side restaurant. And a cigar in Harlan's breast pocket.

"Does P. Diddy smoke cigars?" I ask him.

"You know, I'm not sure. It just seemed to go with the outfit. But I could have my details confused. Should I get rid of it?"

"Well, don't give it to me," Bruce says. "I can't take that foul thing off your hands. My training prohibits such vices. I'm a clean machine, entrusted with protecting and preserving democracy, and spreading it to other countries whether they like it or not. I am your son, your father, your brother. I am the face of America. And I'm reporting for duty!"

"Oh, God help us all," Harlan sighs.

Bruce reaches over and messes up my hair. "You gotta keep this hair unkempt looking, honey," he tells me. "For authenticity. Remember, Hillary does not look like she has an intimate relationship with a comb."

"We should work out some kind of signal between us when someone wants to leave," Harlan says.

Bruce leans across me and looks at Harlan. "How about, hi, are you ready to go?"

"I was going for subtlety."

"I don't have to be subtle. I'm a soldier. What about you, Hillary? Any exit strategy?"

"I think you'll know when I'm ready to leave," I tell them.

When we turn onto the Brentwood street where I used to live, I can already see evidence of the party—cars are lining the street, a sign says Valet Parking Ahead.

Harlan leans forward to speak to the driver. "Just let us off at the entrance and give me your number so I can call you when we're ready to leave."

"Yes, sir."

As we pull up to the gates, I notice security people with clipboards. Panic bolts through me. "We have to come up with a name for me. An actual name—I didn't even think of that!"

"Already taken care of," Harlan assures me.

We wait behind Dorothy and the Tin Man so we can give our names to the uniformed security men and I try my best to stand with Hillary's self-assurance. Shoulders back, I tell myself, chin tilted up— she always does that and it makes her look so confident.

Harlan steps up to the security guards. "Harlan Brandt, Bruce Devore and Susan Boyle," he says smoothly.

They check our names on their list and wave us in. I wait until we're safely past them, walking down the softly-lit driveway before I say anything. "Harlan, you told Thomas you were bringing Susan Boyle?"

"Oh, don't worry. I doubt he'll ask you to sing. I couldn't think of anyone else. It was a spur of the moment thing."

"Susan Boyle as Hillary Clinton," Bruce says, laughing. "This just gets better and better."

The house is already crowded and the guests have definitely taken the "costume preferred" message seriously. I scan the room and spot Thomas—his body language gives him away. He's dressed as Captain Hook, and hanging onto his arm is a young blonde woman in a long white nightgown.

"There's our host," I tell Harlan and Bruce.

"Who's his companion?" Bruce asks me. "I'm assuming she's supposed to be Wendy?"

"I don't know."

Bruce gives me a conspiratorial look. "Is this why you wanted to come? To see who he's shacking up with?"

"Actually, no."

We've reached the apparently happy couple and Harlan takes the lead. He shakes Thomas' hand, then the blonde's, who immediately giggles and asks, "Are you Colonel Sanders?"

Harlan looks terribly disappointed. "No. I'm P. Diddy."

Wendy scrunches up her face. I notice she's put freckles on with eyebrow pencil. "But he's black," she says in a vaguely valley-girl way.

"True, but I thought that would be insensitive. I was concerned about a backlash."

"I knew exactly who you were dressed as," Thomas/Captain Hook says.

Yeah, right.

Bruce shakes their hands, and then points to his Don't ask, Don't tell button. "I'm self-explanatory," he tells them.

My turn. I shake my ex-husband's hand, then his playmate's and lower the register of my voice. "Uh, Hillary Clinton."

I'm hoping to make a fast getaway to the bar but Thomas takes a step toward me. "There's a wonderful piano player here tonight," he says in the voice he uses when he wants something—low in the throat, seductive. "If you get inspired, I mean. He's dressed in a sombrero and work clothes—as Juan Valdez or something. Anyway, we'd be very honored."

I nod curtly—the way I think Hillary would. "Uh-huh."

We wind our way to the bar where I notice that many drinks are being served with straws to accommodate those of us who are encumbered by masks. Harlan pokes me in the back. "Now just don't drink too much and start singing," he says to me. "That would be a dead giveaway."

I get a glass of white wine and a straw. The house is getting more crowded. People are striking up conversations with Harlan and Bruce. Waiters are maneuvering their way through with trays of canapés, which of course only the unmasked can properly eat. A woman in an elaborate Elizabethan costume, carrying a head under her arm, approaches me. I notice that the decapitated head resembles the woman's real head.

"Mrs. Clinton," she says to me in an exaggerated British accent, "I so wish you'd been around in my day. I might have been able to keep my head." She laughs at her own joke and I giggle politely, although I'm pretty sure Hillary wouldn't have.

"And why exactly did you lose your head?"

"I'm Anne Boleyn. That bastard Henry VIII just couldn't see anything beyond the length of his own dick."

"Ah. Yes. I'm familiar with the story. And with that type of man. I can assure you if I'm elected president, they'll all be walking around carrying their dicks under their arms."

She laughs so loudly several people turn around and stare, which makes me nervous. "Would you excuse me?" I ask her. "I have to go find my friends."

I leave Anne with her two heads and move off into a corner where I can scan the room. I don't see Harlan or Bruce at first, but then it's hard to see past some of the guests—the woman dressed as a large martini glass, Count Dracula whose cape-flinging is going to take out someone's eye before the night is done, and someone in a bumblebee suit. Then I spot Harlan talking to a man dressed as Joan Crawford, complete with wire coat hangers looped over his/her arm. Thomas and his faithful sidekick Wendy are chatting with the Pope who is making short work of his drink.

I suddenly feel light-headed. Maybe it's the wine, but more likely it's fear. I slip out through the glass French doors, across the back patio where a few costumed guests are mingling in the yellow glow of Thomas' tasteful outdoor lighting. I head for the shelter of trees and a small stone bench that I always liked sitting on. The cool night air feels good and I wish I could take off my mask, but I obviously can't. I am Hillary, hear me roar.

After a few minutes, I see Bruce come outside and look around. Assuming he's looking for me, I call out from the shadows, "Over here, soldier boy."

"There you are," he says, striding over to me and sitting down beside me. "I thought I saw you come out here. You okay?"

"Yeah. A little overwhelmed, but…Bruce, I need to get upstairs. By the back stairs, which are off the pantry. Which is off the kitchen."

He gives me a wide-eyed look. "Jesus, Joseph and Mary, what are you going to steal?"

"Nothing." His look tells me I'm not going to get away with such a stupid lie. I have to confide in him. "Okay. I'll tell you. Marjorie told me that Thomas has been writing stuff down about the day Nathan died, trying to remember…you know…everything. Like who left the door unlocked. I want to read what he's written. I need to get up to his study."

Bruce nods and looks toward the house as if he's memorizing the architectural layout of the place. But he's probably just mulling over the architecture of my thinking.

"So if you find what you're looking for, then what? Are you going to hang out there?" he asks finally. "Sit in there and read? Or run out with a computer disk tucked in your pants suit?"

"I have no idea."

"Oh. Well. Good planning, Hillary."

"Bruce, how could I plan something when I don't know how or where he's been writing this down, or where he's put it…or anything? I just have to try. So, will you help me?"

He stands up, motions for me to do the same. "Okay. But if Harlan yells at me, I'm putting all the blame on you. What do you want me to do? Flirt with the chef? Trip a waiter?"

"Divert whoever is passing through the pantry."

Moments later we're at the back entrance of the pantry—Hillary Clinton and her gay soldier—waiting for a clear shot at the stairs. These are the servants' stairs. Members of the Berendon family do not take them. I, of course, did—feeling more comfortable there than on the grand front stairs—closer to my roots. Maids ascend these steps and enter the private world of the second floor. Once there they change bed linens, clean bathrooms, pick up stray pieces of tossed clothing. They remove discarded prescription bottles, condoms tossed in wastebaskets, crumpled papers they surely take a peek at— who wouldn't? They know more about the residents of a home than the residents know about each other. Life along the back stairs is full of secrets—that's another reason I liked them.

I start toward them but just then one of the catering staff comes hurrying out of the kitchen with a tray of canapés. I duck into the shadows and Bruce works his magic.

"Hi," he says effusively to the slim dark-haired man carrying a silver tray piled with flaky-crust finger food. The man stops and smiles at the handsome soldier. "I was wondering," Bruce continues in a low, secretive voice, "if there's any way you could find out which of these foods have peanut oil in them. I noticed a vaguely Chinese theme to the food, and I'm terribly allergic to peanuts. Ugly reaction—swelling, my breathing gets labored. Could you maybe find out for me so we can avoid an embarrassing scene?"

The young man smiles, clearly anxious to help. "Oh, sure. No problem. Wait here."

He vanishes back into the kitchen and I vanish up the stairs.

In the elegant hush of the upstairs hallway, I listen for sounds, movement, and hear nothing. Only my own heartbeat, which I know isn't usually this loud. The swell of noise and voices from downstairs seems suddenly far away.

I tiptoe down the hallway where once I walked as lady-of-the-house. Now I'm creeping along like a thief—the daughter of a thief, I think. My father's voice trickles in—chip off the old block, he whispers. Fuck you, is my response.

The door to Thomas' study is heavy oak, carved around the edges as if a vine is growing around it. I know this door. It was my portal into another world—a world of books and knowledge, things I wasn't born with any entitlement to. No one who was afforded an education, who sat in well-lit classrooms at shiny school desks, bought books with their parents' money and never thought twice about it can understand how the hunger to learn can burn you up inside. That hunger is the legacy of people like me, who were tossed the crumbs of the educational system and told to make do. I've listened to rich, bored people laugh about how they used to cut classes, cheat on tests, even hire other students to write their papers for them. Ingrates, I've thought. You have no idea how precious knowledge is. You can converse about Dickens because you glanced at the Cliff Notes, but you know nothing about the life that exists between the covers of his books. The riches. The gates to imagination.

I craved all of that and more as I wandered late at night in my husband's house and found myself here, in this dark green room with so many books I'd never be able to get to all of them even if I lived to a hundred. It was hypnotic, those hours in here. I didn't mind the lack of sleep.

I peel off my Hillary mask and wish that I were here to curl up with Faulkner or Dylan Thomas, rather than search for Thomas Berendon's confessions.

I go first to his computer. He didn't used to have it password-protected; Thomas was never a terribly savvy computer person; he doesn't need to be since his assistant takes care of important files at the office. To my relief, he still isn't that savvy; there is nothing blocking my entrance into his files and documents. But I find nothing, only business-related ideas and some saved articles about other department store chains.

His mahogany desk is large and ornate. I start with one of the two lower drawers that are deep enough to be file cabinets. The drawer slides open smoothly and the files are neatly marked in alphabetical order. Would he file something like this, though? And under what? Nathan? The date of his death? There are tax years, financial investments, insurance, charitable donations…which makes me quietly laugh. Thomas trying to help the world? Maybe he just wanted the tax break. I scan the carefully marked files. There's nothing I want in this drawer. I slide it closed, swivel the high-backed leather chair and open the twin drawer on the other side.

The sound of the door opening should be louder, but it isn't. Thomas is suddenly standing in the doorway staring at me. It would be funny under other circumstances—a grown man dressed as Captain Hook, complete with a long black wig and a plastic hook over one of his hands. But of course there is nothing funny about this moment. He steps into the room, closes the door behind him, still staring at me. My throat is dry as sand.

"And I was so looking forward to hearing one of the songs from your latest CD, Susan," he says, walking slowly toward me.

He takes off his hat, which leaves him with the silly looking black wig plastered to his head. Then he strips that off. "What are you looking for, Isabelle? Money? Have I not given you enough money?"

I shake my head no. I want to speak, but my throat won't open enough.

"You'd better start explaining yourself. I can have the security guards come up and forcibly remove you."

I squeeze my voice out. "Marjorie said you've been writing about it."

He nods slowly, moves even closer to me. I should stand up, but my legs are shaking so much I don't know if they'll support me. What if he hits me? Would he? I'm not sure. There's a letter opener on the desk. Would he stab me? Claim self-defense?

"About the day Nathan died," he says—a statement, no question mark at the end.

"Yes."

He just stands there, towering over me, barely two feet from the chair. I suddenly think about Hillary. She would never just sit here trembling. Didn't she once throw a lamp at Bill's head? Hillary would rise to her feet, stand her ground, strip off her opponent's skin with the blaze of her eyes. I do manage to stand up, but I can't quite muster the shoulders-back, chin-up Hillary posture, and forget about the eye thing.

Thomas takes another step toward me and I move to the side. He goes to the bookshelves just behind the desk and I take a large step back. I'm putting nothing past him—a pearl-handled revolver? Chloroform? But he pulls a thin leather-bound book from a shelf—one of those blank-page books that people always give to writers for Christmas even though no writer I've ever heard of uses things like that. He hands it to me and I take it, seeing something in his eyes that I've never seen before—a soft wilt of sadness.

"I was going to share this with you at some point," he says in a low, flat tone. "Take this home with you and read it. Then after you have, we should talk."

"It was you, wasn't it?"

He gives me nothing, just a long steady gaze. "Just read it, Isabelle. And then call me."

I hold the slim book in my hands and suddenly I'm not at all sure I want to know what's written on its pages.

Thomas puts his black wig back on, then his hat. He adjusts his hook hand, reassembling himself as Captain Hook. Hillary's face is on the desk. I reach for it, knowing I'll have to put it back on before going downstairs.

"Now I'd like you to leave the house," Thomas tells me.

"By the back stairs or the front?"

He walks over to the door, opens it as if he's a gallant gentleman using this formally polite gesture to impress a woman he has his sights set on. "Put your mask on and walk down the stairs," he tells me in a calm, even voice.

I do and as I descend the stairs, once more as Hillary, I realize he isn't behind me. I glance back and the door to the study is closed. I wonder what he's doing in there. There is still a photograph of Nathan on one of the bookshelves. Is he staring at it? Fighting back tears? I have the book tucked into the waistband of my slacks—it's pressing into the small of my back.

I see Bruce first—he's talking to Joan Crawford who has discarded the wire coat hangers somewhere, probably in a potted plant judging by the way Joan is weaving and sloshing his/her drink. When Bruce spots me, he leaves Mommy Dearest and edges around several people to get to me.

"So? Did you find what you were looking for?"

"No," I lie. I don't know why I shy away from telling him. All I want to do is go home.

"Where's Harlan? Would you mind if we left now?" I ask him.

On the limo ride home, I listen to Harlan and Bruce as if from a million miles away. The edges of the book are denting my skin but I welcome the pain. It seems appropriate.

"Did you have a good time, Hillary?" Harlan asks me.

"It was interesting."

Bruce leans forward and looks at me. "At least she knows who her ex is screwing these days."

Thanks, Bruce, I think to myself. I know he won't tell Harlan anything. He'll wait for me to do it. He'll let Harlan think that's the reason I wanted to go to Thomas' party—to check out the future Mrs. Berendon.

Everyone is asleep when I get home. Even Iris. Trick-or-treating can be exhausting, especially from inside a cat costume. I walk softly through the house, turning off lights. There is something comforting about being the only one awake. I feel sleep all around me, breathing in and out of rooms, making the air seem heavy and slow.

I strip Hillary from me, silently thanking her for her inspiration. Sometimes it doesn't take a village, it just takes a mask and a wig. The book goes into my sweater drawer, unopened. And when I slide into bed beside Iris, who stirs a little at the familiar movement of my body next to her, I imagine months going by without my hand turning the pages of the book that will tell me more about the day my son died. I wanted to know so badly; now I'm not at all sure.

25.

"So, you're just going to keep it and not look at it?" Iris asks me.

We're sitting out on the deck and the morning sky is filling up with clouds. The forecast is for rain later. Earlier, Marjorie asked if Delba and my mother could drive her to school this morning.

"You guys look tired," she said to me and Iris.

"Well, I certainly am," Iris answered. "Spending the evening inside a cat suit is not as fun as I'd thought it would be."

I give Delba the keys to my car and wait until they've driven away before I try to answer Iris' question.

"I don't know what I'm going to do," I tell her. "I kept trying to read the look on Thomas' face and I couldn't. Except for sadness—I saw that. Suddenly I wasn't so sure about any of it. I just started questioning the wisdom of what I'd done."

Iris stares into her coffee cup. "But you said he was planning on talking to you about it."

"Yeah. Maybe it's his generosity that's throwing me off. Anyway, I just don't know. I'm confused."

"Well, that's an okay place to be—confusion," Iris says. "I think sometimes it can be a productive place. I heard some country and western singer say in an interview that his daddy told him one of the most important things ever. He said if you're lost in the woods and you don't know where you are, stand still."

I'm not sure what to do with this, but it does make some kind of crazy sense. "Okay. Cowboy wisdom. That works for me."

I think about the small leather-bound book often during the day. I even open my sweater drawer and look at it. It's resting on top of a pale green cashmere sweater as if it's always been there. I stretch my hand toward it—practicing. But I can't move any closer. Something won't let me.

By early afternoon, the sky is billowing with storm clouds. I find my mother in the living room watching a show on the Discovery Channel about outer space. As I sit down beside her, the man on the television is saying, "In outer space, the further you look, the further back in time you go." In life, too, I think. Maybe I just can't bring myself to return to that bright yellow morning and my child's body floating limp in all that water. It must have looked like an ocean to him. Maybe I don't want him to die again. And if I open that book, he will.

"How was your evening?" my mother asks me, her gaze straying to the gathering clouds outside the window before locking on my eyes. "You haven't told me about it."

She deserves the truth. I shouldn't have kept it from her and now it seems silly that I did.

"I went to Thomas' party. That's where Harlan and Bruce were going. And…I asked them to take me along."

She nods slowly. "Ah," she says. Just that, nothing more. Had she already figured it out? I wait for her to ask me why, but she doesn't so I tell her anyway.

"Marjorie told me that Thomas had been writing down his memories of the morning Nathan died. His shrink told him to write it again and again until he remembered everything…the point being that he could then move on, I guess. I wanted to read what he'd written. I wanted…want…to know…I think."

My mother is watching me so calmly it's making me nervous. "She told me too," she finally says. "About her father writing things down."

"Did she say anything else?"

"No," my mother tells me, looking out the window again as the first raindrops fall. "Just that he was doing that. So, did you find his writings?"

"No. Well, yes. Sort of. I didn't actually find them, but...he caught me in his study and gave me a book—one of those blank books you get at a stationery store. I haven't looked at it yet. I can't. I don't know why..."

Before my mother can answer, Delba comes out of the kitchen with a tray and three cups of steaming tea on it. "Hot tea on a rainy day seemed like a good idea," she tells us.

My mother stands up and walks to the window. "I want to go outside first. Remember, Isabelle, when we went to the beach on that rainy day and danced on the sand? Your father was so unpleasant but you and I had so much fun."

"I do remember. Of course I do."

Delba offers to get umbrellas for us but my mother won't hear of it. She takes off her shoes, instructs me to do the same and we walk outside, across the damp deck and onto the sand. Once she's out there, I see her lengthen her body and expand her chest, breathing in as much air as she can hold. She extends her arms to me and I take her hands. Slowly, tentatively, we swing around in a circle—an older version of our dance so long ago. We once spun around like gypsies. Now we're like figures in a music box who turn more slowly as the music winds down.

Harlan and Bruce come out to their deck, zipped up in rain par-kas. "Have you two lost your minds?" Harlan calls out over the wind and the silken sheets of mist. But he's laughing so I know what he's really thinking is, we're being beautifully and completely sane.

"Yes!" my mother calls out, and lifts her face to the quilted sky. She opens her mouth to catch raindrops—everything in her is grab-bing hold of this single moment. A soft, rainy moment dancing with her daughter on the beach like they once did long ago. She gets winded and stops. The clouds have been moving quickly across the sky. The color of the day changes to white—a sheath between one cloud bank and the next. Gray billows are drifting in from the east and will be over us soon. But right now it's the pale in-between. We walk through deep sand back toward the house, but before we go up the steps to the deck, my mother looks at the sky again.

"This is what I think it will look like," she says.

"What?"

"Dying. Your father came to me in a dream the other night. The sky was this color in my dream and he was there, and he told me that's what it's like. He said it's a long climb to a high, white sky. I'm sure he said that, Isabelle, because I woke up with those words in my head."

I lead her back into the house where steam is still curling up from the mugs of tea on the coffee table. I could say so many things to my mother right now. I could say I never knew my father to be that poetic. Or I could say that I had a visit in dreamtime, too. Nathan came to me—under a different sky, but still...

I say nothing. We sip hot tea and watch the next bank of gray clouds move over us and explode into raindrops. The silence is soothing, comfortable.

Someday, when hot summer winds blow, when thin white curtains billow around open windows and we wait for cool blue evening to stretch over us, I'll think of this day. I'll smell the mist and feel it on my skin. I'll see my mother's mouth opening to taste the rain and feel her hands in mine. And I'll know that for a few moments, we danced away time.

26.

For two days, the sky has stayed white. My mother is quiet much of the time, never far from a window. She sits staring out at the veil of clouds and the gray sea. It makes me wonder if people can time their own death from some deep place in the soul. I've heard of that happening. I once talked to a woman who said her father, in the early stages of dementia, announced one morning that he was going to die that day. Then he went to his favorite chair, sat down, and before the sun had moved across the sky, he was dead.

Marjorie senses something, I think. But she hasn't asked to go to Crista's house, so I'm encouraged by that. Often, she trails her grandmother from room to room or sits quietly beside her with a book.

"Did you increase the morphine dosage?" I asked Delba one day when we were alone. I thought that might be the reason for my mother's placidity.

"Only at night, but just a little," Delba answered.

As Saturday gets closer, I wonder if Thomas will ask me whether or not I've read the book I plotted so hard to get. If I haven't opened it by then, I obviously can't lie to him. Maybe it's time. The not-knowing is starting to tug at me again.

It's early afternoon, but the pale sky tells no time of day. Marjorie is still in school and my mother is taking a nap. I can hear Delba in the kitchen and I saw Iris go upstairs a little while ago. I don't know why exactly, but I decide this is the moment. Something about the white lull of the day and the quiet house makes me feel safe and brave.

As I start upstairs, the phone rings and someone—Iris, I'm sure—picks it up on the second ring. I hear her when I get closer to our bedroom.

"Just stop calling!" she says, and her voice sounds splintery. "I don't want to talk to you. I don't want to hear your voice. You just need to leave me alone!" The sharp clack of the phone being slammed down follows.

Well, I'm pretty sure who that was.

I hesitate outside the bedroom door, which is slightly ajar. Then I push it open gently.

"Iris? Can I come in?"

The sound of crying answers me. She's sitting on the bed, her knees pulled up against her and she's crying harder than I ever thought Iris could. As I go to her and angle her knees so I can put my arms around her, I realize how even the people we think we know can surprise us. Her tears are the choking kind, her face is crumpled like a young girl's and her chest is heaving with the effort to get air in past the sobs.

"Iris…" I don't know what else to say beyond her name as I rock her and wait for the waves of tears to ease up.

Finally they do. She wipes her face with both hands—her cheeks are red and splotchy. "That was my mother," she says.

"Yeah, I kind of guessed that."

She laughs then, and so do I. It probably wasn't that funny; my guess is we just needed to break the mood.

"I thought she couldn't get to me anymore. The night of the fire when I was telling you about her? I really believed I was finally immune to her. But hearing her voice just then—I just curled up inside."

"You're asking a lot of yourself, Iris. You don't have to be immune."

She shakes her head as if trying to dislodge a memory. "She broke something in me so long ago. Before I had any chance to head her off and protect myself. I was the ugly kid, not what she'd imagined or wanted. Or chosen. I was too skinny, too tall, only good for one thing—to be married off to a man richer than my parents so they wouldn't have to think about me too much. And just then when she called and I heard her voice…I was that kid again."

"Your mother said you were ugly?" It's so hard to fathom. Iris walks into a room and both men and women get whiplash turning to look at her.

"It was always about power. Only that. She needed to make me as small and insignificant as she could."

"I know you feel like she broke something in you," I tell her. "I understand that. But I don't think you're broken, Iris. That's not what I see."

"Trust me. Way down deep? It gets dark down there."

I pull her into me again. "Well, not forever. Broken places heal. I believe that."

"Do you?"

"Yeah. And you don't have to have anything to do with someone who's hurt you. You have a family now."

She unwinds her legs and stands up. "I'm going to wash my face. I must look like shit."

"And you never look like shit. Trust me."

When she goes into the bathroom, I open my sweater drawer and lift out the leather book. I sit on the bed where Iris just was; the warmth of her body is still there. I'm holding the book, still unopened, when she comes back into the room.

"Speaking of broken places," she says.

"Yeah. That's what I was coming up here for. I think it's time I looked at this."

"Do you want to be alone?"

I shrug as if it doesn't matter but the truth is, I do want to be alone and Iris knows it. She glances at her watch. "It's almost time to pick up Marjorie. I'll go get her."

Thomas' handwriting is an even, careful slant. His writing is like his sock drawer—everything neatly lined up in perfect rows. Actually, every drawer of his is like that, and so his life. He's filled a lot of pages in the book and, looking at the first entries it's obvious that to him the morning began with Nathan's drowning. But of course it didn't, and that was the point of his therapist's instructions.

I start thumbing through the pages, scanning them, looking for the point at which he began at the beginning. And I start to see clues in the way he's stumbled through memories, impressions, snapshots that appeared in his mind.

The sun shining down on the water. An orange butterfly in the pool. A rescue by small hands…

Oh God, no, I think and almost close the book. But it's too late. This is Bluebeard's Chamber. There is no turning back. I turn more pages and find the last entry.

"I remember how bright the sunlight was on the pool. Strange because it was still early—it's going to be a hot day is what I thought. I saw Marjorie kneeling down at the side of the pool, reaching for something in the water. I was on my way to talk to the contractor and I stopped and asked what she was doing. She came running over to me with an orange butterfly in her hands. 'He was drowning and I saved him,' she said. Then she told me she was going to put him in the bushes on a big leaf so he could dry off and fly away. I said something like, Good for you. Or, That's nice. I don't know what I said. But what I didn't say was, remember to lock the screen. Because she always did. Always. Marjorie was so attentive to Nathan, she was always check-ing his toys, making sure there wasn't anything loose or torn that he could swallow. I didn't see her come back in, but I remember calling out goodbye to her when she left for a friend's birthday party a little while later. If I'd reminded her to close the screen, would my son still be alive? Maybe. Possibly. But if I'd checked on it after I saw her out there he would be too. I should have checked. Then Nathan wouldn't have drowned. I'd have discovered the mistake. That's what it was, it had to be. A mistake. A terrible, fatal mistake. Does Marjorie even remember the butterfly that morning? Does she remember going outside and failing to lock the screen when she came back in? I don't know.

I don't know. I don't know. I don't know. I don't know. I don't know. I don't know. I don't know."

The last stream of words is as hard for me to read as everything that went before. I imagine him writing 'I don't know' all those times to keep himself afloat—away from the murky bottom, the currents pulling him down like determined arms. I imagine him finally giving up and sinking, down and down and down to a place so deep and hurting it feels like forever.

I close the book, dry-eyed. There are caves in the world of grief, some sealed off from tears. A long-ago part of me softens toward Thomas—I did once feel something resembling love for him. Now we've been hurled together in the awful truth that Nathan is dead because Marjorie didn't remember to lock the screen door that morning. One child's careless hand, another child's life ended.

I feel emptied out. Numb. I know this place—this cavern deep inside. I was trapped here after Nathan died. A terrible familiarity takes over. Then a rush of images sweeps through my mind. Marjorie's Barbie doll at the bottom of the pool. Her drawings of dark water and her brother's body. Her eyes watching me intently as she talked about Nathan in heaven, riding on the wind and sitting in the laps of angels. Somewhere in her the memory must be there— buried, obscured, but there. Children are adept at burying traumatic events—denying what's too painful to look at. But eventually doesn't everything surface?

I don't know what to do.

The front door opens and closes. Marjorie's voice fills the house.

"Where's Mommy? Is she home? I want to show her the drawing I did."

"I think she might be taking a nap," I hear Iris say.

Thank you, Iris. For who you are. For who you don't even know you are. How am I going to look at Marjorie? I'm not ready yet. I have to compose a face, a mask…I need time. But I'm not going to be given time. Marjorie's footsteps clomp up the stairs. Being told a parent is napping can't stop a child who has something exciting to share. I slip the book into the nightstand drawer and act as if I've just woken up.

"Hi, were you asleep?" she says, bursting through the door and leaping onto the bed beside me, a piece of white drawing paper in her hands.

"Nope. Wide awake. What do you have there?" I ask her, trying to make my voice sound normal. I'm hoping that my face and eyes give away nothing. A sharp dread slices into my midsection. What if she's done another drawing of Nathan?

Smiling, she shows her drawing to me. A gray dolphin is swimming in blue water with a purple rabbit balanced on its back. My breath mercifully fills up the spot where seconds ago there was only fear.

"That's beautiful, Marjorie. Really. They look like they're having so much fun."

She points to the rabbit and frowns a little. "I know rabbits aren't purple. But I couldn't make it white 'cause the paper's white. And, besides, I like purple."

"I think a purple rabbit is just fine. How did he get on the dolphin's back?" I'm hoping she doesn't say that the rabbit was drowning and was rescued.

"He just wanted to go for a ride on the waves." She takes the paper from me and looks at it again. "They're friends." She scrambles off the bed then. "I'm going to go show it to Grandma and Delba."

"Okay."

The room closes in around me when she leaves. There is one thought—so cold and dark I don't even want to touch its edges. But I have to. Could it be that Marjorie does remember and doesn't really care? Could she feel comfortable, relieved, in having gotten away with something this awful? No—as soon as the possibility forms in my head I know it can't be. I would have to hate her then, I would have to see her as a heartless, even cruel child. No part of me believes that about her. She's a child who made a terrible mistake. But then so did we—by forgetting that she was a child.

And yet...and yet...there is a flutter of hatred in me. Not for who she is but for what she did. I know I can't keep it out. It streams through the cracks and fissures in my soul with icy persistence. I will never look at Marjorie the same way again. The love I've been building, reinforcing, is fractured. But I do still love her. I bleed for what she doesn't remember, for what she may someday recall. Love and rage twist inside me. She is both innocent and guilty. She's a child. I'm an adult. And I'm helpless. I have no idea what to do with this changing tide inside me.

I'm in a fog for the rest of the evening. I know Iris is wondering what I discovered in Thomas' book, but she has the sense to not ask. At moments, while we're eating dinner, I feel my mother's eyes search my face and I avoid meeting her gaze. I have to tell her, too, and I wonder how many times I can endure repeating what I never thought I'd discover. Delba's eyes seem to pass across me as well with an unusual scrutiny, but I might be imagining that. Delba's attention is primarily focused on my mother—on whether or not she's eating and swallowing properly. She studies my mother's hands for tremors, looks for signs of pain. Delba is everything you would want a nurse to be—everything we grew up thinking Florence Nightingale was. I'm not sure about the real Florence—history might have embellished her—but I trust in who Delba is.

Marjorie doesn't appear to sense anything. She's full of news about ballet class, about Crista maybe getting a puppy, about her arithmetic teacher who, according to Marjorie, wears ugly shoes and has bad breath. There are times when Marjorie seems to absorb everything around her, when she strips every adult down to bone-raw honesty. Thankfully, this is not one of those times.

When it's time to put her to bed, I ask Iris if she'll do it, prompting another questioning look. "I have a couple of phone calls to make," I say, loudly enough for Marjorie to hear. Iris knows I'm lying, but I don't think Marjorie does.

My mother and Delba are in the living room watching some reality show with has-been actors and actresses dancing around in spangly costumes, grinning for the camera and giving it their all. Aristotle is on my mother's lap, also staring at the television screen.

"When Iris finishes putting Marjorie to bed," I tell them, "I need to talk to all of you about something."

Delba and my mother both turn to me with wide, worried eyes. "I have something to tell you and I don't think I can say it more than once, so…if I can just tell everyone at the same time…" I add.

They nod and I see that I've now pulled them into my numbness. We all turn our attention to the television screen, but none of us are really watching it. We're all waiting for the sound of Iris' footsteps. When she finally comes back downstairs and sees us turn in unison toward her, she doesn't seem surprised. She sits down on the couch beside me, slides her arm around my shoulders and gives me a steady, searching look.

"Okay, Isabelle."

I reach for the remote control and turn off the TV. I know I have to fill up the silence over us—and I do—but I'm unprepared for the strange monotone quality of my voice.

"I read what Thomas wrote about the morning Nathan died. He's been trying to remember everything, and…he has. It was Marjorie. She went outside to pick up a butterfly. To rescue a butterfly, as ironic as that seems. He saw her. He spoke to her. She was the last one to go through the screen door."

Iris' arm tightens around me. Delba's eyes are calm and kind, but I think I see tears pooling at the edges. My mother lowers her head, nods slowly and whispers, "Yes." It's her I focus on.

"Did you know that?" I ask her.

"No, dear. But I thought it might be possible. She's a child. I know she's mature for her years, but she's still a child. And children make mistakes. Children are careless."

Careless. It seems like such an inappropriate word for what happened. But I can't stay with the word. I need something from these women who surround me. I need them to be a fleet of boats, I need them to rescue me from this dark sea where I can so easily drown.

There are all kinds of drowning. And all kinds of rescues. I need them to lift me to the surface and help me float there.

"I don't know what to do," I say to them—all of them. "I'm sure she's blocked out the memory. Do I unearth it for her? Take her back to that morning?"

Iris shifts her weight, moves her hand from my shoulder to push my hair back from my face—her palm is cool and reassuring on my forehead. "No," she says emphatically.

I wait for more. She leans forward, puts her elbows on her knees. "A couple of months ago, a woman and her son came to the center. They'd run away from her abusive husband—made their way here from Arizona, staying in motels. Only the thing is, when they first fled the home, there were three of them. She had a baby girl. Four months old. In one of the motels, the baby was crying and crying, and the boy—he was five—tried to pick her up. He dropped her and she died. He wouldn't talk about it—actually, he hardly talked at all. He'd retreated into this…silent place. The counselors at the center got children's books for the woman to read to him, about mistakes that sometimes happen and bad things that can result from those mistakes, and how important it is to remember they're still mistakes. Believe me, Isabelle, they have children's books for every kind of situation now. The counselors told her to talk to him about real life events where someone has been careless or negligent—not bad or mean, just careless—so he could learn that there's a difference between being bad and making a mistake. That's what we need to do with Marjorie—create an environment that feels protective, understanding. Just having that cocoon around her might lead her to the memory. And if she does remember, she'll already—hopefully—have a soft place to fall. But she has to go there on her own."

"I think that's right," Delba says. "It's too brutal to force her to remember."

"Are you going to talk to Thomas about this?" my mother asks. Her look is direct and uncompromising. She is, at this moment, my mother and she's about to tell me what to do.

"Yes, of course. We may be divorced, but this belongs to both of us. We have to be united in how we deal with it."

My mother nods slowly. Then she says, "Good. Because she will probably remember. Someday. The two of you need to agree on this now. On how to handle it, I mean."

No one says anything for what seems like a long time, but probably isn't. We're each lost in our own thoughts, our own questions.

Finally my mother lifts Aristotle from her lap and stands up. She crosses over to the couch, sits down beside me and puts her hands over mine. "Isabelle, I know that when she does remember, you'll give her all the love she needs. You're not sure about that right now—I can see that. But you're my daughter. In some ways I know you better than you know yourself. I might be gone already when the time comes that Marjorie remembers, so I want you to hear from me now how much I trust you. How sure I am that you'll do whatever you can to help her not blame herself. You're going to handle this with love, no matter what else comes into your mind."

My mother feels so frail when I put my arms around her. I want to hold her tightly, but I'm afraid she'll splinter. I can feel her leaving. But what she's told me will remain alive even after she's gone. It's one of the mysteries of death—how so much life stays behind.

27.

In blackness, I've slipped out of bed just before three in the morning—to sit by the window in our bedroom and look out at the calm satiny sea, the sky punched with stars. I let myself dive down to the darkest place inside me—where Marjorie's face floats alongside Nathan's—where they will be linked forever in a dance of death. Her small careless hand, his small unformed life.

I shudder when I hear Iris roll over. I know she's woken up. She gets out of bed and crosses the room. I don't want her here with me at this moment, which is something I never thought I'd feel. But I'm so ashamed of who I am right now. I'm raging inside at a child for causing the death of my child.

"Isabelle?" She slips in beside me in the double-wide armchair.

I don't say anything to her.

"Isabelle, talk to me."

"I can't."

She loops her legs over mine. "Yes, you can. There's nothing you can say to me that I can't handle."

Oh God, she knows. She knows where I've gone to. The soul can take slippery turns and I've taken one of them.

"I'm so afraid I might hate her," I tell Iris—my love, my rescuer—but who can rescue me from this?

"I understand," she says, with nothing but a warm breeze behind her voice.

"You do?"

"Of course. Part of me does too. It's what we're going to have to live with, though. And what Marjorie will have to live with someday when she remembers. She's going to have to deal with hating herself. We're partners in this tragedy—all of us. The centerpiece of the tragedy is that Nathan's gone. Hating Marjorie won't bring him back. Nothing will. And the thing is, you don't really hate her. You hate what happened."

"I guess that's true. But it all feels tangled up together. How do I untangle it?"

"You don't," Iris says softly. "You just accept that sometimes life is horribly messy. And love's the messiest part of it. But I think—no, I believe—love can coexist with other feelings—like anger and blame, even moments of hatred. You know in your heart she didn't mean it."

"Yes..."

"You believed for a while that it was you. How were going to forgive yourself? Or were you?"

A stream of wind comes through the window, smelling of the sea. I turn my face to it and realize how hot my skin is. "I don't know. I decided it was me, but I had no memory of going near the door earlier. I think now that I wanted to inflict even more pain on myself—it seemed appropriate to suffer every aspect of Nathan's death, even the responsibility for it. There was always some doubt in my mind... In a way, Thomas and I are both at fault. We gave Marjorie too much responsibility. We should have always been checking up on her."

Iris shakes her head slowly. "Isabelle, this isn't going to help—going back over everything that could have been different. We have to deal with all the tomorrows in front of us."

"I'm never going to look at her the same."

"No, you won't. But you're still going to look at her with love, and eventually with forgiveness. Because that's who you are—I'm with your mother on that one."

28.

Nathan is buried beneath a tree at a cemetery in Westwood. I've not visited his grave since the day his small casket was lowered into the earth, when we stood in a mournful black circle trying not to hate God. Only family members attended. We had no elaborate church service, no gathering of friends afterward milling about tables of food and liquor. Because of the circumstances of his death, we agreed that the standard protocol wouldn't be appropriate. It was the last thing Thomas and I ever agreed upon.

Until today. The cemetery is where we've agreed to meet. He's already there when I arrive. The sky has opened into blue again but the wind is chilly and strong. I suddenly imagine how Nathan might have liked flying a kite on a day like this.

"Have you been here long?" I ask my ex-husband. "I got caught in some traffic."

He looks at me with the eyes I once fell in love with. "Only about ten minutes."

We stand side by side with the wind shivering leaves above us and our heads bowed, parents of the child buried at our feet. The headstone is simple and small, carved with his name and the dates that would break anyone's heart, even a stranger passing by.

"Have you come here before?" I ask Thomas.

"No. It seemed too hard. You?"

"No. Same reason."

The wind curls between us, some yellow leaves skitter across Nathan's grave. We've come here to talk about Marjorie, about what Thomas remembered, but I'm not really sure what we should say to each other. I slide the book out from my purse and hand it to him. He takes it and stares at it.

"What should we do?" he asks me.

I tell him what Iris said about how love can get tangled up in so many other emotions, but it's still there—beating and red and alive. I tell him about the books we need to get for Marjorie, the net we need to weave beneath her so that when the fall comes—when that one singular memory unhinges her—she won't crash onto a hard unforgiving surface.

He nods and we stand there for a few more minutes, watching leaves drift and swirl in patterns across Nathan's grave, brush against the white stone marker and then move to other graves—other lives and deaths.

"There have been moments," Thomas says, "when I've thought I never want to see Marjorie again."

"I know. Me too. We'll have to live with those feelings and never show them to her. Maybe someday they'll fade away—I don't know. I hope so. It's all we can do, Thomas. We can't lose another child."

There are different kinds of deaths. There are things that have to die between people so new life can find its way in. All the anger and resentment I once felt for Thomas has evaporated. We are, as Iris said, partners in tragedy. And that fills up the space between us. As we walk away from the spot where our son is buried I do something I never thought I'd do again—I loop my arm through Thomas'. I lean my head against his shoulder like I used to in another lifetime.

I look behind us at the green field dotted with graves and headstones. "We should come here sometimes," I tell him.

"We should. We will. And we should talk about him a lot—all the ways he was, the things he did. So he stays bright and alive. Do you think—if Marjorie remembers, or when she does—that she'll ever be able to talk about him again after that?"

"I think she'll have to. At some point we're going to need to talk about sending her to a therapist or psychologist. Maybe even soon, but I don't want to frighten her or make her suspicious. We can tell her it's to help her deal with grief…I guess we'll just have to be intuitive about when that time comes. Are you okay, Thomas, about this parenting arrangement? I mean, we really are a trio here when it comes to Marjorie—Iris is her parent, too."

"I know. And yes, I am. Marjorie is happy with you and Iris, and obviously the two of you are happy, so…"

I look away from Thomas because tears are pressing into my eyes and I don't want to cry in front of him. If I start, I might not stop.

He walks me to my car and I sit there for a few minutes, watching him walk away. I imagine him old, his steps slower, his back narrower. I imagine the blue of his eyes fading, the lines around them deepening. And his fingers curving around the memory of his son's tiny hand in his.

We are bound to each other with stories. It's the illusion of divorce. We think when the papers are signed and our lives are separated, when belongings and properties are divided, that nothing remains of the weave that once held us together. But we're wrong. Memories have tight stitches, and children are sewn into our lives with unbreakable threads. Living or gone, they are us—the union we once believed would be forever. And is…in them.

29.

I'm standing in the doorway of the room where my mother will die. It's past midnight. A bright full moon bathes the house in a silver-white glow. Delba sleeps in the living room now; I can hear her breathing behind me. Aristotle is, as usual, curled up against my mother's thin body. He hardly ever leaves her side now. We all stay close to her these days, bringing our meals into this room, sitting in a circle around her, carrying on conversations that she sometimes listens to, shares in. Other times she drifts off to sleep but with a faint smile on her face, as if she feels protected by our presence. She's grown smaller, her skin more transparent, but as the days go by her features seem to smooth out, relax. Delba has told us this happens when the end is near.

Weeks have gone by and life has settled itself into a pattern of watching and waiting. Iris and I look for signs that Marjorie has returned to that yellow morning and is remembering the velvety feel of a butterfly in her palm, the cold aluminum handle of the screen door. So far, we've seen nothing.

"We have to just let things take their course," Iris said to me the other day.

I know she's right and there are times I'm awestruck at the course we've all taken to get here…especially me. The only deliverance for a damaged heart is love. My mother waited her whole life to see me realize that and there are times now when she opens her eyes, looks at me and Iris sitting beside her with such joy on her face I think she might decide to leave right then.

There is something peaceful, even lovely, about waiting for an end we know is coming. Maybe I'm more able to float on the beauty of it because the icy shock of Nathan's death is still scarred on my soul and always will be. But it's Iris who really keeps me afloat. There are nights I wake up crying and roll into her, but my weeping is soft, easy, and she is my harbor. There is nothing else I could want for in this life.

Tonight, standing here alone in the moonlight, I'm far from alone. There is a family around me; their hearts beat rhythmically in the quiet dark. And upstairs, the woman I fell in love with sleeps with me beside her even when I've left our bed to wander through the house.

Earlier, Marjorie didn't want to go to sleep, the moon was so big and tempting.

"Don't close the curtains," she told me as I was doing exactly that.

"Okay." I opened them again. The edge of the moon was peeking in at one corner.

I lay down beside her and turned off the bedside lamp. "One night a really, really long time ago," I told her, "I found your Grandma lying on the floor in the living room right in the beam of moonlight coming through the window. It was a full moon that night, too. I asked her what she was doing and she told me she was bathing her bones. She said the moon's light is magical and if you lie in it your bones will stay white. I stretched out on the floor with her and I told her we were going to have moonbones, and we'd live forever."

Marjorie scrunched closer to me. "Were you my age?"

"A little older."

"So I can have moonbones too?"

"Absolutely. But you have to go to sleep under the moon. Sleep is very important in the whole process."

She turned happily onto her side and closed her eyes. "Okay."

Sometimes I look at her and feel only love for the innocent child she is—for her bright, curious eyes and for the way she sits patiently beside my mother's bed. For her gentle hand stroking Aristotle's back and her watchful gaze as she scans the ocean for dolphins, or watches pelicans soar across the sky. There are other times when I look at the soft flesh of her hand and picture it sliding a screen door shut, neglecting to flip the lock down. I feel rage and blame ignite in me, but then I remind myself that there will come a day when Marjorie's rage toward herself will threaten to immolate her. Iris and I, along with Thomas, will have to pull her back from the flames.

The house I grew up in sold a few days ago. Iris and I were in our usual chairs around my mother's bed when we told her. We were prepared for some sadness, but she just smiled and said my father had visited her in her dream—he was fine with the house going to someone else, she said, and he was fine with her leaving this world because she would be with him soon and he'd missed her.

"Trees are houses in heaven," she said.

I nodded and smiled at Iris as if I knew what she meant, which of course I didn't. Delba told us later it might have been the morphine talking, but I'm not so sure.

Long before Marjorie is a teenager—pouty with lipstick, practicing attitude in the mirror—this room will be restored to what it used to be—a den with a desk and arm chairs, small end tables. The hospital bed will be gone. So will the tray that holds lotion, cotton balls, rubbing alcohol, morphine. The stacks of towels and blankets. But my mother will always linger here. I'll still pass by the doorway and listen for her breathing.

I feel death here as I stand in the pool of moonlight. But it doesn't frighten me. It's not asking for much right now, only that we pay attention. Eventually death asks for everything, but my mother is teaching me that it can be a tender exchange if you're willing. Her sleep is dense, thick. I wonder if she's dreaming. And if so, about what? My father? Trees in heaven? A rainy day on the beach?

Someday Marjorie and I will talk about her grandmother. How she loved her shawls and believed that dancing is not just something you do on a stage—you do it throughout your life. You live as a dancer—and she did.

We'll talk about how she adopted a big lumbering cat who is so loyal he'll lie beside her until her heart goes still and her breathing stops. Even after she's gone he'll wait for her, look for her behind every rainy day, every orange dawn.

Someday I'll tell Marjorie about standing here in this full-moon night while everyone else in the house slept. I'll tell her about knowing I have to let my mother go, but at the same time knowing we never really let anyone go.

I'll tell her that life is strange and unpredictable, but if she can find someone who will meet her soul with theirs—if she can wake up in the morning and go to sleep at night knowing that love is right there next to her—then she'll be living the best life she can.

I will watch her—for months, years if I have to—alert to any sign that her memory has traveled back to a bright Saturday morning and a butterfly she saved from drowning. And if it does, we'll travel back together—to the last day of her brother's life. I'll tell her that I forgive her even though doubt whistles quietly inside me. She doesn't need to know about that. She only needs my love. I'll tell her that people sometimes turn at the wrong moment, or look away, or forget some small gesture that they've always remembered before, and huge terrible things can be the result. But life is about going on even when you think you can't. It's about trusting the people who are traveling beside you—trusting that they won't let you fall.

Sometimes in life you have to turn and go back to figure out how to move forward—I'll tell her that, too.

On rainy days, I'll take her out to the sand and twirl around with her like my mother did with me. I'll hold her hands and think only about their gentleness, not about the one careless moment that scars them.

My mother will be gone soon. But already I can hear the echo of her voice saying, "It only seems that way, dear. I won't really be gone." She'll always pull me out into the rain and dance with me beside the sea.

Our footprints only seem to disappear. The truth is, they stay forever.